To Ko
I hope you love it!

Fyra B. Ginn

Crimson Aria
Edition 2

By

Fyra B. Ginn

This work was created by the author without the use of AI technology. The author did use automated grammar and spelling checks.

ISBN: 979-9-898831-51-9
Published By: Phoenyx Honor Publishing
www.fyrabginn.com

The wind will tell you first.
A slight change, a flicker,
fire's caress.
She wills it to do her bidding.
to carry her heat.
It flows in swirls and rivers
from her fingertips to your skin.

Your ears hear something soft
growing, a crackling
that alerts your skin,
shivers up your spine.
At last, your eyes see the fire bird
as her crimson aria unfolds.

She is alive,
her wingspan is power,
her voice, force,
her speed, honor,
her height, pride.
From the depths of torment, she ascends,
from the bonds of mortal fate, she rises.

Serendipitous day of the phoenix,
daughter of the sun,
the vengeance of ashes.
Soaring, her anger a tool,
burning her enemies,
protecting her people,
to leave nothing but a whispering wind
and small tendrils of smoke.

-From the poetic works of Dr. Gregory Jackson

Chapter 1
Ides of May

...Smoke...

It filled her lungs... making her cough and spew...They burned...aching and raw with her first breath. She heard the crackle of fire... the screaming around her. Too many noises filled her head... kept her from controlling her racing thoughts. *Who am I? Where am I?*

Blinded by the sun's light, her eyes slowly blinked open. Her vision took shape but the harsh glare pierced her eyes. She tried to shield them but pain radiated up half of her body from the movement of her arm. It tore a sound from her throat, halfway between a scream and a moan.

A gentle caress softened the pain then a force pulled her away from the worst of the heat. She rotated her dizzy head and saw blue tones. Her hazy mind struggled to see the face of her rescuer as she came back to reality.

The fear rose in her throat when she remembered. Something had gone horribly wrong. She'd faced death and survived. Snippets of memories fluttered through her mind like nightmare butterflies but were gone as quickly as they entered. A friend's smile.. a phone.. breakfast...

The boy took her to the shade beneath a rock structure. The heat, the light, the intensity all faded, and she could think again. The boy had a name.

She knew his name.

She knew *her* name. Relief flooded her body, the fear washed away for a brief moment.

"Ann..." His voice sounded miles away. How could that be? He stood, cupping her face in his hands. She laid hers on top of his and focused while he tried again. "Ann! Can you hear me?"

She couldn't answer. A secondary explosion deafened them as he covered her head. Her ears rang from the force of it. She struggled to control her breathing as the fear rose high in her throat, cutting off the air to her compromised lungs.

With breath came the horrid smells. Burnt rubber, smoke, and dark, charred figures lay around them in three directions. Stillness occupied them, their thoughts heavy, until her rescuer stood to leave and she grabbed his hand as panic tore an awkward squeak from her voice box.

Don't leave me alone! She tried to form the words, but her words were gone. He knelt and slowly removed her hand. His smile and mannerisms melted away most of the panic. She nodded to him. The boy abruptly left to search for other survivors and she inhaled deeply then released the breath slowly. Then she did it again. And again.

Starting at her toes, she moved each muscle, working her way up her legs, hips, core and arms. She sucked air in sharply as she felt pain radiate through her left arm again. Looking down, she saw a black and yellow piece of metal piercing the upper arm. She glared at it, the strange shape bringing a hysterical laugh at her ludicrous situation. *Well, that doesn't belong there.*

She grew somber, attempting to stand. She fell, her legs unsure of themselves. How did this work, again? The second time she stood, her knees locked so she wouldn't fall. She dared to lift her vision, the scene before her desolate. The black and yellow metal belonged to the school bus she'd ridden on. More quick flashes of memory gave her pause. A field trip, someone shoving past her on the bus, choosing her outfit for the day. The harder she tried to hold on to a memory, the faster it slipped away.

The smoke billowed around what remained of it. Sections of the bus were scattered along both sides of the highway. She put one foot forward, testing her knees, before she made her way closer to the wreckage.

Her rescuer had secured another survivor. He ran past her, carrying a girl, small in frame, in his arms. He set the limp girl down in the shade and walked back, struggling to breathe. *At least you're not alone.*

"Ann, you good? I could…use the help." He followed her gaze to the unconscious girl. "Joy is alive, but out cold." She heard his voice tremble despite his bravery. She touched his arm gently. He smiled at her silently. She looked over the scene and despaired. Where was the driver, and the teacher?

"I'm good." She found her voice at last, though it was strange, rough and sore. "What did you need help with Seth?" Seth, Joy and Ann. Those were their names.

He stared off to the other side of the horror before them. When he looked at her again, his voice broke even more, his brown eyes hopeless. "The bus driver and Mr. Huber are… d-gone. Joy's safe. I'm still trying to find any- "

A low-pitched scream brought back the tension in her body, and she leaned against Seth for a moment. When she was steady, she looked toward the sound, a muscular figure whose legs were trapped beneath what was previously the emergency exit.

She managed to follow Seth cautiously forward. She felt the fear rise with each scream, louder than the last. As they walked eschew from the flames, she prayed to any listening deity that the explosions were over.

Seth grabbed the bottom. He motioned for her to grab a side. "I lift, then you push, ok?" She nodded, and they lifted the debris off the boy, whose screams turned into harsh breaths. They helped him stand, though his legs shook from the effort. She could feel it as she lifted his arm over her shoulders. She winced as his hand grazed her wound, but she was steady. *I know how you feel, big guy.*

He was tall and fit. She was grateful when he gained his equilibrium after a few steps forward. With shaky legs of her own, carrying an athlete was out of the question.

Seth, the slender of the two, still helped the larger man to the shade, releasing him as he sat next to Joy. He placed a hand firmly on her good shoulder, a silent thank you for her help. She smiled back as best she could. A glimmer of hope shone in her eyes. Maybe there were others? Maybe she could help.

"Connor." The boy's eyes rested on Seth. "Connor Owsen, right?" Seth placed his hand on Connor's shoulder.

"Yeah…" He coughed and breathed deeply. Ann knew how he felt. "What… h-happened?"

"Something exploded…" Her sarcastic humor went unappreciated, however, as Connor ignored it, and Seth narrowed his eyes. She shrugged back at him, but the action shot pain down her left arm. *Bad timing on the sarcasm, self.*

Connor continued with questions as Seth looked over her wound. "Well, obviously, but how? Where *is* everyone?"

"Just the four of us so far." Seth grabbed cloth out of his pocket and wrapped her arm tightly above the wound. It stung, but she understood what he was doing. "I'll keep looking for others. How are your legs?"

Connor nodded and the two rose to leave. "Ann, do me a favor and watch over Joy."

Relief came quickly. She didn't want to stand again so soon. "On it."

As they walked away, she looked over her bandaged arm. She was tempted to take out the chunk of bus, but some vague recollection of a boring lecture cautioned her against it. She could bleed out.

Instead, she focused on Joy. She could see no broken bones, no burns. Physically, she was in better shape than Ann. Her breathing was slow and even. Ann took this as a sign that her body was functioning at least that much. She looked around Joy's head for signs of any trauma but found nothing, no blood. She wondered if she should elevate her, or leave her be?

Seth returned to them before she could decide. Connor followed, straining with another boy limp in his grasp. He set him on the ground, Ann between the two reclining survivors.

"I don't know him. Do you?"

Seth shook his head. Ann looked down at his face, noting his breathing was uneven. She gently brushed the sand off his face, his skin several shades darker than her own.

"He's safe, that's what's important. Is there anyone else?"

She looked to Seth, her rescuer, with a hopeful expression, but he refused to meet her gaze. Connor waited in silence until he seemed to realize Seth couldn't say it.

He knelt beside Ann and gently drew her to him, whispering a single word. "*No.*"

Hope fled her. Her breath caught, but the sorrow she should feel didn't pass the shock. She focused on the unconscious boy, saying, "I don't see any blood on him, either."

His eyes suddenly opened, dark and wide with fear. His lightning-fast hands reached around her throat and squeezed tightly before she could utter a word. Red filled her vision as she lost sight for a moment, the dark sweeping in. She regained consciousness quickly, her sore lungs heaved as she coughed and wheezed, the red haze fading. Seth and Connor were wrestling the boy away from her.

"Calm down. We're here to help you." Connor half shoved, half dropped the boy on the ground, guarding Ann.

Seth stepped between the two, calm and composed. "You're safe now. You're okay."

The boy tried to stand, took a step back, tripped and toppled to the ground. Scooting away he said, "Stay back! Just…" His head hit the ground, and he stopped moving.

Seth rushed to check his pulse, his breathing. "He's alive," he uttered in relief.

He headed toward her then tilted her chin so he could feel her neck. "Can you breathe? Are you okay?"

Her emotional roller coaster continued as rage filled her, suddenly. "Yeah, I'm okay. Just dandy. Someone tries to choke me to death, someone blows up the bus I'm on, but hell, it's a bright sunny day! When can we get out of here?"

Seth suppressed a smile. "We have to stay with the bus."

Connor and Ann both groaned. "Really? I say we start walking. We know the way to St. Blaise."

Seth sighed, frustrated with them. "The bus and the fire can be seen from miles away. You stay with the big objects so rescue workers don't have to look all over the desert for you."

"That makes sense." Ann's voice was still hoarse. "Besides, we've got two down. We can't leave them to die." She brushed the hair away from Joy's face.

Connor spoke softly. "We don't even know when someone will come by. How are we going to let emergency services know that we're alive?" He reached into his pocket, pulling out a melted smartphone. "I don't know about yours, but mine's fried." Ann grew afraid again. What would they do without a smartphone?

Seth nodded. "The bus driver would have to check in. The school will know something isn't right when we don't make our destination, but we could use help now." He surveyed the scene before him and said, "Connor, check the backpacks on the right. I'll check over here."

They left, busy with their work. Ann checked both of the unconscious students again before she stood, hoping her legs would hold. Walking around, her brain tried to process what she was seeing, but it was so egregiously horrific that she couldn't. She stepped to avoid someone's arm and tripped over something, falling to the hot ground.

She rubbed her head and lay still for a moment as the world swam inside her mind. Opening her eyes, she froze, face to face with someone once familiar, but gone. Curly dark hair, light eyes. Her body was free of burns. If she didn't know better, she would say she was merely asleep, but her eyes held the blank stare of death. Ann knew her…

The two girls walked up to the front of the school where a bus was parked, the engine humming softly. Marie turned to Ann and smiled broadly. They laughed at some untold joke, their merry nature due to the field trip of the day. A muscular boy shoved himself between them, his narcissism apparent.

"Excuse you!" Marie said it loudly, but he kept walking onto the bus.

"Rude."

"Ladies." Seth walked in front of them, facing away from the bus entrance. "Best day ever?"

Marie punched him. "Right Seth."

"Same field trip we take every year. Same boring museum."

He shrugged his shoulders before placing an arm around each of them. "Beats math."

They waited their turn, boarding the bus. Ann chose a seat near the center. Seth sat in front of her, Marie next to her.

"How was your weekend with your dad, Marie?" Every other weekend her friend got to spend time in the nearest city, where her father lived and worked.

"It was great. He was promoted at work, because of a project he's working on, we had to stay at his apartment instead of the house. The building has room service and everything. I never had to leave."

"That sounds extravagant but isolating."

"Yeah, but he loves it. Keeps saying the same thing. 'We're making lives better.' He thinks I should major in biology."

"Well, it's in your blood." Marie's smile caused envy in her friend. Ann didn't know anything about her birth parents.

"My dad's pretty great. Don't know why mom divorced him."

"Oh, hey! Does this mean you've given up on your childhood dreams of becoming a tap-dancing clown?"

Marie glared at her. "I was five. I can't believe my mother showed you those pics."

Ann chuckled. "I wish I had been there. I'd have taken so, so many pics. And some videos. To document the whole thing."

Marie giggled as she shoved her shoulder into Ann's body. They sat back as Mr. Huber took roll call. Two more students rushed to the back of the bus as they conversed in Spanish. Mr. Huber let them pass before calling off more names.

Everything set, the bus began to move slowly into the street. Ann nudged Marie.

"Top secret government facility. Must have been something exciting about it, right?"

"It was impressive, other than the freak-out drama after I misplaced my bag."

"Huh?"

"The whole place went on lockdown. Found my bag an hour later."

"So, a secure facility locks down over a backpack gone missing?"

"Right? I thought it was overkill." Marie reached into the front pocket of her backpack, removing a laminated key card. "Look at this."

Ann took it. Marie Bethany Cline. *It was official looking, with a picture ID and a data chip. She had an image of Marie in the future, working for a company like this. Pride swelled in her chest at her friend's intelligence.*

"What's the green strip for?"

"That's my clearance level. Green is the bottom level. Black is the top. My dad's is black. Not many people have that kind of access to the building." She beamed with pride.

"Just your dad?"

"My dad, the head researcher, and the Director."

"The 'Director?' Sounds very official."

"Super serious. He walked by me in the hall after my backpack had been found, told me to watch my stuff more carefully next time. Like a principal on steroids."

"Creeper…"

"Totally."

A hand in front of her brought her back. Seth gently closed her friend's eyes. Lifting Ann, he hugged her tightly. Amidst the shock flooding her system, a few tears still managed to escape her eyes, cascading down her cheeks to end on his shoulder. Her chest heaved as the pain of loss constricted her heart. He whispered, "*I'm so sorry. She was gone when I got to her.*"

Ann pulled herself together and let go, refusing to wallow in thoughts of misery until she was safe. She walked away slowly, shallowly contemplating the end of a kismet friendship through the shock and adrenaline flooding her body. She quickly found herself at the edge of the concrete road, looking off into the distance. She tried to remember more, but strain as she might, her memory after that instant would not coalesce. What had gone so incredibly wrong between their normal morning and now?

She spun around, feeling useless, with nothing to do but walk to the shade and rest. She sat beside Joy and checked her breathing again. Still even.

"No, this is not a prank call…" Seth was trying to convince some operator that they were indeed in peril. "I understand that I can be expelled for calling in a fake explosion… No, I didn't blow the bus up! Listen, I have four survivors here with me. Please help us."

She could only half listen to the conversation through the fog in her brain. Her adrenaline rush waned, and every bone began to hurt. The pain stole her thoughts. She was so sleepy.

Connor knelt beside her, looking her in the eye. "Don't pass out. You have to stay awake as long as possible." He then continued moving bodies. His words galvanized her to fight the heaviness saturating her being.

"If you just look for the big puff of smoke, you'll find us. No, not the interstate, the old highway. Fine." He hung up and relaxed beside her. She rested her head on his shoulder, and he let her. "What's the plan now Seth? You're the expert here."

"Looking for water wouldn't hurt in case they take their sweet time getting here." He stood and walked to Connor, motioning for him to follow. Seth was a survivalist. His dad was into hiking, living off the land. Although he was raised away from the culture, he had strong First Nation roots, that showed in his love and respect of the land. On a dare, he'd once prepared squirrel for her to eat. She shivered at the thought.

The moments alone stretched on, as she fought the urge to fall asleep. She began listing all the reasons she knew of to remain conscious, reciting them like a prayer until the boys came back, sooner than she expected.

Connor patted Seth's back, the two laughing. Ann didn't get the joke. Her anger rose again.

"What could possibly be amusing?" She asked it when they were close enough to hear.

Connor smiled wide. "Seth found water. I need to find a container. I thought that would take longer, but it's like he just knew where to look."

Seth knelt beside her. "We got lucky."

She laughed, maniacally. "Sure, we did. Today is the best day ever."

He chuckled with her for a moment before saying, "I'm serious though. We survived. That's a good thing."

"Marie didn't…" She said it so softly, she wasn't sure if he'd heard.

Seth said nothing for a moment. Connor waved to him, but before he left, he found the words. "Marie would be rooting for us to make it, don't you think?"

He walked away before Ann could form an angry retort he hadn't earned. She watched how excited they became at finding a couple of water bottles. Though the lids were blown off, they could still hold water. They left, as Ann recited her mantra again. When Seth came back, he handed her water, which she graciously accepted.

"Sip it slowly. We don't know how long they'll take."

That gave her pause, even though she was very thirsty. She followed instructions, only sipping every so often. The boys sat down next to her in the shade, the work they could do finished.

"Seth told me your best friend was on the bus." Connor looked at his feet. "All of mine are back at school. Sorry for your loss." He placed a hand on her shoulder.

"It's not your fault."

"I can still be sorry."

She took another sip of water, noting how dirty it tasted. As much as she knew the truth, knew these horrible events had just occurred, her mind struggled to process everything and failed. Marie was gone. Marie.... was.... gone. Marie was gone? No amount of prosody would help alleviate the disbelief.

"Huh." This came from Seth, who was staring at the smoke.

She looked at him. "What is it?"

"That's odd." Connor pointed to the crash.

Ann's brain could suddenly take in the details. She thought she'd seen everything, but she was wrong. She gasped when she realized why they'd been alarmed. She stared at what she thought was black smoke, saw it flicker, move, consuming whatever it touched.

That isn't smoke. It's black fire.

Officer Benjamin Ryan was on another goose chase. This had to be a prank call. Exploding bus in the middle of nowhere? Right. They thought they were so clever, but if he didn't find anything, he'd call the principal, get his cooperation in tracking down the caller. End of the school year, kids did silly things, especially seniors, but in this day and age, calling in a threat wasn't a prank or a joke.

Grabbing a sip of his sixth cup of coffee for the overtime shift, he focused on the pay he'd get. His wife was on maternity leave, so the more time he clocked, the more they had to live on. Prices rose every day and there was never quite enough to go around. This call would help.

Ryan let his mind wander as he drove the winding path. He took a curve to the left, sharply, a little too fast, and swerved a bit to correct after seeing the plume of smoke. Grabbing the radio, he was all business as he called it in.

"Dispatch, get more men out here now!"

He drove to the scene, bodies lined neatly on the side of the road. "I need all emergency services here. I got a bus in pieces, but someone survived to move the bodies."

The operator answered back as he slammed on his brakes. He walked out of his patrol car, scanning the area. The fire had died, only traces of its destruction evident. Priority one was finding survivors, though. He looked for the most probable location to hide and wait. Eyeing a large rock structure, he sprinted forward. *That's where I'd go.*

Rounding the structure, he saw two boys, and three unconscious teens. They were sweating, breathing heavily. He knelt beside them and checked their pulses. Steady, but fast.

"I'm Officer Ryan. We got your call."

One boy smiled at him. "I'm Connor."

"Seth."

"Connor, Seth, I'm here to help you. Ambulances are on their way."

"Do you have water?"

"In my car. I'll drive it over."

Racing back, he used his radio one last time. "Dispatch, put a rush on that bus."

He entered his vehicle, and disregarding protocol, he drove off the highway, kicking up dirt. He heard a couple of bumps, knew his lieutenant would probably dock his pay. Didn't matter, these kids needed to get out of the heat, *now.*

Emergency services arrived, taking the most seriously injured to the hospital first. Loading Ann and Joy in the back, they took off, squealing tires toward the nearest city, still some forty minutes away.

She was in and out of consciousness for the whole ride. She felt so hot. The paramedics must have noticed, or maybe she had said something aloud, because they placed cooling blankets over her. She glimpsed Joy before her eyes grew heavy and she fell into the black again.

> She stood with Joy, next to the accident. Wasn't she just in an ambulance? This was strange, but a feeling of calm enveloped her as she saw her friend, awake and alert, next to her. Her eyes glowed brighter than normal, her hair reflecting a thousand strands of light. Joy reached out, touching her hand.
>
> "Don't be afraid, my friend." Joy's voice seemed to echo slightly. Ann tilted her head. She wasn't afraid, she was calm.
>
> As they watched, time backtracked. The bus, the scene disappeared down the street, only to reappear a moment later. It launched down the highway toward its doom.
>
> "Stop!" Ann tried to yell, but nothing came out. Her voice was gone.
>
> Joy wouldn't let go, her grip strong, unbreakable. "You will not die today." Her voice echoed with an authority she normally didn't possess.
>
> Ann struggled against the arms that held her, to try and warn the bus, but it was little use, as the accident happened again, as if in slow

motion, with a clarity she hadn't possessed on scene.

She began to cry, confused by the events in front of her. Joy didn't allow a reprieve, however. She shook Ann's shoulders. "No, not now. Now you look around. What do you see?"

She faced Joy, ready to admonish her friend, when she saw what Joy intended. In the back of the scene, a shadow moved, as if human, in the desert. It sat, watching the destruction, watching as they struggled to live. When it'd learned all it could, it vanished, but not before its cold gaze landed on her, chilling her soul.

She woke from the nightmare, tears streaming down her face. The EMT next to her held paddles in her hands. Seeing Ann awake, she smiled down at the girl.

"You're back. Thank God."

Ann was confused. Had she…died?

The trauma unit on call got the radio signal that the first were arriving. Everyone sprang into action quickly, among them a young doctor in the second year of her residency. Blonde hair pulled back, she locked her attention on the first patient, an unconscious female with a shard of metal embedded in her left triceps.

The EMT gave her the info she needed. "Revived once in the field, in and out, only visible injury on left arm. Fever, possible heat exhaustion."

Wills took the lead and hustled the victim inside. After her boss looked the girl over, she was told to follow through with care, and what order to treat her symptoms. She nodded, remembering the list. She began to bark orders for supplies to be brought.

There was sudden pressure on her arm. She looked down, saw the girl staring back at her. A moment later, and she was back out. Wills hurried forward, the procedure automatic now as she tended to her patient.

"You're not dying on my watch."

Lucky Seth never fell asleep. He was awake, given water and taken to the hospital, where they found nothing wrong with him. An hour later, as he sat in a waiting room, Connor was dismissed as well. The two boys sat back-to-back, as others whispered around them.

Officer Ryan found them quickly after checking in. He shook their hands and squatted next to them. "How are you feeling?"

Seth simply nodded.

"Well, I'm great. Good to be alive and out of that heat." Connor smiled wide.

"They give you water?"

"Tons. Can't drink anymore. They said I have to watch my temperature, make sure I drink water for the next couple of days. Down electrolytes."

"Heat exhaustion is no joke. Take their advice. Listen, I was wondering if I could ask you two a few questions. Would that be alright? You have the option of waiting for your parents, but they were just called, and the sooner I wrap this up, get to the site, figure out what's wrong, the sooner I can give your friends justice. Can you help me out?"

Connor looked at Seth, who shrugged. "What do you need to know?"

Wills was called in on an emergent situation with one of the survivors, a boy that'd been unconscious upon arrival. She ran to the room, among screams and shouts to "restrain him!"

Nurses were surrounding the boy, whose wide eyes looked distant. "Situation?"

"He woke and started to freak out. Took out Jenny with a shove. Girl's on the floor."

She asked for a strong sedative and prepared a syringe. "Hold him down."

"Trying, doctor. He's strong for his body type."

She found a vein and jabbed, the liquid flowing into his arm. His tense body slowly relaxed. As it did, she placed a gentle hand on his forehead. She saw a tear stream down his cheek, and said, "Don't worry. I've got you."

The hospital room was dark. She lifted her body as she woke, sitting up in the hospital bed. Ann surveyed her surroundings, machines beeping softly. Her arm was wrapped in a flexible cast. Her right arm was attached to a saline bag. It took her a few moments to let the memories return, another few to try futilely to remember. Unable to think of anything else to do, she carefully reached for the TV remote. Hitting the power button, the local news came on.

"The crash is still under investigation. We do not know at this time if it was an unfortunate accident, or malicious bombing. However, several representatives from the hospital have confirmed that five survivors have been brought to St. Blaise General. They are reportedly all in stable condition at the moment, though several remain unconscious and in intensive care. Thirteen people have been pronounced dead, including the teacher and bus driver, plus eleven students. Names are being withheld until family can be notified. Our hearts go out to those suffering through this tragedy. We at Channel 23 news are grieving with you. Stay tuned for periodic updates…"

Ann wanted to stay awake, but the darkness beckoned. She was asleep moments later. From the corner of the room, a shadow seemed to flicker for just a moment, before resetting to normal.

Officer Ryan pulled into the hospital after revisiting the crash site, barely missing the large mass of reporters waiting for word. He blended in nonchalantly with several employees so he could enter without questions. He had to go over the scene one more time with the boys.

Entering a small side room, he noted the local police had already asked them for another interview. He nodded to hospital security, who said, "Officer Ryan, guardians gave permission. You're welcome to ask your questions in here."

"Thank you." He walked in, shutting the door softly. This whole situation was a mess. While his gut told him that none of the survivors had malevolent intent, the evidence was piling up and it didn't make any sense.

"Can you go over it one more time for me, son?"

Connor looked at Seth, who shrugged. "Look, we told you everything we know. We can tell you again, if you'd like, but I don't know how much more we can help you."

He tilted his hat, rubbed his five o'clock shadow. He needed a shave. "Look, I got the basics, but when some flags pop up, as they did on the scene and in our conversation, I have a duty to ask. Do you mind if I bring up a couple of questions about your statements from earlier?"

"Go ahead." Connor was very poised and collected for someone who'd just been through hell. He made a note of it on his pad.

"The thing that concerns me most is the description of the fire. Now both of you told me that as you sat there, you watched black…" he circled the word, "black flame. Now this is a flag, because I'll be honest, flames don't burn black."

Seth shrugged, and Connor sat confused. "Yeah, but it was."

"What I'm trying to get at, is that it's possible you could have been hallucinating. You suffered a trauma after all. Think back on it, try to clear your mind. You sure you saw *black* flames?"

They took the moment, which was good. Meant they were trying. Seth gave a nod and Connor answered for the both of them. "We're sure. Ann saw it too, but you haven't talked to her yet."

"I'll do that, as soon as she's stable. Next question…." He underlined it in his notepad. "Now, you said the five of you were inside the bus, when it exploded?"

"We…assume so."

"What exactly do you mean?" He placed his hands joined on the table, a sign that he was relaxed. He needed the truth.

"We…don't remember."

"Right, but you were on the bus prior?"

"We both remember boarding the bus at the school, but after we left home, we…can't remember anything."

"Is it possible you stopped for some reason?"

"I suppose we could have. Why?"

"Well, you've given me your positions on the bus. I…I have to be honest with the two of you. You couldn't have been inside the bus when it exploded."

"Why not?"

"I looked over the site myself, talked to the inspectors. They were…surprised to find out that there were five survivors. Things don't add up in this investigation."

"Why?" Connor tilted his head, still confused.

"Look, you two saw the bodies, right? And yet, the five of you, while some of you were injured, you're all missing something you should have if you'd been on that bus."

"What?" Connor still didn't see it.

Seth finally spoke. "No burns."

Officer Ryan looked him over, gauging his reaction, or lack thereof. "Exactly, son. Not one of you was admitted with even minor burns. Your clothes, sure, but none of you. That's a big flag. What's even more interesting is the presence of a sixth victim in unusual circumstances. Two human adults were found and identified with severe burns. Ten burn victims that are your age. Then there's the last. She was dead upon arrival, but like the five of you, had no burns. Care to explain that?"

"We…can't. We don't remember." Connor mimicked his movements, placing his hands on the table. He picked up quick. "What do you need from us? We want you to find out who did this."

"See, and I'm not sure what I need to put the pieces together, because right now it seems like you were saved by your guardian angels. Which is why I asked you to go over the whole thing, one more time."

Seth sighed, and Connor put his head down. Officer Ryan wrote down everything. "Just one more time."

He walked out of the room an hour later, satisfied that they weren't lying, yet. He nodded to their guardians and sat down, looking through his notes. He hadn't lied to them. Some things about this situation didn't add up.

He looked over the inspector's quote when he told them of the survivors. "No way anyone human was on that bus and walked away. None. They should be dead."

He didn't see the point of scaring the teens, so he hadn't phrased it so roughly. None of those teens should be alive, yet they were. The inspectors had bagged trace evidence at the scene, trying to pin down what type of explosives were used, the point of origin. For now, it looked like the explosion came from the middle of the vehicle. Where three of the survivors had been sitting.

He'd already placed the call into his lieutenant. He'd be put up in a hotel across the street for the night, fully paid, so he could wrap this up. This madness never happened in their small town, and he was playing it mostly by ear. It was on him to figure this out. Assuming of course, that it didn't warrant federal attention. They had crossed state lines before the bus exploded.

His mind drifted for a moment to his home and his comfy bed, his wife's cold feet touching his leg…

"Shit!" He said it too loud. The guardians all looked at him, worried. "Nothing to do with the case folks. I just need to make a call."

Stepping into an empty room, dread plain on his face, he called her.

She picked up on the first ring. "What. The. Hell. Ben?"

He sighed. "I'm sorry, Ellie."

"Oh, you will be when you get home." Her voice dripped with the venomous threat.

"I was called in on an emergency. Getting overtime pay."

That seemed to calm her. "I was just…so worried."

"I'm sorry that I forgot to call." Her tears made him feel guilty though he'd called her at the first opportunity. He sighed gently and began to explain everything.

Chapter 2
Day 2

Dr. Wills walked through the hallway near the victims' rooms. She'd just checked on number 1, Joy. Still unconscious, though it defied explanation. Her temperature was good, vitals were good, no blood in the catheter, no signs of heat stroke or exhaustion. She was, just, asleep. Wills knew the statistics. The longer she remained out, the more likely she wouldn't wake. Still, maybe she was just recovering.

She looked down at her watch. It'd been exactly twenty-four hours since they first arrived at the hospital, as of five minutes ago. She assessed the next victim, walking into the room, taking her vitals. She looked over her chart, satisfied that Ann was stable, that she'd done all she could. They'd matched the description of the girl while calling parents. They knew her name was Ann Smith, Caucasian female, five six, currently resting. Wills checked her cast, satisfied with the result.

"I told you, I got you, Ann. Sleep tight."

She walked to the last victim's room, a bit uncertain. This was the sedated boy. The one who'd taken several nurses out yesterday while they were trying to heal him. She opened the door slowly, noting his name on the chart. Julius Reyes. Hispanic boy, five foot nine. His parents were here, waiting eagerly for their son to wake.

Neither was in the room at the moment, so she rounded the bed, checking the restraints. She recorded normal vitals and prepared to go, when she looked down and jumped. His deep eyes were locked on hers.

"Julius?" She asked it softly, afraid he would hurt her. "Is your name Julius?"

He didn't answer, but he did nod. "Okay. You're lucid. That's good. I'm Dr. Wills. You're in the hospital. You were in an accident, but you are alive and well. Would you like me to find your parents for you?"

He nodded again. "Sit tight. I'll be right back."

He watched her leave, then when she was out of sight, he put his plan into motion. He pulled on his restraints, but when they didn't budge, he sighed, and lowered his head to chew through them. He had a strange feeling. This building smelled of death, and despair. He couldn't stay here a moment longer. He had to get out.

His hand came loose faster than expected. His teeth felt stronger than normal. Once one was loose, he released the other, then paused, hearing footsteps coming. Feigning sleep, he lay down until they passed by. When they'd gone, he freed himself and stood, shaky at first. He used his ears to listen. Everything was quiet on this floor, save beeping machines and talking nurses.

When he was sure the coast was clear, he bolted out the door, heading right. He raced down the hallway until he smelled someone coming. They reeked of sweat and odor. He almost puked but managed to control himself. Instead, he hid in the nearest room until Stinky McNurse was gone.

He sighed with relief, but it was short lived. He smelled it. The crash, the strange metallic odor. It was in this room with him. He slowly rotated his body, to see…her, and he… remembered.

He sat next to Marcus at the back of the bus as it chugged down the old highway. Bright rays of sunshine beamed through open windows, the soft breeze cooling their skin. They bounced merrily along as they talked of their plans for the weekend.

Marcus shoved him. "How lame is this trip, huh?"

Julius nodded, looking down at his smartphone. "No homework, though."

Marcus relaxed in his seat. "I'm just bored. Can I still come to your place after school?"

Julius laughed.

"What?" Marcus looked at him funny.

He looked up and stared his best friend in the eye. "You want to come over? To do what?"

"Play video games, man. Pizza. In person. It'll be fun."

He looked back down at his smartphone. "Sure. Nothing to do with my sister, right?"

Marcus chuckled. "No, I respect you, man. I wouldn't go there."

"Because you know what would happen to you, if you end up in her DMs?"

They both laughed. Julius looked up to the front of the bus. He put his phone away for now. He had time to look forward once more before the black smoke exploded from the middle of the bus. The darkness leapt at him, so quickly, then everything was gone.

Breathing heavy, he looked at the girl in front of him. She lay on the bed, sleeping softly. She smelled of the crash, of death, of destruction. He walked toward her, a little afraid, but she didn't move. *Fire death girl.* He remembered waking, remembered what he'd done. He checked her neck, noting some minor bruising, but she seemed to be breathing fine.

Feeling guilty, but scared, he smelled her hair. She hadn't washed it yet. It smelled of that strange metal but also like her. She began to stir, and he tensed away. The nurse was gone, and he was afraid. He went with instinct, opened the door, and ran across the catwalk to the stairs.

Ann dreamt of her friend, Joy. They were playing in a park, the sunshine bright and comforting against her skin. It captured Joy's golden hair, highlighting it with energy. She swirled around and threw a ball to her bestie. Her left arm, free of the cast, let the ball glide gracefully forward. Ann looked down, the hospital gown a surprise to her. Why was she wearing this?

Before she could debate longer, the clouds began to roll forward, blocking the comfy sun. *It's going to storm.* Usually she loved storms, but not *now*. Not while she was in the park with Joy. She ran forward as the rain began to fall.

She gasped as she reached Joy. A halo glow surrounded her friend, keeping her dry despite the storm. When Ann touched her shoulder, the glow extended around her too, a comfortable feeling of security enveloping her.

Joy gave her a long, hard squeeze, before whispering softly to her. "*I'm dreaming, but I need to be right now. It's safe for me here. You, my friend, are not safe. You need to wake up.*"

She snorted. "I don't want to." She was comfy and warm, saw no reason to leave.

"Ann," she began apprehensively, "it's safe for me, but you're a whole other story."

"Who will play catch with you if I go?"

Joy looked to the forest, where another figure was running toward the girls. Ann tilted her head but couldn't quite make out who it was.

"Marie and I can visit, but you need to go, now. Wake up."

Marie's face came into focus just as she felt herself slip away.

The rolling thunder of the storm jostled her body into consciousness. She lay in the bed, confused, groggy. What had she dreamt of? Sitting up, she saw activity around her. Nurses, cops, security, doctors. Everyone was running, everywhere. Her cast ached from sitting up.

With her good arm, she pressed the call button. She didn't know what was happening, but she wouldn't let herself be forgotten. Waiting for a response, she powered on the TV. More incredibly convenient news coverage.

"This is Channel 23 news coming to you live from the hospital where several teens are recovering after the infamous bus crash that left thirteen dead, eleven of them, high school seniors. We have received word from the hospital that one survivor has been…lost? Hospital staff are searching everywhere for the troubled teen. One victim remains comatose, three in good health. I'm here now, with Officer Ryan, who was first on scene.

"Officer, this is obviously a horrible situation for these teenagers and their families. What, if anything, can you tell us of the accident?" She shoved the microphone into his face. He couldn't leave if he wanted to. Ann felt a small grin form at the edges of her mouth.

"Unfortunately, we can't discuss many of the details of this case until it's been closed. As it's still under investigation, you can understand my position, but I will tell you what I can. While we initially leaned toward an accident, we now suspect that someone deliberately sabotaged the bus. That's all I can say at this time as no formal charges have been issued. We are asking the public to respect the rights of the families and allow them to enter and exit the hospital to see their children without incident."

"Officer Ryan, do you suspect that the missing student is connected to the case?"

"As it is an ongoing investigation, I can't say one way or the other. It's peculiar that a teen would leave a safe environment after suffering such trauma, but while it may appear suspicious, it definitely does *not* imply guilt."

"Thank you, Officer Ryan. We have reports of several helicopters flying to the hospital at this time. Folks, whatever this was, it has caught national attention. Stay tuned to your local Channel 23 News for continuing coverage of this tragedy. Moving on to other news, police are still searching for a man that has killed five victims by stabbing injuries. They are comfortable at this time with calling this a serial killer. The internet has already named him 'Stabby Steve,' believe it or not. Please be advised…"

National attention sounded bad. More government sounded bad. Growing up in the system, she contained what she considered to be a healthy distrust of authority. She knew most people looked out for themselves. It was interesting that, though there'd been excellent news coverage about the crash, no one was interested in her. Not her fosters, not her friends, not even a reporter or two.

Her mind drifted to Seth and Joy. She'd known them since the first day of seventh grade. She'd walked into the classroom and locked eyes with Joy, Seth and Marie, knowing somehow that those were "her" people. Was Joy still unconscious?

Struggling to remember her dream, she only recalled fleeting tidbits of happiness. She remembered the aura of sunlight, that her friend had said…something…important, hadn't she? What was it?

After minutes of contemplation, a nurse walked into her room. "Good morning, Ann." She smiled professionally as she glanced at her chart. "I hear you had quite the experience yesterday."

She gave a weak half smile to the nurse. "Yeah."

Her voice, still rough and raw, was not as solid as she'd hoped it would be. She cleared her throat and spoke with more volume. "Where are my friends?"

The nurse helped her sit up, adjusting the bed. "Two of your classmates are at home, recovering with their families. You are not cleared to leave yet. We just want to run a few more tests on your arm. Joy is still sleeping and we don't know where Julius went. We have security and police looking for him. Can you tell me anything that might help us narrow the search?"

He's not going to come in here with me.

She shook her head, softly. "I don't know him personally. Sorry."

"I understand. Please wait here while I see if your parents have arrived. They'll be thrilled to know their daughter is awake, I'm sure. I'll be happy to share the good news with them."

She sighed, disheartened. She was no one's daughter. She'd grown up in foster care. She couldn't even remember her first home. These fosters didn't care past the price she cost them.

They'd come in complaining of hospital bills, like Ann was personally responsible for the bus crash. She'd have to get a part time job to pay them back. Remembering the bad homes, she resigned herself. As much as she complained, they didn't beat or starve her. Six weeks, then she was free. Interesting that her arm would be bound for six weeks as well.

She looked over the rest of her person, assessing the damage. She remembered the bus chunk in her left arm, but nothing else. She looked at her clothes; mere rags singed from the flame of the blast. How were her clothes so badly fire frayed if her body suffered no burns? Shouldn't she be burnt?

She gave a silent plea, hoping her fosters remembered some clothes. The singed rags had been one of the few outfits she could still wear. She looked around the room. Through the open door, she could hear the hum of machines, followed by shouts and voices in the hallway. To her left was a view of a catwalk that crossed the entrance of the hospital. On the balcony stood several suits staring in her direction. A doctor with bright blonde hair was with them. While she seemed rather pleased with herself, the suits she talked to didn't give away anything. That warned her that they were government suits. System suits. *Just what I need. Probably wondering if I did it.*

She pivoted her head away from the system suits and the nice cheery doctor. Nonchalantly, she resumed doing nothing intently. She wasn't going to give them any reason to talk to her. During her time in foster care, she'd learned to distrust officials of the state. Some were decent, but most were in it for themselves. If her real parents had thrown her away, didn't protect her, then no one would.

Before the suits could enter, her fosters came in with flair, dressed in their nicest clothes. They'd bought them with money that was supposed to go to her wardrobe, but Ann wasn't going to complain. They stood with fake smiles plastered on two-sided faces. Giving the whole routine their all, they dialed up the charm.

"Oh, Ann!" Mrs. Miller came to her, hugging her close, a little too tightly for Ann to be comforted. "We were so worried, Dear."

Ann knew this routine. It was the same one they used when the social worker came to visit. She knew her role but couldn't bring herself to play the respectful daughter today. They were ridiculous, and her best friend was dead.

Grabbing her by the arm, Mr. Miller leaned in to whisper, "*you almost gave us a heart attack.*" The words, though sweetly phrased, were a tainted honey. Her rage grew suddenly as she thought of all she'd suffered in her short life.

They pulled their hands away immediately. "You're burning up!"

They called in the nurse, who took her temperature. A curious frown played on her face. "Sorry, this must…be broken? Let me get a manual one."

She left as the suits entered, and Ann's rage morphed to apprehension. She didn't trust system suits. The nurse came back shortly, recording her temperature. "Perfectly normal, now. 97.9." She walked back out quietly.

The bigger suit was just there to look scary. That was their job, so she looked to the small man that must have half a brain. He smiled at her, and sat down on the edge of the bed, a respectful distance away. Her face remained blank.

"Ann Smith" he began, "sorry, do you have a middle name?"

She glared at him silently as her fosters answered for her. "No, just plain Ann."

He nodded, making a note. "We're here to talk to you about the events that led to your hospitalization yesterday. I'm sure you understand that the more information you give us, the more we can help wrap this all up so it's over." *More likely the more info I give, the more you have on me and the more you can use to falsely accuse me.*

"I'm sorry…"

"Agent White."

Sure, whatever… "Agent White but I seem to be suffering from amnesia. I can't remember anything beyond boarding the bus that morning."

"That was at…nine a.m.?"

She nodded. Mrs. Miller, eager beaver that she was, placed a firm hand on Ann's shoulder. "I'm sure if you just give her a moment, that Dear Ann will remember. She's a good girl, aren't you?"

Ann eyed her blankly. Agent White cleared his throat loudly. "Mr. and Mrs. Miller, I'm sure that this hasn't been easy on you- "

"-It hasn't."

"-My poor baby!"

The agent tried again. "With all due respect, however, you were not the ones to go through the accident. Ann was. My questions are for her alone. You're welcome to remain, but for the sake of the investigation, Ann needs to be able to speak for herself."

Ann couldn't help it. Half a brain had managed to impress her. She felt a smile worming its way onto her face. She respected anyone that told her fosters where to go.

"Ann, could you describe the events as best you can for me?" His pad and pen were poised in his hand, waiting for her words.

She sighed, frustratedly, and started at the beginning....

Chapter 3
Day 3

Far away from the explosion, untouched by technology or the corporate capitalism that dominated West Coast American culture, a small lake lay pristine against a single mountain. The flora and fauna flourished far away from the effects of man. The birds sang sweetly around the lake, their offspring ever hungry. A deer stopped by the lake to drink its fresh clear water.

The peace was disturbed as a head emerged from the middle of the lake. The deer froze, the birds ceased their song. With a deep breath, the man rose from the depths and began to swim to the dock. The birds continued, used to him, and unperturbed.

He pulled himself out of the water and rubbed his body down with a towel, starting at his red hair, over his face set with turquoise eyes, and down his bullet scarred torso. When he was dry enough, he pulled on a rope and two trout were slung over his shoulder.

Whistling loudly, he walked to the only building on the property, a small, ancient cabin in the middle of the wilderness. This was family land. Three hundred years ago, this property was a large farm. Famine and drought dictated a change, so a lake was envisioned, as a campground getaway close to big cities. Now, it was his land, and no visitors would come, today or any other day. He liked the quiet, the solitude.

Placing the fish on the counter inside the cabin, he opened the fridge and scratched his head. Giving up, he grabbed a remote and flicked on the small TV, complete with rabbit ears for better reception. As he half listened, half whistled, he prepared breakfast.

"...News about the deadly crash that happened two days ago..."

Wishing he'd had something to cook the fish in, he made a short grocery list on an old receipt. Shoving it in his pocket, he took out all he had, salt and pepper.

"As I've stated, eye-witness statements from the victims may or may not be accurate..."

He began to gut and prepare the fish, his small frying pan already on the stove.

"Two teens have left the hospital. Of the three that should remain, one is missing, one is awake, and one is still comatose."

He tried lighting the stove but the pilot was out. Searching the drawers, he looked for a match.

"There are several questions being asked by investigators at this time. It is curious that none of the five suffered from serious burn injuries. Other peculiar facts include..."

Ah! Matches! He lit one, but it went out. The second didn't light. On the third try, he was successful.

"The last being the congruent accounts from three victims that the fire was black. Yes, you heard that correctly, the victims claim that the fire in the crash was black or greyish in color."

He froze, so still someone might think him a wax statue. He moved again when the match burnt his skin. Cursing, he rubbed his fingers together and increased the volume on the TV.

"Yes. That's correct. Black fire. I assumed they were referring to the smoke, as fire by its very nature of reflecting light cannot burn black. Trauma can indeed impair the mind's ability to remember details correctly."

He ran out the door, breakfast dripping off the counter, the TV blaring. At least he hadn't left the stove on.

◆ ◆ ◆

Day 4

Officer Ryan may not know who they worked for, but he recognized agents when they threw their authority around. One stood facing him right now, in fact, and he knew the speech and what the appropriate response would be. Honestly, he was kind of glad. He wanted to go home to his pregnant wife.

"Officer Ryan, let me first congratulate you for the thorough handling of this case. I'm authorized by the president to tell you that the investigation is now formally an issue of homeland security."

Ryan held up a hand. "Listen, I know where all this is going. You're in, I'm out. I'm not allowed to talk about it, blah blah." The agent looked momentarily uncomfortable. Ryan hid a smile. *Good.*

A card with a fake name was handed to him and he was free to leave. He knew better than to argue with him. He knew everything about the case. If he needed to, he could still look into it.

He couldn't help but overhear another agent taking a doctor to task. "Mrs. Wells."

"It's Wills- "

"First I'd like to congratulate you for your hard work and dedication…"

Sucks to be Wills. Ryan chuckled as he walked out to the parking garage. He made his way to his vehicle and unlocked it, stepping inside. He set his notebook down on the passenger seat. He glanced at a pair of eyes in the mirror before something struck him and his vision faded.

Ann couldn't help but be a bit excited. Today she would go home. A home with fosters, crowded rooms and no privacy, but that wasn't the reason for the excitement. She felt an urge to see the other survivors, to make sure they were okay. She couldn't wait to talk to Seth with her head clear, though the amnesia hadn't receded.

She finished changing into a pair of clothes given to her by the nurses here. Her fosters had, *surprise, surprise,* forgotten that she needed those to leave the hospital. Several of the nurses, upon hearing that, made some calls and she found herself with a brand-new outfit that actually hugged her curves instead of crushing them.

She placed her hospital gown on the bed, folding the sheets around it as she'd been instructed. Before she could leave, her breathless doctor came. "Ann! Good. Listen, before you go, I need one more blood sample."

"Mess up at the lab again? This is the third time."

She shook her head. "I'm so sorry. It really is important. Do you mind if I take one vial?"

Ann sighed. "Go for it." Personally, she felt the incompetent person should reimburse her for all the poking. Wills quickly drew the blood and left again, without a word. Ann tilted her head after the woman. *That was odd.*

Her fosters entered on cue. "Ready to go home, Ann?"

Your home, not mine. "Sure. Can I see Joy before I go? Make sure she's okay?"

They both sighed overdramatically. "Ann, we're quite busy. Besides, she isn't awake yet. You can see her when she goes back to school."

The rage came. It wasn't as if she'd asked for a trip to Mars. They could afford the five-minute detour. A few deep breaths and, without the shock of trauma, she could control it, as she'd been doing her whole life. "Fine. Let's go." She sauntered out without looking back, mimicking her fosters. They were so engaged in their conversation that they didn't catch on. As she walked down the stairs, she felt something pull at her, so much so that her eyes moved to the right of their own accord and locked eyes with the boy who'd tried to choke her. The fear crept in but she kept her face carefully blank. Blinking slowly, she focused on keeping her pace even and turning her head away from his stare. Strange, but she felt something else as well. Fear, but also a profound urge to help him, and he wouldn't appreciate that. Besides, she didn't owe him anything.

He could still smell the fire and death around her, even with the door closed. She was leaving, and that helped him relax immediately. He sat across from Agent White, arms folded, wondering how the agent could function through the smell of coffee and the stench of cigarettes. It was almost gagging him. *The new fragrance for men. Cigarette Coffee, by Agent White.*

"I was at the back of the bus with my best friend, Marcus."

"You were in such an advantageous position, seems odd that you couldn't help more. You clearly remember the event more accurately than the other survivors. Are you sure there's nothing you can tell me?"

He didn't trust this guy farther than he could throw him. "No. I was looking at Marcus when the bomb exploded." A little, necessary lie. He wasn't about to give away what he knew. He was no snitch.

"And what can you remember after the explosion."

"Apparently, I woke and choked the girl…"

"Ann. Yes, but you have no memory of that, yes?"

"No. I'd apologize but she just left. I was out of my mind. I don't raise my hand to women. My Madre taught me better than that."

"I believe you. The explosion, it was… inconsistent in some ways."

"I don't have any burns."

"Yes."

He shrugged his shoulders. "Your guess is as good as mine. I was at the back, maybe I went through the back window?"

"Then you'd have glass shards in your back. You don't have those either."

This guy can fish. Julius threw up his hands. "Dude, what do *you* think happened?"

Agent White gave him his best professional smile as he stated clearly and loudly, "I have no idea."

"Listen, Marcus's funeral is today. I'd like to leave to say goodbye. What can I say to get out of here?"

"Just the truth."

"I don't remember the truth."

"Why don't we…" he circled a couple of words on his pad. "Why don't we take it from the top, starting at that morning, once more. Then you can go say goodbye."

Julius sighed, complying, careful to use the same words as the first time. The Agent, far from satisfied, was still true to his word and allowed him to leave.

He walked out of the room, the sun not halfway through its journey, yet he was already exhausted. His parents waited patiently at the end of the hallway. He hugged his mother, seeing her for the first time since the accident. She smelled as she always did, of roses, earth and fertilizer, but the scent was stronger than normal today. Lines were beginning to show on her face, especially when she smiled. She gave him a big, wide one.

"I'm glad you're safe." She kissed his cheek. Then, a frown appeared. "I don't remember signing a permission slip for this trip, m'hijo."

Damn, he'd forgotten that. "At least I'm alive, mama?"

Her eyes narrowed, as she looked down at her flip flops. "We'll see if you still are when we get home."

His head down, he followed his parents out.

Dr. Wills crept into Joy's room. Producing a syringe, she drew her blood. She looked over her vitals one last time, observed even breathing. That was auspicious, though she was still asleep. She removed the syringe and spun to leave, concealing it in her arm. She missed the healing that instantly took place on Joy's skin.

She swirled, suddenly face to face with an agent in front of her. "Dr. Wills, you're no longer authorized to be in this room. I must ask you to leave."

"You don't want me to finish her charts for you? Fine." She started to leave when he grabbed her arm. She eyed him down, worried she'd been made.

"Please sign it before you go."

"What I was doing in the first place." She took the chart, wrote the final set of vitals down and signed. She handed it ceremonially to the agent. "Your chart, good sir."

"The sarcasm is not appreciated."

"Neither is your attitude. These kids need to heal, not to be probed for information."

He cleared his throat and motioned to the door. She was free to go. Rounding the corner, she took a few deep breaths in and out. She kept an even pace until she was in the resident's lounge. She opened the fridge to see random containers with sticky notes like, "Jordan, I know you're stealing my sandwich," and "Touch and Die!"

She didn't care about those. She looked at the back of the fridge for a label that said, "Liver and Onions." Smiling wide, she checked the room. Alone, she took the small cooler out and opened it. She labeled the vial, "#1." She placed it inside the cooler, closing the lid sharply.

She grabbed her belongings and walked out, container in hand. If they thought she'd just stop, they were crazy. The lab results were confusing to say the least. They'd been run multiple times with different results. Something was wrong with these teens, something big, that no one wanted to admit, and she'd be damned if anyone else found out before she did.

"Hey, Wills. Wait up!" She rolled her eyes and sighed. "What is it, Jones?"

"Wanna get a drink now that your shift is over?"

She continued walking forward to the parking garage elevator. "No."

"That's okay. You look tired. I'll walk you to your car. Want me to carry anything for you?" He reached a hand out to take her cooler, and she spun away from him, saying, "no, I got it."

He seemed taken aback. "Sorry?"

"I don't need an escort either. I'm not interested. You should go." Though he looked a bit hurt, she stared him down until he took the hint and walked away slowly.

She waited for him to leave before hitting the elevator button. She rode it solo and walked quickly to her car. Getting in, she set the cooler on the floor and started the engine. A gloved hand snaked around. She smelled something sweet before she was gone.

Connor and his older brother, Damien entered his apartment. The ride home had been silent and awkward. The door shut quietly and his brother, six years his senior, looked him in the eye.

"If mom were alive, she'd have a heart attack."

"I didn't cause the crash."

Damien grabbed the back of Connor's neck, but the anger quickly subsided, replaced with tears. "I know, but... they died in a car accident, then the call…"

Connor hugged his brother tightly, smacking his back. "I'm okay. They were looking out for me."

"Right, cause a deadbeat like you wouldn't just walk away, right?" His brother punched him in the shoulder, playfully. His brother opened the fridge, took out a beer. "Sorry, I know I said no alcohol in the house, but I need one right now."

Connor looked at him. "Shades of dad?"

"I'm not getting behind the wheel tonight; I just want one."

Connor nodded. "I get it. Can I have one?"

Damien stared him down. "No. It's late, go to bed. School tomorrow."

Connor walked to the smaller of two bedrooms. Laying down, he saw the faces of his parents, remembered the day they'd left the earth. Tears formed, but he didn't let one fall. His brother had stepped up after, was obsessed with his education. He worked hard, and after this, Connor could allow him a night to blow off steam.

Had his parents protected him today? Did he have a couple of guardian angels looking out for him? He was seriously considering the possibility, especially after the talk with that cop. How was he alive when so many lay dead? Survivor's guilt came and went, as he drifted off to sleep.

Damien checked on him some hours later, opening the door softly, closing it again. Underneath the bed a ruby necklace appeared from thin air.

Day 5

Ann woke, startled, the following morning. She didn't remember what she had dreamed of, just the intense terror it created in her. The memory of a voice softly echoed, "say nothing. Tell no one."

Well, duh. Like she'd just start blabbing about her personal business. Even if she did remember, which she still didn't, she wasn't giving it away to anyone that could use it against her. She was at heart a survivor, always had been. She'd survive this too.

The clock told her how early it was, so she shut off her alarm and walked into the bathroom. A nice, long shower would help her think, clear her head before her first day back. She locked the door for privacy, an action frowned upon by her fosters. *Like I care right now.*

She rotated the valves so the water began to flow. She brushed her teeth as it warmed, still contemplating the message. Finding no answers when she was finished, she cleaned the brush and removed her clothes, entering the shower.

She rotated the water to cool. It was already hot outside. The lukewarm water calmed her, as she envisioned herself underneath a waterfall, surrounded by serene, natural beauty.

The pounding door brought her instantly back. "Ann! Other people need to shower, too."

Ann knew how early it was. There was plenty of time for the other children. Mrs. Miller wasn't concerned about them, but she was terrified of the large water bill. "I just got in!"

"You've got five minutes before I find the key and drag you out."

What was she, five? Ann closed her eyes, trying to control the sudden, intense rage that filled her. All she wanted was peace and quiet for a few moments, and in this house, she could never seem to find that. The rage came back when Mrs. Miller knocked a final time.

"I meant it, Ann."

She sighed aloud and finished washing. Turning the stream off, she stepped out, surprised to see the room full of steam. She hadn't had the water that hot…

Mrs. Miller opened the door just as she wrapped the towel around her. "Get out!"

Ann eyed her but complied. At least she'd gotten a few minutes in. Walking to her bedroom, she did her best to rise above the angry woman who said, "no breakfast for you this morning."

You'd think pure gold was coming out of that faucet. Ann slammed her door and dressed for the day in the new outfit from the hospital. She'd taken it off when she arrived at home yesterday, as she wanted it to be clean for her first day back.

Admiring the clothing in the reflection of the window, she smiled softly. She almost looked pretty. *Almost.*

She walked down, noting the full plates of food that Mr. And Mrs. Miller were downing while she went hungry. *Great parenting.*

She gave them her back, preparing lunches for the three younger foster children that lived with them. Carefully, she put an extra snack in all their bags. Their miserly fosters would have to deal.

In a rare, seemingly caring moment, Mr. Miller stopped her as she was about to walk to her bus stop. "I'll drive you."

She glared at him. "Why?"

He glared back. "What, I can't be nice? You were just in a bus crash. You shouldn't have to ride one today."

She debated the truth until they reached the school grounds, where she received her answer. Reporters stood outside, snapping photos, huge cameras trained on them. *He wants the attention.*

The car came to a stop and he was instantly out the door, rounding the hood so he could open hers. *How chivalrous.* She rolled her eyes and stood. He placed a hand on her shoulder, too firm to be a tender gesture and walked her inside. As soon as she could, she left him to the cameras. She didn't want anything to do with them today.

Seth watched the whole charade from the dumpsters to the side of the school. He waited patiently until Ann joined him, smiling broadly a few moments later.

She hugged him tightly, a bit longer than normal. He hadn't been allowed to see either of the girls while at the hospital. He'd asked permission several times, and the security had always denied access.

"It's so good to see you again!"

"I know, right? How have you been?"

"I'm…alive."

She nodded, silently in agreement. She knew what he was thinking. People were supposed to be here that weren't. People that would never be here, anymore. The pain swelled in her chest again, a pain she wasn't entirely certain she could control.

"Look, it's okay to feel guilty." Seth softly touched her shoulder. "I feel it too, but I'm also happy I'm alive."

"I get it, it's just…hard."

He let her have some contemplative silent moments before he interrupted. "Listen, I hate to change the subject, but…how have you been feeling, physically?"

She tilted her head. "Huh?"

"Has anything…strange happened to you? Lately? Since the accident, I mean?"

She thought of the cold sauna. "No, nothing."

He was disappointed. He'd hoped she would trust him. "Really? Nothing?"

"Anything strange happen to you?"

He smiled widely. "Plenty, but the bell's about to ring. We'll talk later."

He swirled around and the bell did in fact, ring. He had perfect timing. *That's new.*

Ann struggled to pay attention, but it wasn't entirely her fault. Around her were constant whispers, stares and condolences. Even several angry glares from friends of the unfortunate. Her teachers were no better, with their fake remorse. Most of them had ignored her all year, yet now they wanted to bond? She didn't trust that.

She was grateful when Seth sat next to her in last period, though it was hard to see Marie's usual spot so…empty. She smiled at him as class began, the teacher continuing from yesterday as if something horrible hadn't occurred. Yet the tension in her body betrayed her true feelings. *Yeah, this is awkward.*

She began to doodle Marie's full name in her notebook, her own way of dealing with grief. She placed roses and flowers around it, using different colored pens. It calmed her. It wasn't until Seth dropped an old-fashioned note on top of the notebook that she looked up.

Why hadn't he just texted her? She leaned back, carefully unfolding the paper.

Ann,

In a few minutes someone will come to get me. Do not speak, do not give them any reason to take you, too. I'll be fine.

Seth

Well, that was…strange. She put the paper in her notebook and looked at her friend, but he just kept watching the clock. The teacher called on him to answer a question, and he was correct. She marveled at how fortuitous his life had been since the accident.

Five minutes later, two system suits walked into the room. The teacher stopped what she was doing, looking immediately at the two of them. The students stared as well, as if the day needed to be more socially uncomfortable for her. She kept her head down, doodling.

The agents silently walked through the room, standing directly behind the two of them. She kept her breathing even, but her rage was slowly growing. They were wasting time questioning them instead of finding out who the culprit was. The bad guy that killed her best friend was out there, not in here. An agent reached out with one hand to touch her. She sensed it, saw the edges of the paper beneath her start to smolder.

Then Seth stood, silèntly, eyeing them both. He took his backpack and walked out without another word. The agents followed him out, then shut the classroom door. Her teacher absurdly resumed the lesson, as if a student had not just been taken, possibly kidnapped. Her audible sigh of frustration went unacknowledged. *She owed him one.*

She assumed with Seth's luck that he'd be okay. She'd been playing the events through her mind since it happened. She wondered who, and why, and why them? Thinking of Joy still in the coma, alone, possibly scared when she woke, not understanding the situation… She wiped away a tear from her eye and glanced at the clock. Only five minutes left, then she was free.

Connor was waiting outside her classroom when the bell rang. She'd hugged Seth that morning, a natural reaction to a close friend. Connor, she didn't know, yet he squeezed her tightly as if they were old comrades. Worse, it didn't feel as strange as it should. She'd never so much as given this student a handshake, yet he felt somehow familiar.

"How are you feeling?"

"I'm okay. You?" It was polite, after all. She noticed several fan girls glaring, but she ignored them. Connor was their quarterback. Everyone knew he was going to St. Blaise University with a full ride.

"I'm…different, since the accident. Do you feel…different at all, too?"

She did. "Don't quite know what you mean."

He placed an arm around her shoulder and walked forward, whispering to her. "*I mean, has anything…strange happened to you?*"

She thought of the smoldering paper and the cold sauna. "Not really."

One of his teammates high fived him as he walked by. "Listen, I already heard they took Seth. Just…don't talk to anyone unless it's one of us. Something weird happens, you tell me or Seth. Okay?"

She wondered why he was so protective of her. Maybe he felt that strange familiarity too? "I can do that."

"Great." He smiled at her. "Meet me by the dumpsters in the morning. I have some things to tell you."

He walked away as she rounded the corner. How did he know about their spot? Stepping out into the May heat, she saw the buses had left. She also saw no car waiting for her. She sighed as she started the long walk home. Apparently, that courtesy had only been good for as long as the news coverage lasted.

This wasn't the first time she'd had to walk home by herself. She knew the streets well. She took her usual route, focused on the concerns she had around the trauma. She was so in her head that she missed the steady sound of footsteps following in pace with her.

Her phone began to ring seconds later. Seeing it was Seth, she hit answer, but the call was dropped. Confused, she put her phone away. He'd either hung up or the service was dropped, and she usually didn't have a problem with service in town. She began walking again, but this time, she was very aware that she was being followed.

Seth put the phone back in between his sock and his foot, just as the agent opened the door. He was more than lucky. His gut had been telling him things, leading him toward the right choices. He'd just had a sudden urge to call Ann, and knew if he hadn't, she might die. So, he did.

The agent sat down next to him; his arms folded neatly. An unopened file with a large stack of papers sat next to him. His gut told him not to worry, to be as laconic as possible.

"Mr. Seth Gorski, I'm Agent Brown. I was hoping you could recount the incident one more time for me."

"I already gave the police my full statement. Why did you need to see me again?"

The agent cleared his throat. "Mr. Gorski, the investigation has been moved to another department. We work directly with Homeland Security. They want a fine-toothed comb ran over this investigation. That involves information and eyewitness testimony. You're not a suspect at this time, we would just like to go through it once more, if you don't mind."

Seth wasn't an idiot. His gut was screaming that something was off about this investigation. Still, they were between him and the only exit, so sighing softly, he began again.

Meanwhile, Ann grew more nervous every minute. She deviated from her path, rounding as many corners as possible, trying to lose the tail. It was pointless, as the footfalls always found her again. She didn't have any way to defend herself, either.

Picking up her smartphone, she dialed, hoping she'd answer quickly. She wasn't disappointed.

"Where the hell are you? Why weren't you on the bus?"

"I missed it."

"So, where are you?"

"On my way home. I'm almost at the gas station."

"Oh." Pause. "Then why are you calling? The cell phone you have is prepaid and the family shares it."

"I just wondered if you wanted anything on my way." At least she knew where she was.

"Thank you, but no. I'd just prefer to have the money returned to me that you didn't spend."

Of course, she would. Ann rolled her eyes and said, "Fine. I'll be home shortly."

"I hope so. You have chores to do." Mrs. Miller hung up.

She placed the phone in her front pocket and walked into the small establishment. Using the mirrors, she kept track of the movements of her stalker, a large man wearing black with a ball cap covering his face. He stayed out of view, an aisle over. She grabbed a glass bottle of soda, thinking she could use it as a weapon, and walked to the counter to pay.

"Nice weather, huh?" The attendant smiled widely at her.

"I don't think it is." She was trying to let her know something was amiss, but the worker just rang her up.

"Anything else?"

She only had a couple of dollars. "No, just the soda." This guy was clueless and wouldn't be helpful to her.

The attendant read off the total and she paid, taking her sweet time, hoping the stalker would give up. Still, no luck. She frustratedly sighed and left, making a split decision. She walked a few steps, waiting until she had a straight shot home. Three blocks, three stoplights, and she would be safe. She took a deep breath and sprinted for it.

The footsteps sounded behind her. Fortuitously, the light changed to red as she approached the first street, and she crossed safely. His pace was quicker than hers. She could tell he would catch her if she stopped.

The next light didn't cooperate, and she ran through anyway, to the honking of several angry drivers. Still, she made it across. *One more and you'll be home.* Her lungs, still weak from the trauma, were aching as she stubbornly focused on each step forward. *Just keep going…*

Hands grabbed her around the waist and mouth so she couldn't scream. She was constricted, unable to struggle. He walked into the alleyway, and she tried to reach for the glass bottle. With a terrified sigh she realized that it was stuck, that she couldn't defend herself. She bit at the hand covering her mouth and flailed about, throwing her attacker off balance, but he recovered and tightened his grip.

But her nature was survival. Her life flashed before her eyes as she realized she may perish, here in an alley, seconds from home. Thinking about the unfairness of it all, she summoned her rage. It came, sudden and potent, and she let it wash over her. Like lava, the heat spread until it touched him, until he released her. She rounded on him, looking at her attempted kidnapper. He lunged at her with a knife.

Her rage guided her hand. It flowed from her fingertips easily. As she watched, red flames circled the man. She watched the whole event. Watched him fight the flame, his screams a distant, inconsequential annoyance. The smell of burning flesh was foreign to her, but still, her will persisted, until he stopped moving, until his body was nothing but carbon.

I'm safe now. With that thought, her rage vanished, the hypnotizing state gone. She stared at the man before her, at her hand in disbelief. Several long, eternal moments of silence passed before she started to shake, to panic. Realizing what she'd done, she looked away, the smell and sight too much for her. She puked into a dumpster nearby. When her stomach stopped heaving, she looked back. The knife still lay on the ground, curved and bloodied, but she couldn't bring herself to touch it.

Walking away, worried she'd go to jail for murder, she paced her steps home deliberately. She walked into the front door to the sound of complaining adults and children, unconcerned with her chore list. She walked straight into the bathroom and placed the shower on high, amid objections from her fosters. Apathy fogged her mind.

Getting in, fully clothed, she let the water wash over her as she tried to clear her opaque thoughts. She convinced herself that she'd hallucinated. She looked down at her hands, unsinged. If she'd burned him, she would have suffered as well. Her hands would be charred. No way she could barbecue someone. No one could create fire out of thin air. No one could burn someone to a crisp like that. She'd momentarily hallucinated, some strange coping mechanism from the real trauma, the bus crash. She had clearly concocted a false memory like she did with the black flame.

She turned the water, which had run cold, off. Stepping out of the bathroom, Mrs. Miller grabbed her good arm. "What did I tell you about taking long showers?" The parsimonious woman was red faced with anger. "No dinner, and I expect you to do double the chores before you go to bed."

Ann's rage was ready, as she thought about what she'd been through, her life worth so much more than the few dollars that shower would cost them. Mrs. Miller backed away suddenly.

"Ouch!" She glared at Ann, who just shrugged her shoulders. Feeling better, she walked into her room and shut the door. She placed a chair under the handle, despite the yelling fosters. Alone, safe, she changed into her pajamas, climbing into her bed. The covers wrapped tight, she switched on the TV. Her eyes went wide.

"I'm standing here at the corner of Michigan and Arizona Ave, where a gruesome scene lies behind me." She increased the volume, unable to change the channel. "Evidence points to some vigilante, a private citizen who took justice into their own hands. Behind me, are the remains of what police believe could be the notorious serial killer, Stabby Steve."

She shut the TV off, and rocked back and forth, her brain contemplating too much to hang on to any given thought. She'd…murdered…had to be a mistake. Had to be…crazy. No one could do this. She'd done it. She wasn't a murderer.

She stopped when it hit her. Her eyes welled with tears, over what she'd done. She'd killed Stabby Steve.

Chapter 4
Day 6

She walked into the school entrance, no cameras flashing today. They were preoccupied with another matter. She didn't even think the name out loud, for fear she'd give herself away. She was a freak, some odd creature that masqueraded as human for years. No one could ever know.

She was so busy concentrating that she missed the stares directed her way, cared nothing for the whispers of her classmates. She was inside her head so much that she missed the note that fell to the floor as she opened her locker.

A sympathetic voice penetrated her brain fog. She rotated, blinking, a familiar face in view. It took a couple seconds for recognition to occur.

"I'm sorry, Connor, what did you just say?"

"This fell out of your locker." There was a note in his hands. She took it, giving him a modest smile.

"You…weren't at the dumpster, so I came to find you. How are you feeling?"

She thought of the burning flesh of the man she'd taken out. "Fine. You?"

"Practice yesterday went great. It was like, I was flying across that field instead of running. My throwing arm was so accurate, I didn't miss one throw. I feel amazing."

Another football player walked by and high fived him. "Man, you were on fire yesterday!"

Ann froze for a moment before grabbing his arm. "You weren't really on fire, were you?"

He gave her a look. "No, it's just a figure of speech."

Of course, it was. "It was a joke."

"Oh." He laughed politely, though it was obvious that he didn't find it funny. "Listen, I know we weren't friends before the accident, but…things have changed."

He was right about that. "So?"

"So, I…" he fumbled for the words. "Look, it's like we're part of a support group, now. You know, the only survivors of something awful. I want to make sure you're okay, and if you're not, feel free to come see me. Where's your phone?"

She handed it to him while he typed in his number. Several onlookers began to whisper. When Ann looked at them, they glared back with acrimony. She rolled her eyes.

"There you go, just so you have it."

"Thanks."

"So, have you been okay?"

She was conflicted. Her experience told her not to trust him, but the comradery of the event pulled her to do so. "No, no I haven't, but…" she looked at the glaring girls. "I don't want to discuss it here." Tears came, inappropriate and uncalled for. She immediately embraced him to hide their fall.

"Whoa, Ann, it's okay." He rubbed her back and squeezed tightly. "You're okay."

She whispered, so only he could hear. *"Nothing has been okay since the bus."*

After a moment of silence, he whispered back. *"I know."*

He let her go and abruptly walked away. She contemplated his tone. It was as if he knew. He wasn't saying anything though, and this wasn't a safe place to talk. She shut her locker and headed to class. A commotion down the hall stalled her progress.

"I know you took it, and I know it's in your bag." Julius stood, his face inches away from another boy. "Give it back, now."

"I don't know what you're talking about, bruh."

While she watched, Julius shoved the boy, who fell to the ground, then wrestled his backpack from him. "Hey!"

Opening the bag, he found what belonged to him and shoved the bag back in the boy's face. "Don't take my stuff."

The boy ran off, and Julius looked down at his smartphone. He began to walk toward her, but there were so many people around that she couldn't move out of the way. When he bumped into her, his eyes locked onto hers.

He jumped back, frightened. She looked at him and said, "Watch where you're going, okay? You almost knocked me over."

Swallowing hard, his hands moved to block her. "Hey, I don't want any trouble. I just wanted my phone back. I'm just, on my way to class, same as you." He backed away slowly.

"Why are you so freaked? Do you remember me?"

He laughed, then leaned in close to her. "Yeah, *fenix,* I remember you. I remember everything. The cops, tried to get me to snitch, but I know better. They wouldn't believe me anyway. You don't have to worry, I kept my mouth shut."

She tilted her head, confused. "Okay, just chill."

He stared at her for a moment before he busted out laughing. "You? Telling me to chill? Hilarious." He walked away before she could ask him what he meant.

She sighed as the bell rang, walking to the office for a tardy slip. When she was safely in her assigned seat, lectured by the teacher about the importance of good timing, she opened the note.

I'm fine. I won't be back at school today.
Tell no one.

Seth

P.S. you may want to destroy this note, possibly with fire?

The panic rose inside her. Did he know? For the rest of the day, she fixated on it. She tried to destroy the note at lunchtime, but no matter how hard she concentrated, the flames didn't come. This only reinforced her belief that she was crazy.

The end of the day brought another moment of panic, as she glared at the bus in front of her. The trauma played over and over in her head, and her breathing came quickly. Still, she didn't want to hurt anyone else walking home. She forced her feet forward until she was through the door, then to the front, middle and back of the bus where she sat rigidly, attempting to control her breathing through the intense fear.

She looked out the window to take her mind off her emotions and saw Connor getting into a black sedan with system suits. First Seth, now Connor? The pull to help him was strong, but the bus began to move away. As the scene grew smaller with distance, she fixed her eyes on the black sedan, until it was completely out of sight. Alone with her thoughts, her only goal was to keep from having a panic attack. Were they coming for her next?

Wills felt something soft beneath her body, then the pain in her head. She had a massive headache. Slowly opening her eyes, she was surrounded by the dark. Laying on a bed, correction, cot, she slowly pushed herself up to a sitting position.

Her memory caught up, what transpired replaying in her mind. *I've been kidnapped!*

Who would want to? She was a doctor. She saved lives. Her eyes widened when she remembered the serial killer preying on women in her area. Foolish! She let a serial killer take her.

Placing her feet slowly on the floor, she felt the uneven grain of wood beneath her. Distributing her weight evenly, she slowly applied pressure, hoping the boards wouldn't squeak beneath her weight. They didn't.

She sprang into action, feeling around in the dark for a weapon until her eyes adjusted and she could see. Another cot with another victim lay across the room from her. The doctor in her wanted to assess them but her survival was more important. *You can't help anyone if you're dead.*

She scoured the room for a weapon. Finding a plastic flashlight, she shook her head. It was better than the pillows or the sheets. She walked to the other body and placed a hand beneath their nose. Breathing evenly. She saw the large chest, confused. This was a man. The serial killer had only targeted women. *Or only women had been found.*

His head had been bandaged, and he began to move. How would she get him out of here? She moved toward the small sliver of light near the ground, the way out. With the plastic flashlight in her hand, she slowly reached for the knob.

The door opened as she touched it, and she jumped back, screaming. A dark figure appeared, a shadow in the harsh light. The flashlight swished wildly forward and was swatted away. A moment later, the light in the room flickered, and her vision was gone again.

She braced for an attack that never came. She heard a moan from the other cot. He needed medical attention, so she needed to be brave. Determined, she glared at her attacker.

He was tall, built, with red hair and light eyes. She placed her hands on her hips and said, "I'm not afraid of you!" To her chagrin, her voice squeaked when she was trying to be fierce.

Tyrus stared at the doctor in front of him. He gave her a soft, sympathetic smile that didn't help his case. Instead, he checked on Ben Ryan, who was now awake.

"Sorry about this, Corporal Ryan. Cameras are everywhere these days, and you've got yourself mixed up in some real crap here." He held out a hand and Ryan shook it.

"Sergeant Keating? Tyrus! How you been?" They shook, one arm patting each other's backs.

"Better than you. Sorry about the head. It'll be fine. I bandaged you up."

"Could have just told me."

"I wish it were that simple." They both heard angry pounding on the front door. "Help! Someone please help me!" The doctor was trying to leave.

Ben stood up quickly. "What did you do?"

Tyrus shrugged. "Arrest me if you want. I needed the both of you and I needed it to be undocumented by media."

Ben nodded and walked to the doctor. "Ma'am? I'm Officer Ryan."

She looked at him with wild eyes. "I want this kidnapper arrested."

"You do?"

"YES! NOW!"

Ben shrugged at Tyrus, took his handcuffs and tossed them at him. "Put these on."

Tyrus did so, securing them tightly. Ben tilted his head and said, "is that what you wanted, Ma'am?"

She eyed them both. "You're working together." She began to move toward the kitchenette, probably to find a knife. It would be up to Ben to deescalate the situation before it became dangerous.

"Ma'am, I assure you, I am no kidnapper, and normally…" he gave Tyrus a look, "normally he isn't either."

"You're just saying that because I'm near the weapons."

"No, I'm not, Ms. Wills…" That's right. "You're the doctor from the hospital with the bus explosion. You treated Ann, Joy and Julius."

It took a few seconds for her to remember him. "Oh, *that* Officer Ryan." Her posture relaxed, and she stopped moving toward the knives. "What exactly is going on?"

"I don't know yet, but I'm sure Tyrus will explain. Care to sit?"

"No, I'll stand."

"Suit yourself." Ben went to the mini fridge, took out a beer and removed the top with his bare hand. "I'm sitting."

He plopped on the couch, Tyrus next to him. Wills eventually faced the two. Tyrus waited until he was sure he had their attention, let Ben finish his beer. "Sorry about the way this happened, but you both had so many tails and bugs that this was…the only way for us to talk without being caught."

"Caught doing what?"

He sighed. "We have a huge…problem."

"You mean other than the assault and abduction charges you're facing?" Wills eyed him coldly.

"More like a mix of sabotage, guerilla warfare and possibly good, old-fashioned thirst for power. I'm sorry you're involved, but there's some things you should know before you make the call to turn me in."

"Does this have to do with the strange medical results from the survivors of that bomb?"

Ben interceded. "What strange results?"

Tyrus held up a hand. "We don't have much time. If we want to save these kids, we have to act quickly."

"Save them? From what?"

He sighed and shook his head. "From…" He looked as if he was searching for a word. "…from a terrible fate."

Ann couldn't remember the last time she'd eaten dinner. She seemed to be surviving on school lunches and adrenaline. Pacing in her room, she convinced herself that the agents were on their way. They'd be there any minute now, to take her like they'd taken the others. She couldn't calm down. She couldn't sleep. Though she felt especially ravenous, she couldn't eat.

She jumped when her phone went off, a sound too shrill and disturbing in the silence. Crossing to it, she felt her muscles relax as she saw "Seth" on her screen. She picked it up, answering.

"Where the hell are you? Are you okay? What did they want?" It all came out rather quickly.

"Well, hello to you too, friend."

She grew irate. "I've been worried sick about the two of you."

"I know. That's why I'm calling, to tell you I'm ok and to eat something. Then get some rest. You'll need it."

"What are you talking about?"

"There's some ice cream hidden in the laundry room in the extra freezer. Chocolate, your favorite. Down that and try to sleep. We can't talk on the phone. We'll talk at the dumpsters in the morning. Oh, bring snacks." He hung up on her. She felt like she was going to scream. She grabbed a pillow, releasing her frustration. When she lifted her head, the pillow was on fire.

◆ ◆ ◆

Day 7

She stepped off the bus and rounded the school to their spot. Finding it empty, she wondered if this was some sort of ruse, until she saw a star-shaped note between the two dumpsters. She unfolded it quickly.

Come to Joy's. Don't go to school.

Seth

She sighed as she walked away, fast enough to look like she didn't care, but slow enough not to draw suspicion. Skipping school was the least of her worries. As she walked, she thought about the burning pillow the night before. She'd kept the house safe by tossing it out the window. It was ashes seconds later, falling silently to the grass below. She also wanted to know how he knew about the ice cream. It had been delicious, especially knowing that she was taking something back from her fosters.

They'd want to talk about "it". That was the last activity she wanted to engage in, but nonetheless, it would happen, so she went over what she would say and what she would conceal. Joy's house wasn't far away, and she reached it before she'd ironed out her speech. Her parents' car was gone. *Good.* She wouldn't be using the front door anyway.

Joy's room was a converted attic, large enough to hold all her artwork. The house had a large back porch complete with roofing; a tree placed conveniently close. She looked it over, the marks from their childhood showing, the bark worn away from their weight. *Same routine as always.*

She climbed the tree, walked across the roof of the porch and climbed up a rope ladder to an open window in the attic. They'd spend many hours inside Joy's room, with Marie. That saddened her, enough that she paused a moment to focus on the good memories. They wrapped themselves as a cocoon around her aching heart.

Feeling stable, she continued up, until she'd reached the window. Without warning, the boys grabbed her under her arms and lifted her through, placing her safely inside the room. "Thanks?"

Connor sat on a bean bag chair, she took the bed and Seth sat in a desk chair. For a moment, no one spoke as she looked around the room, imprints of her BFF everywhere. Joy's talent was exceptional. Ann had always been envious of her ability to draw, something she couldn't do. Who knows, maybe if she'd been raised in a loving home with two parents, she'd have more skills like Joy.

Smiling at the boys, she shrugged her shoulders, as if to say, "What now?"

They shared a look before Seth began. "We wanted to meet to talk about…well, the accident and the effects of it."

Connor nodded in agreement. "Something has changed in each of us."

Ann laughed. She couldn't help it. "Yeah. Seth gets to read fortunes; you get to go pro and me? I'm literally on fire half the time."

A noise outside the window tensed her body. "What was that?"

Julius locked eyes with her and froze for a moment. When she moved, he jumped, and began to climb back down.

"Julius, wait!" Connor ran to the window.

"You said we were safe, man!"

"Come on, we're all in this together. We need to figure this out and we need you to do it."

"I'll stay if you keep fire death girl away from me."

Ann moved away from the window. Seth gave her the chair, standing instead. Julius took the bed.

"Now that most of us are here," Connor began, "we need to talk, compare notes on our lives since the accident. All of us have changed, and I'm not talking emotionally."

"I agree," Seth kept his arms folded. "Something strange happened to us that day. No one knows what it is, and we came here to try to figure it out, before…" He paused for a moment. "Before we hurt someone, or someone hurts us."

She chuckled, dryly. "Too late."

Julius stood quickly. "*Fenix,* you come at me, and I swear- "

"Slow down Julius." Connor stood. "She isn't going to hurt any of us. I'm not even sure she can."

That calmed him and he sat.

Seth continued. "All of us have been through some exceptionally twisted situations. What I want us to do is to compare those experiences, so we get that it's happening to all of us. Maybe, between the four of us, we can figure out what changed us a week ago."

He handed out pens and paper. "Why not just use our phones?"

Seth looked at her. "I hate to sound like a conspiracy theorist, but we're being watched, and phones are tech that's hackable. Pen and paper, not so much."

Ann stared at her piece of blank paper. They exchanged glances for a moment, before they collectively began to write. She focused on herself and wrote down what she could.

Extreme fevers.
Bad Dreams talking to Joy and Marie
Cold sauna shower
Burned a pillow w/ no match
Fire everywhere, especially when I'm angry

She paused before she bravely wrote the last one.

Barbequing Stabby Steve, who so deserved it anyway.

She sighed, relief at getting her secret out. The chips would fall where they willed. She watched as the others finished, as Seth stepped up, taking their papers and shuffling. Then he handed out the lists, no one receiving their own. "This way, we don't have to read our own. When you're ready, go ahead and read it out loud."

She glanced at her list, trying to place the symptoms with one of the boys in the room. It was odd.

Better eyesight
I feel like I have wings when I run.
My accuracy at throwing is perfect.
I have a strong urge to protect everyone.
I dream of Joy telling me strange things, even though I haven't met her.

She knew she had Connor's after the second sentence. Ann looked over at him, but he was looking to Julius, who looked at Seth. That meant…

Her gaze fell to her friend. His eyes were wet, his face apologetic. *Yep, he has mine.*

Clearing his throat, Julius spoke first. "Okay, this one says, my gut is never wrong, I feel something about to happen, then it does. I know the exact time without checking a clock. I'm lucky. I won three classroom contests this week. Keep dreaming about meadows."

Seth walked forward. "That's me. I know it doesn't sound like much, but it's already saved my life. A car almost hit me yesterday, but it blew a tire with enough force to avoid me. I didn't get a single scratch. I'm *very* lucky."

"But we're all lucky," Connor said. We survived." Silence fell as everyone thought of the awful loss of life.

Connor went next. "This one says, I have an overactive sense of smell. I can sense emotions people try to hide, as long as they're strong enough. I dream of running with a pack of others like me, sometimes in places that are dark, some so bright I can't see well."

"That's me. Lately, I think I might be part wolf, you know, figuratively."

Ann went next, reading the list in front of her.

"That's mine." Connor rubbed his neck. "I have improved so much the coach checked me for steroid use. I was always good, but now, I'm…unstoppable. And look." He pulled out the ruby necklace. "I have no clue who this belongs to, but I found it while I was cleaning my room. I don't remember taking it, and I'm afraid what will happen when my brother finds out."

Seth checked it out. "Looks genuine. Worth a bit of money." He tossed it toward Ann. "Hang on to it." He smiled at her, almost as if he were waiting for permission to read hers.

The three of them looked at her. "It's okay, Seth. Read mine." She sounded courageous, but her panic was quickly pressing down on her chest.

He read all but the last. He paused for a long moment, as if he were debating the consequences. "Barbequing Stabby Steve, who so deserved it anyway."

Julius reacted first, breathing heavily. "Stay. Away. From. Me."

Ann faced him. "I didn't mean to do it. I don't want to harm anybody. It happened to me, but I still can't…understand what I did. I'm…" her voice broke. "So scared that I'll hurt someone innocent."

Seth knelt in front of her. "Ann? Do you not remember the fire? Really?"

She shook her head. "I do." Julius began. "It came from your friend's seat."

That shocked her, but her memory chose that moment to come back, and her eyes closed.

She sat in the middle of the bus, on the left side, next to Marie. They laughed and talked about a planned sleepover for that night. Marie got a call on her cell. Before she could answer, Ann took it, playfully, ready to give some smart greeting to the caller. She knew them. She tapped the green button to answer the call and…

She opened her eyes to the waiting boys. She was at the origin of the blast. Had she not answered, Marie would still be alive. Connor offered her a tissue. She used it out of habit, but she didn't really care. Numbness crept over her, along with apathy.

After a moment she whispered, *"I'm the reason they died."*

Chapter 5

Wills finished washing the black dye out of her hair in the tiny sink. She stared at her face in the mirror. Her skin looked too pale now, the contrast too striking. She looked like a vampire. She'd have to make sure she got more sun to make this look work.

Brushing her hair with the only thing she could find, a comb, she strode out of the bathroom to a bustle of activity. Tyrus was packing, Ryan was talking to his wife. She laughed as she heard him tiptoe around his location. She supposed if she were on the other end, she'd be upset as well.

"No, Ellie, I have more to do on this case." He paced back and forth. "It came up suddenly, listen, do you trust me or not?"

She must have hung up because he looked at his phone in disbelief. Sighing, he sat down, rubbing the bridge of his nose. Tyrus came back from the storage room with more supplies, shoving them unceremoniously into black duffel bags.

"Give her time, Ben."

"Yeah, you need any help?"

"No, this is it."

They both looked at her. She finished combing her hair. "When do we leave?"

"Now." He handed her a duffel bag. "The sooner we get there, the sooner we can figure this out, help these teenagers."

"I'm still not sure I understand all of this."

"It will sink in eventually." He opened the front door holding three bags. Ben walked ahead of her with two. She carried one. As she passed him, he elaborated. "Then you might wish you weren't on shift to save them."

Ann stood in the shadows at their local bus stop, waiting for Seth to purchase the tickets. It was almost time to board. She had a panic attack thinking about another bombing, but she recovered as he approached her. She was still processing that they were here, leaving, dealing with the events that had gone down.

"I'm the reason they're dead." She broke down crying. Julius stood, pacing back and forth in the large attic bedroom.

"I knew it," he said, shaking his head. "It was you, huh? I smell the flames and death all over you. I'm gone."

He turned to exit, but Connor blocked his path. "We're not leaving Ann to deal with this alone. We're in this together. That means you stay too."

Julius let out a strange growl. Connor folded his arms in front of him. Seth began to whistle, a tune that somehow washed calm over them. The growl stopped and he sat on the bed, eyeing Ann.

"She needs to tell us what she remembers."

Seth took her hands in his and said, "can you do that?"

The song had cleared her mind. "Yes. Sorry, I didn't mean…" Sighing, she organized her thoughts. "Someone called on Marie's phone. The explosives must have been in her backpack. If I hadn't stolen it and answered, then she'd still be alive. They all would."

Julius was the only one brave enough to ask, "so it was Marie?"

She glared at him. Fear entered his eyes, so she calmed herself. "No, Marie was a sweetheart. It was wired to explode when her smartphone was answered. The person on the other end of the call was responsible."

"Who was it?"

Protecting someone, Ann said, "I don't remember. That's blank, still."

"Question," Connor began, "I was right in front of Marie and Ann. Seth was to the side. We all survived, though we were at the epicenter of the explosion."

"That's odd." Seth softly implied.

"Only person who should be alive is Julius, who was at the back of the bus."

"Yeah, but Marcus, right next to me, he died too."

"This doesn't add up."

"That's what that cop said." Connor's eyes grew wide. "The cop knew. The one that saved us."

"He seemed just as confused."

"Yeah, but what if he figured something out between then and now?"

"Seemed like a decent guy. If he knew what was wrong with us, he'd probably tell us."

"Assuming he doesn't come to the conclusion that we were responsible."

No one could provide an answer. They sat there for several silent minutes, so wrapped up in their own thoughts that the slamming of a car door below caused them to jump in concert. Seth stood, checking the window.

He held a finger to his mouth, implying they should remain silent. A few seconds later, they heard the chirping of a smartphone.

"Hello?" It was Joy's father. "Yeah. We can…come back."

"Who was that?"

"Hospital. They think Joy's about to wake soon. They'd like us to come back."

"My baby!" Joy's mother slammed her door, and a couple seconds later, another slam. Then the car pulled out of the driveway.

"You knew that was going to happen?" Julius asked Seth, who nodded. "Man, give me some lotto numbers then."

Seth laughed, but they grew somber quickly. "We need a plan."

The others nodded while Ann spoke. "Seth, you're the lucky one. You tell us what happens next."

She jumped at Seth's gentle touch of her shoulder. He held tickets in his hand. "Ready to go?"

She nodded. "Are you?"

He looked his friend straight in the eye and said, "No. Let's board." They left the shadows, Seth grabbing the bags. Ann pulled her cap lower over her face. The call had already gone out. They were runaways. They sat at the back, their bags beneath them. Ann relaxed into the seat as Seth put an arm around her. Her mind wandered backward.

"We find out why."

"How are we going to accomplish that? We already said the police don't even know."

"We find out why we're still alive first."

"The hospital…had to take multiple blood samples, something about the lab messing up. Three times. Maybe the records are still there? Maybe someone can tell us what happened." Ann looked at Seth. "I say we go there."

Julius voiced his concern. "This is loco. How will we get there? Our parents will put out a call the instant we don't get home from school. I only boarded that bus to get out of a math test. I'm leaving."

Connor blocked him again. "I can't let you. Like I said, we're a unit now, and we stick together."

The jostling bus began to move. Ann surveyed its passengers, worrying for a moment. Seth massaged her shoulder and smiled.

"You guys having a hard time being on a bus, too?"

She looked behind her and saw Connor's deep eyes, a little too wide. She nodded, hoping the bus wouldn't blow.

Julius stared Connor down. "So, that's it, I'm out voted so I need to go with you?"

"Something like that."

"We need you, Julius." Seth locked eyes with him. "Your abilities, they're powerful. If you don't go, we may not make it through this."

"Whoa, whoa." Julius paused. "You're saying if I don't go, you all die?"

Seth shrugged. "It's a possibility."

"And how do I know you're not lying?"

Seth took a moment, thinking to himself. "You don't."

Julius sighed, heavily, pacing back and forth. He took several strides to think it through before he stopped. "Fine, but I'm only coming because I don't want someone else's death on my conscience."

"How are we getting to the city? Anyone have a car?"

They all shook their heads. Connor gave an answer. "The bus?"

"We really want to board another bus so soon?"

"I get it, it's just…less security than the train. Not like we can fly there. Unless someone knows how to hotwire a car."

Ann decided. "We take the bus. We'll figure it out. Hey, we made it through one crash. Maybe we aren't cursed, maybe we're chosen."

Yeah, "Julius argued, "but you need money for the bus. I don't have any."

"Me either."

Seth cleared his throat and took out a wad of twenties from his pocket. Passing out some to each person, he explained. "I put a twenty in there this morning. It keeps…reproducing in my pockets."

"I've got this." Connor held out the ruby necklace. "I could pawn it."

"No, you should let Ann hang on to that for you." Seth didn't add to his cryptic request.

Connor held it out to her. "Want a necklace?"

"Sure." She took it, placing it around her neck. "Shiny!" She smiled at Connor, who looked awkward. "Thanks."

"No problem."

"Connor and Julius, you need to leave to get to your houses. I'll go with Ann. We board the ten pm bus to St. Blaise."

"Why ten pm?"

"Switching shifts. Go. Now."

"See ya." The two left quickly. Ann tilted her head. "Seth?"

"Yes?"

"Why am I wearing this?"

"Because one day, not today, it'll save your life."

"Oh." She looked down, getting lost in the jewel. As she watched its center, she thought she saw a spark, a flame in the crystal facets, but that was impossible.

Ann woke after a short nap. They were about halfway through their journey to the city. Seth was gone. She swiveled her head around, until Julius sat down next to her.

"Your boy's in the bathroom."

"He's not my boy."

"What's with all the touching then? Him and Connor?"

She shrugged. That was a good question. "It's platonic."

"Well, then," he placed his arm around her shoulder, taking it away a few seconds later. "Nope. Can't do it, Fenix."

She laughed, making him smile. "Listen, sorry about assuming it was you."

"Your sense of smell was helping you survive. Nothing to apologize for. Besides, I keep thinking if I hadn't answered that call…"

He took her hand as tears formed, refusing to fall. "But you didn't know, you know?"

She looked out the window, squeezing his gently. "I know."

Seth's house was close to Joy's, so it was relatively easy to enter. He had the key, and both his parents worked the day shift, so they were able to stay there for the rest of the afternoon, playing games and acting as if things were normal. Five thirty rolled around and he said, "We need to go now."

They grabbed his backpack full of clothes and snacks, leaving quickly. They meandered through the city streets until six pm, when they arrived at her foster's house.

She took a deep breath. "You're welcome to take the lead."

He did just that. "Follow me, exactly so we don't get caught."

"We'll have to avoid the other kids. They're snitches."

"I know. Don't go in the front." He motioned to the back door. "They're in the kitchen stealing snacks."

They walked around to the back entrance, which opened into a washroom. They crept inside, careful to tiptoe. From here, a hallway led to the kitchen and stairs, while another led to the rest of the floor.

Seth shoved her against the wall suddenly, as a foster came inside the room, tossed their clothes into the washer and left, his back to them the entire time. She breathed silently with relief.

Ann became bewildered as Seth chose the hallway to the living room. It was quicker through the kitchen, but she followed behind him. They ducked behind the couch as two fosters began to play, then argue near the TV. A few seconds later, they moved back to the kitchen and up the stairs. The back door suddenly slammed, and the children raced into the washroom to greet the Millers, coming home.

They hustled into the kitchen and up the stairs, shutting the door to her room. "Hurry."

She nodded, grabbing clothes that fit and shoving them into her bag. A toothbrush followed, because hygiene, then a small silver bracelet, the only possession she'd received from her birth parents. She turned to the window, ready to climb down, but Seth stopped her.

"No." He grabbed her arm firmly. "Not one more step. Fate shifted somehow. We have to do this the hard way, Ann."

Steps on the stairs, then shouting fosters entered the room. Mrs. Miller stood with her hands on her hips, her face red with anger.

"I was going to ask you about skipping school, but it seems that's the least of our problems. After everything we've done for you, the roof over your head, paying your medical bills, you decide to slut yourself out with some boy, in our house? I don't think so."

"What's in the bag, son?" Mr. Miller tried to take it from Seth, who tossed it out the window. Mr. Miller swung, but Seth's gut knew where it would land. He avoided the force with grace, running out the door and down the stairs. The Millers and Ann followed behind. Seth ran out the front door. Ann ran to the back, Mrs. Miller on her heels. "Just where do you think you're going, you little brat?"

She grabbed Ann by the hair and pulled. The pain triggered rage, suddenly, so much that she couldn't control it, nor did she want to. She rounded on the older woman and let the flame dance from her hand to her assailant. Mrs. Miller, who wore a lot of hairspray, was quickly aflame, her pretty curly perm burning. Ann used that moment to leave. Seth found her and they ran away.

In the distance, she heard Mr. Miller shout, "Don't you ever come back here, you ungrateful slut."

Seth came back from the restroom, tapping Julius's shoulder. The other boy moved and Seth took his place. Ann placed her head on his shoulder. "Seth?"

"Yeah?"

"Why the hell didn't we just go out the window?"

He put his arm around her. "Had we done that, you would have tripped, fallen and broken your neck. You'd be dead. Besides, how funny was it to light that woman's hair on fire? Especially considering her colorful, completely false language."

She chuckled, but the harsh words couldn't help but penetrate her soul. *They just don't know me.* Maybe she'd believe it if she repeated it to herself, a lot.

Joy, blissful and jubilant, locked hands with Marie. The two of them spun until they were so dizzy, then fell to the ground. Laughing, Marie lifted her body to talk to Joy.

"It's been great having you here."

"I've enjoyed it. It's so…peaceful. Now, anyway." Her eyes veered off in the direction of something dark. Eventually, it wouldn't be so sunny.

"You realize it's time to go back."

Joy frowned. "Yeah, I know."

"You can come visit again, I'm sure, but Ann needs you."

"Right. Fate of the world and such."

"It's important, Joy."

"I know. I know." She sighed. "It's just…a lot."

"We both know it only gets worse the longer you stay."

Joy nodded gravely. She'd seen the alternate timelines. "How will I know what to tell them, and what not to?"

"Trust me, you'll just know."

"What will you do?"

She looked toward the small city below. "I'll prepare from this side. You have to go, now, before they find you."

Joy sighed again, glaring at the storm. "Fine." She stood, brushing off her dress. "See ya!"

Joy woke to the beeping of machines. Stretching, she gave herself only a moment to remember what it was like to have a body. It felt so… slow, restrictive. Then she stood. She looked down at her hospital gown, frowning. This wouldn't do. Closing her eyes, she saw the clothes that she wanted to wear. A warm glow surrounded her as her hospital gown changed.

When she opened her eyes, she was dressed in color, purple, pink and blue. Nodding, she skipped merrily out into the hallway. She slid and skipped her way to the elevator, contemplating a moment. No, she didn't take the elevator now, she took the stairs.

Ooh! Stairs have railings!

Whistling a jaunty tune she wrote herself, she opened the door to the stairwell and began to descend, letting out a "yippee!" as she slid down the railing. As the door shut softly, the elevator opened, revealing nurses, her parents and several agents, headed to her room.

They reached the edge of the city by nightfall, booking rooms at a small, rundown motel. Tyrus handed them keys after checking in.

"We'll meet at 600 hours."

"6 am?"

He smiled at Wills. "Yeah. Military time."

"No, I get it, once a marine, always a marine."

Ryan carried the bags out of the car. "Where should I set all this?"

"Uh, my room. Here." Tyrus helped his friend situate everything neatly inside the middle room. Wills came in and sat on the bed.

"I'm hungry."

"I can order a pizza."

"Yeah, it'd be great. We didn't eat before we left."

"I'm starving too." Ryan sat across from her. "You mind, Tyrus?"

He chuckled, "No, I suppose since I brought you in, the least I can do is get you a pizza." He opened his smartphone and began to dial.

Ryan locked eyes with Wills. "Those agents…"

"The ones that took over the investigation?"

"Yeah. They seem…strange to you?"

"Agents taking patients is strange. What exactly do you mean?"

"You become a cop; you deal with other law enforcement. They…have a distinctive walk, FBI. These guys seemed to…loose with their stride."

"Then who were they?"

"I'm not sure. I'm just not convinced that they worked for the department they said they worked for. I'm wondering about the pieces that don't fit. Wondering if they're connected."

"Who would pretend to be government unless they had to?"

He shrugged. "List is long. Foreign nationals, spies, someone cleaning up the mess they made. Private security. Could be anyone involved in the bombing."

"That makes this investigation much more…hazardous." She shivered, thinking about a company that would have the gall to destroy a bus full of young adults.

"Exactly."

Ann and her companions grew more anxious the closer they came to downtown St. Blaise. By the time they arrived at the bus stop, she was fighting another panic attack. She felt the jilt of the stopping vehicle, then the door opening, and just as she was about to sigh with relief, Seth said, "duck!"

They did so, a round glow of light coming from the outside window. Someone was on the lookout for runaways, possibly the four of them. A police officer came onto the bus with his phone opened, thumbing through pictures, matching them to people as they were let off.

A few rows from their seats, the policeman's radio sounded. "I think I've got them. Inside." He exited quickly, and the four of them grabbed their bags and bolted. Following Seth, they walked down the alleyway, ignoring the station. They walked right and waited in the next alley for a police car to pass by.

Ann was impressed. "Was all of that you?"

He just shrugged. Satisfied, he looked at his friends and said, "From this point, we'll have to run for a while. Are we all ready?"

Ann frowned at him but nodded. Julius jumped up and down. "Let's do this. I'm ready after that bus ride."

"Keep pace with me, stay behind, and follow, got it?" Seth seemed to count in his head, then he ran out of the alley. Julius, Ann then Connor followed, through the dark streets toward the old heart of the city.

The pizza came and went, the three adjourning to their respective rooms. Tyrus took a long, hot shower and dressed for bed. He hit the lights, falling face first exhausted onto the soft mattress. For a few hours he tossed and turned, trying to sleep, until a knock on his door at one a.m. caused him to rise quickly.

Grabbing his firearm, he looked through the peephole and saw a blonde…girl.

She stood with her hands on her hips and smiled. Confused, he opened the door a crack. "Can I help you, miss?"

Her smile became a frown. "Yeah, you can. You can tell me why you stopped here instead of going where you were supposed to go."

He tilted his head. "Huh?"

"You stopped at the wrong hotel, Tyrus."

He rubbed his eyes. "Have we met before?"

She looked at him like *he* was the crazy one. "No."

He sighed. "Then how do you-"

"Fate, Tyrus." She placed her hands on her hips. "Are you going to remember your manners and invite me inside or not?"

Something within him wanted to trust the crazy girl in front of him. He unlocked the door, let her inside, but kept it open. She grabbed an extra piece of pizza and began to eat. "I tell you what, being in a coma makes you hungry."

"You were in a coma?"

"Duh!" She rolled her eyes at him as she devoured all of the remaining slices while he watched confused. "So," she continued, rolling over onto her stomach and crossing her ankles in the air. She placed her hands under her chin and smiled. "What's the plan?"

"What plan?"

She looked at him, suddenly serious. "The plan to help me and my friends."

Day 8

They ran until their lungs ached, stopping only when needed. They ran until their muscles refused to cooperate. St. Blaise was a large city, and they hadn't made their destination by the time the sun was beginning its journey over the horizon.

Ann stopped, exhausted. "We…" *breath*, "need," *breath*, "to stop."

"We haven't made the hospital yet." Julius felt fine.

"We aren't making the hospital. Not today." Seth pointed toward a neon sign across the street. "We're staying there for four days."

"Why so long?" Connor placed his hands behind his neck.

"Trust me. I'll be back."

Seth walked toward the entrance as the others struggled to regulate their breathing. They were too tired to make small talk, so they dealt with the awkward silence.

When Seth returned, he said, "Two rooms. Ann gets her own." He handed her a key. "Let's get to the rooms, rest, recuperate. Take naps."

"I…prefer to snuggle with girls…" Julius looked uncomfortable for a moment then winked at Ann, who rolled her eyes.

Seth laughed. "I already got a cot. We'll switch who has to sleep on it."

They walked to the hotel, crossing the street together. Connor made sure to stand between her and traffic. When they reached their rooms, they walked in unceremoniously and shut their doors.

Ann, alone for the first time in days, sighed, and headed straight for the shower. She was gross from the run, and she needed to fix that. Had she known how much running she'd have to do, she'd have tried harder in P.E.

Stepping into the stream, awkwardly trying to avoid getting her cast wet, she felt frustration well up within her. She wished she could just remove it already. It was itchy, too. Reaching down, she tried to scratch, but couldn't get in far enough. The rage came on suddenly. As she watched, her cast burned slowly from the tips of her fingers to the top of her arm. She watched the ashes float down the drain.

"Huh." She moved her arm, noting it was completely healed, save a scar where the bus shard had been. "That's new."

She finished and walked out, wearing a towel, searching for pajamas. As soon as they were covering her, a knock sounded at the door. She answered, seeing Seth with a full ice bucket. "Trade me." She obliged, handing him her empty bucket. Grabbing the cold one quickly, she chomped on the pieces of ice. She was thirsty, and hungry.

Another knock sounded, and Seth was again at her door. With snacks. "Have I told you how much I love you?" She smiled from ear to ear.

He chuckled. "Just eat and get some rest."

She grabbed all the snacks and shut the door. Too overwhelmed by the change in her life, she decided to process her emotions later, when she had brainpower left. Powering on the TV, she switched channels until she came upon a cartoon they commonly watched as children. She finished the snacks in record time and slowly drifted off.

Chapter 6

I'm fired. "Agent White" approached the Director's office, sweating underneath his suit. *So fired.* He'd tell him what happened, how he'd lost the kids, in a small town of all places, and then the Director would fire him. He didn't know what he was going to say, but if he had any shot at a reference, he needed to tell the truth. The Director had a way of knowing when someone was lying.

He felt his heart pump so hard he thought his chest would explode. The sweat dripped down his back as he waited in the chair, patiently, professionally. He still had his pride, for the time being.

He'd introduced himself to the Director's colorful personal assistant and was waiting his fate. After a buzz and a quick, "send him in," the assistant sympathetically gestured to the double doors.

"You may go see him, now."

He walked slowly forward, opening the doors to see the Director of the Project for the first and last time.

Day 9

It was Seth's turn to take out the trash. Ann would do so tomorrow. He knocked and she answered with her trash in hand. "Thanks." She shut the door again softly.

They'd have to find a grocery store or a good restaurant soon. Eating junk was fun, but it was making them lethargic and sluggish. He walked around the hotel to the dumpster, placing the trash bags inside it. As he did so, a black SUV pulled up to the hotel. Dressed suspiciously in clothing designed to escape notice, a red headed man exited the vehicle, walking to the front desk. Seth walked around the back of the motel, the longer but secluded way. He didn't know who they were, but his gut, famous for keeping him alive, was suddenly silent, and he didn't like that at all.

◆ ◆ ◆

"Stay here. Keep your heads low and forward." Tyrus stepped out of the driver's side and walked to the front office, smiling at the attendant.

He was grateful Joy had finally found a place worth staying at, though he was perplexed by her choice. They'd passed numerous, more acceptable options before she excitedly steered them here. Third hotel he'd have to rent. Good thing they all took credit. Good thing he had forged credit cards under an alias. It wouldn't be impossible to track his movements, but someone would have to want to work for it, very badly.

The attendant opened the small hole in the window. "Yeah?"

"Got a couple of rooms for the night?"

The attendant eyed him. "The whole night?"

Tyrus narrowed his eyes at him. Joy chose that inopportune moment to not listen.

"We'd like rooms 20 and 21. And we're staying for three nights."

He gave her a look, but she eyed the playground equipment nearby. "Ooh! Swings!" She skipped away before he could reprimand her.

The attendant gave him a look. He let anger fill his eyes. "It's my niece, okay?"

The attendant relented. "Cash or credit, sir?"

Tyrus hated being called, 'sir.' "Credit." He handed the attendant his card. A few moments later, he came back, with keys to rooms 20 and 21.

He motioned to Joy, who returned to him, skipping. "Here you go."

She looked at her key to room 20 and frowned. "No."

"I thought you said-"

"I did, but this is your room. The girls will take room 21, thank you." She switched the keys without asking and ran toward the door. Wills and Ryan followed Tyrus to their rooms.

When Wills entered, Joy had an ear to the room next door. "Joy, if you want to spy on the guys, you've got the wrong wall."

She knew what she was doing. "Take a shower. I'm good."

Wills shook her head at the strange teen and walked into the bathroom, shutting the door.

The four teens congregated in Ann's room, 22. Talking strategy, Ann leaned against the wall. Julius and Seth sat, one on each bed while Connor paced back and forth.

"We're sitting ducks here. We should keep moving." Connor's drive to keep them safe put a lot of stress on him. Seth began to whistle, and Connor faced him. "Stop that."

"I need to run." Julius stretched on the bed. "Seriously, the hours that we spent running felt so *great*."

"So, go running. No one's stopping you." Ann gave him a look. "I will not be joining you though. One night of running was enough for my lifetime."

Julius locked eyes reluctantly with Connor. "You felt it too, right?"

Connor nodded. "Felt great."

"See? Running is good. Let's go."

"What do you think Seth? Will they draw too much attention?"

Seth thought for a moment before concluding, "I'm sorry this is frustrating. I know it's not in your nature to do nothing, Connor. Maybe the two of you can run in the morning to relieve your stress. See who's faster? If you go before the sun is up, it feels to me like it'd be safe.

"As for the stay here, I'm sorry but my gut is still saying to continue with the plan. If it makes you feel more comfortable, we can scout the perimeter, make sure we don't see any drones like at home."

Ann narrowed her eyes at him. "What are you talking about?"

He looked at her. "Drones, agents. I felt them at home. That's part of the reason I suggested leaving."

"I smelled them."

"I saw them." Connor stopped pacing. "You didn't sense them, Ann?"

The only person she'd seen following her was the serial killer. She shivered as she relived the last moments of Stabby Steve. "Looks like I drew the short straw."

Julius snorted. "Seriously? Right, the chick that can make fire got the short straw." He shook his head at her.

"So, you aren't stealthy," Connor began, "but you're powerful."

She sarcastically chided them. "Right. If I can ever figure out how to control this, I'd make some wicked s'mores."

Seth's face was serious. "Or you might save our lives." The room fell silent, and Seth realized he may have said the wrong thing. "Hey, that was a joke." He punched her arm playfully. She punched back. His eyes lit up. "That's what we should do."

He walked over to the window and opened it, pointing. "That old, abandoned building? Perfect place to test our powers."

Ann heard a familiar, merry giggle from the next room, but she couldn't quite place it. The boys were continuing the conversation, leaving her no time to contemplate it.

"Up for it Ann? Give you a chance to practice without the stress of hurting anyone."

She nodded. That was exactly what she needed. "Sure, but when? What's the plan, Seth?"

Wills came back after she showered to find Joy still listening at the wrong wall. "Your turn."

Joy skipped into the bathroom without a word. Wills shook her head at the strange girl. Sitting on the bed, she thought about the next few days, her part in it all. The blood samples were long gone, too much time had passed for them to be viable. She was hoping that some new samples could still give her answers.

However, she'd been vetoed every time, something more urgent needing tending. Joy was a powerhouse for such a sweet individual, refusing to allow them to deviate in the slightest from her agenda. A strange girl, still she was able to observe some behaviors. While in the car, the teen had been surprisingly possessive of Tyrus, as well as controlling over the radio. She had an uncanny ability to find the same song on different channels. She shivered, wondering if she'd ever get the melody out of her brain.

She got dressed quickly, in old clothes from Tyrus that almost fit, mostly neutral colors. Taking the ball cap, she pulled it low over her face and left Joy alone in the room, shutting the door securely behind her. She was staring at her feet, trying to be incognito, when she bumped into another resident. "Sorry," she said, moving around him and knocking on Tyrus's door.

Julius recovered from the shove, the familiar scent of the woman invading his senses. He couldn't place it, but he knew she'd recently dyed her hair. Had she been here yesterday? Something tugged at the back of his mind, but it refused to coalesce, so he continued around the woman to buy snacks at the convenience store across the street.

Wills shut the door behind her. Ryan was in the bathroom, shouting at someone over the phone. Wills assumed it was his wife. Tyrus gave her a weary smile, sitting uncomfortably on one of the queen beds. She sat on the other and waited, patiently trying not to listen.

"Yes, I understand…" *pause.* "No, that's not what this is. Yes, you remember Tyrus?" Pause. "No, you don't get to imply…" *Pause.* "Yes, Dear."

He walked out of the bathroom and Wills could hear yelling coming through the smartphone. He handed it to Tyrus, who looked at it as if he would die by touching it.

"She wants to talk to you."

Tyrus slowly took the phone among the yelling sounds and held it up to his ear, clearing his throat. "Hello, Ellie."

The voice sounded suddenly pleasant. "Yeah, I'm consulting on the case. Ryan is doing the best he can. I would love that. How's the baby?" *Pause.* "I'll have to visit after she's born."

He handed the phone back to Ryan, saying, "here you go." He smiled as he did so.

Ryan frowned at him and took the phone. "Yes, Ellie." The yelling began anew. He walked back into the bathroom and shut the door.

Tyrus looked at Wills. "He may be a few minutes longer."

"No problem. Any time frame you can give for me to ask for new samples? Documenting what's happening is important. I have some supplies at my apartment. Am I free to go get them?"

"I'm aware, we have to deal with one issue at a time. After Ryan calms her down, you can go tonight. I'll stay here and hold down the fort with Joy."

"She's so…odd."

You have no idea. He nodded. "Get used to it." She chuckled but his face grew serious. "They're victims, of something they don't understand. That's why we need to find them as quickly as possible. Get your supplies, come back, so we can figure it out and see what can be done to help them."

"I'll…need a sample from you as well."

"I'm not going anywhere. You get back, you can test mine too. I just know I'm too far gone to be helped."

"I'll do the best with what I have. I just wish there was an untraceable fully functional laboratory I could use instead."

"Can't risk it."

"Yeah, I know. Eyes everywhere."

"I don't know if there are, but we don't want to do anything to jeopardize the safety of these teens. You…don't know what's happened to others like them."

A red-faced Ryan left the bathroom, giving them both an apologetic look. "She'll understand."

Tyrus stood, shaking hands with Wills, then Ryan. "Good luck to the both of you."

"You as well."

"I've got the easier job."

Wills laughed. "Right. Still, good luck."

He smiled as they left. When they did, he rubbed his face in his hands and sighed. The motel phone rang. Picking it up, he said, "Yeah?"

"It's Joy."

"I figured. What do you need?"

"Uhm, food."

"What do you want for food?"

"Uh…I'll call you back."

He cleared his throat, alone with his thoughts for a few moments. It was times like this, when things were too quiet, that he worried.

Seth watched them leave, knowing that they'd split up. That meant at least one of them was still here. His instinct was telling him to leave, his gut forcing him to stay. He was confused and didn't understand the big picture. While his friends believed he could *see* the future, he could only feel positive and negative outcomes of events occurring soon. More of a feeling than a vision.

He walked back into his room where the others waited, shutting the door behind him.

"We go tonight. Julius gets the supplies, and we'll go into the building tonight." Connor repeated it as if he were trying to convince himself that it was a good idea.

"I'm still worried." Ann pictured charred flesh every time she thought of using her powers.

"You'll be worried until you can control it." Seth handed her a juice, which she downed. She was hungry and thirsty more than usual.

"How many hours till sundown?"

"A few yet. I say we nap while we can, so we're renewed while we test ourselves. When the alarm sounds, we get up, Connor and I will check it out, and Ann and Julius will join us when it's safe."

They all nodded, getting ready to pass out. Ann walked back to her room, shutting the door behind her. As it closed, Joy came out of hers and grabbed the food from the delivery guy. "The guy in this room will pay you." She shut her door as Julius walked out, getting supplies before his nap. He nodded at the delivery man as he passed, who nodded back.

"Didn't know there was delivery here."

"Yeah. On apps and from the restaurant. Here's a menu."

Julius took it, eager for something other than snacks. "Thanks man."

"No problem."

Julius continued his walk, strange familiar smells filling his senses again. He just couldn't place it. Looking around, he convinced himself he was just imagining it, then moved on.

Tyrus awoke suddenly, a feeling of dread spreading through him. The smell of thick smoke warned him of an ensuing blaze. Rhythmic knocking on his door signaled Joy. He stood, opening it, his gaze widening at the building engulfed in light across the street.

He started to head out, but Joy's hands around his arm stopped him. "No. You don't go; you call the police now."

Looking at the colorful girl, whose eyes weren't quite as bright, he said, "alright, but you need to-"

"Lights off and hide. I know."

"Would you let me finish my thoughts please? It's rude to interrupt."

"Sorry." She kicked her feet. "You need to call now, and I got impatient. I'll go hide."

"Draw the-"

"-shades. I know." She sounded very annoyed.

He locked his door after he saw her close her own. Then, dialing 911, he waited and said, "yes, I'd like to report a fire."

A few minutes prior to the blaze, the four teens stood awkwardly inside the abandoned building on the third floor. Long moments of silence ticked by as they looked at each other, unsure of themselves, until Connor stepped up. "Well, someone has to go first. I'm it." They moved away from him for space, unsure of his intent.

He closed his eyes, and when he opened them, they'd taken on an animalistic quality, like a lion or an eagle, glowing in the dim light. "I can see farther."

Ann commented, "Your eyes changed." Her voice sounded breathy.

He nodded. "Yeah. But when they're like this, I can see…five blocks away from here. Helped me throw the ball accurately."

"What else?"

He took out a small ring. "This appeared, under my bed this morning. Should I give this to Ann too?"

Seth looked it over. "No, I'll take that." Ann frowned as she watched his face turn a little red, igniting the curiosity inside her. What was that ring supposed to be for?

"Why does jewelry keep randomly appearing under my bed?"

Everyone shrugged. Seth spoke after the ring was placed on his pinky. "What else?"

"When one of the guys went to tackle me, I was able to evade it. Julius, come at me, like we're playing football."

Julius snorted. "What you and I call football is different."

"American football."

"Lame, but whatever. You want to get your butt kicked, happy to help." He waited a moment, then lunged at Connor. It happened so quickly that Ann wasn't sure she could follow it all, but it appeared that Connor somehow floated around him.

"Hey, that's not fair."

"I know, right? Like, half flying or something. And the last thing…" He paused, rubbing his neck. "I want to protect everyone. Like I'm a knight or a soldier and it's my job to make sure all of you," he looked at them individually, "are okay. It's so intense that I couldn't concentrate at school until I talked to Ann."

They nodded. "Like we're a unit, now."

"Or more like a…" he paused. "I can't think of the word."

"Pack?" Julius asked. "That's how I feel."

"No, more like a…"

"Pride?" Seth folded his hands in front of him.

"Yes. Exactly, but with an even ratio of males and females. And I don't want to kill you guys. Well, sometimes Julius but…" He punched him playfully in the shoulder. "Seth, you're good."

They laughed at the jest. Silence fell until Julius broke it. "I want meat, same as Connor. I'm hungry all the time. I'm fairly certain I can remember people based on their scent. I can tell when it's Ann or Seth or Connor knocking on the door. I feel connected to the wolf in me, you know? Watch this."

He stood in the middle of the room, and as she watched he took in a large, deep breath, his rib cage expanding more than a human chest should. Then he let out a fierce howl. It wrapped around her bones like cold death, gripping her heart tightly until it was over. She breathed heavily as it ended, seeing the others doing the same.

Seth commented. "Breathtaking. Literally. Don't do that again unless you must."

"Yeah, right?" His legs gave out, Connor steadying him. "Takes a lot of energy to do that, though."

Seth stepped forward next. "Well, most of my powers you already know, and they aren't really physical, *per se*, like Connor flying and his…death howl."

"No, but maybe you can do more, if you concentrate."

"I can try." He stepped into the center of the room, and closed his eyes, meditating peacefully. Ann could almost feel the ocean breeze, soft flowers against her skin. When he opened his eyes, though, nothing happened. "Guess not."

He leaned back against a pillar. She watched it shimmer, as if it was there then it wasn't. Seth fell through it and was gone. They looked around, trying to find him. A few seconds later, he reappeared in the same spot.

"What happened? Are you okay?"

He held up a hand, spinning to vomit on the floor. "Yeah, fine now."

"What was that?"

"A…portal? I was in the hotel room, then I came back. My brain was fine, but my stomach didn't like it."

Julius held out a fist. "Ready to rob our first bank!" Seth bumped his fist but shook his head.

Ann, waiting until she could feel all of their eyes on her, then stepped forward. "I still think this is a bad idea."

"We showed off for you. Your turn."

She tried to smile at Connor's words, but it didn't quite work. Seth took her shoulders. "Listen, this is the safest environment possible. Besides, if you screw up, I can portal us out, right? Just try it Ann. Remember the ocean?"

She could still smell the air from his meditation. Closing her eyes, she let the ocean come to her mind, stood in the stillness of the room while the others waited. As she watched, something in the distance approached from the middle of the ocean. Wings flapping, she assumed it was a bird. It grew closer and she could see red fire around it. It was…enchanting.

She opened her eyes, looking straight up. The bird was in the room with her, and at her summons, a single feather dropped from its wings to her hand. When it landed, it changed into a perfect flame, like a candle in the dark.

Seth reached out to touch it, and it burned him. "That's real." He shook his hand. "Now try to put the flame out."

She thought of it, and the bird moved in front of her, fanning the flame with its wings until it had smothered what it had created. Only a thin trail of smoke remained in her hand. The bird left with it, becoming smoke itself.

"She's beautiful."

Seth looked at her. "What?"

"The bird."

"What bird?"

"Drone!" Connor shouted, and they looked out the window to see one eyeing them. A laser sighted them, a camera obviously filming everything they did. Someone was watching them.

Upset by this, reacting more than controlling, Ann threw a flame ball at it. It knocked it down a floor, and the drone crashed into the second story, lighting the dry building quickly aflame.

The others gave her shocked stares. She didn't know what to say. "Oops?"

Making a portal, Seth motioned them through. Connor, then Ann, Julius and finally Seth. Ann felt her stomach twist as she moved instantly from one place to another. They were suddenly back in the boys' room. They looked at each other for a moment, before Ann rushed to secure the toilet before anyone else could. She promptly threw up, while Seth did so in the sink behind her.

Tyrus couldn't bring himself to look away from the flame. Fire triggered him, caused his entire body to fight against the calm that kept him stable. He focused on being mindful, breathing slow and even, trying to convince his parasympathetic nervous system to help calm him. He watched the flame, facing it, while the police arrived, while the firefighters battled to keep the flames contained.

He felt the cold concrete beneath him, the soft, warm breeze from the fire tainted with smoke. *Stay present in the moment.*

The fire fighters fought the flames, steam rising from the site. No one left the building, the ambulance sitting there. Hopefully that meant no one was seriously injured. He watched them work, their hoses dousing the blaze. *Stay in the now.*

The fire finally started to die, and he rotated to go inside his room. To his right, three doors down, the shades drew closed. Making a mental note that the enemy may be closer than they appeared, he kept a blank expression on his face.

The teens were close, as was evident from the blaze. The last time he'd seen that kind of firepower…Well, many could control the flame, but only one was consumed by it. He felt their presence, as did Joy, more than Wills or Ryan would understand. He'd sent his team away hoping they'd feel more comfortable revealing themselves, but they hadn't done so. He thought of his last encounter with flames like that, and looking into the mirror, his eyes glowed with them.

Dr. Gregory D. Jackson stood in his office, receiving the call promptly. He knew before answering who the likely caller was. He powered on his earpiece, a red light signaling a call-in-progress.

"Yes." His voice was soft but firm.

"We found them."

"I trust that this time, you will follow my exact instructions?"

"Yes, sir."

"Good. Surveillance only. I need to know how much exposure these teens have encountered. That will determine how we contain this…situation. Can you accomplish that?"

"Yes sir. We have replacement drones on standby."

He sighed; the mistake obvious to him but oblivious to his employee. "They'll be expecting that. No, we go undercover, with people. Classic car road trip. Hire some actors to mix in with the agents. Tell them no contact. Only smartphone video and pictures." He paused. "Send me the tape of the downed drone. Collect statements from the local police. Find the source of the fire."

"What agency are we from this time?"

"FBI."

"Over and out."

Dr. Jackson ended the call, knowing his work for the evening was not yet complete. "Isaiah," he said over the intercom, "we need to call *her* in."

"Yes, s-sir. Right aw-way." The fear in his assistant's voice was palpable. Isaiah was a soft soul but had always been loyal. He didn't deal well with the more…licentious aspects of the business. She personified that. He hated having to do this, but the teens were proving to be quite sly, escaping his grasp before he'd even tightened it. She was one of the few surviving ones he knew of. If anyone knew what they were going through, it was her. The question was, would they survive her usually dire salutations.

"Sir. She's on the other line."

He switched over and said, simply, "I need you."

The phone clicked dead. He sat in his chair, gazing out at the full moon, wondering what shenanigans the evening would bring, and how he would conquer them.

Chapter 7

Ann was returned to the meadow. Green grass rippled in the soft breeze, caressing her knees so much that it tickled. She looked down to see herself dressed in white, a sash of pink and blue tied around her waist. She focused her gaze down the hill, where flowers of all shades and colors bloomed in the full sunlight, too large in petals.

She heard the sound of distant laughter, so she followed it, running downhill. She ran toward the giggles as they grew louder. She saw Joy and Marie in the distance, dressed as she was, dancing merrily together.

Joy!" She shouted it, loudly. "Joy! Marie!"

They stopped dancing, waving her closer. She thought of the great distance between them, deciding to fly instead of run. Great wings of flame appeared, and she flexed them like an additional pair of arms before trusting them to carry her softly, gracefully, to her companions.

The girls grew more jubilant as she landed next to them. Hugging her hard, they resumed dancing. Around and around they spun until at last they fell to the ground, dizzy with play. After catching their breath, Marie leaned on one arm, her attention on Ann.

"I miss you."

"I know. Your trip is lasting forever."

"There's always summer."

"Summer doesn't last forever."

"It does, just not in the same place."

"Will you make it back by fall?"

"No, I don't think so, Ann."

"Oh." Something flickered at the back of her mind, but she couldn't hang on to the thought.

Joy sat up suddenly. "Marie! Tell her the thing. Quick! She doesn't have much time left. Tell her so she remembers."

"Right." Her face grew serious. "It wasn't me, Ann. I didn't know."

"Know what?"

The scene was changing, growing dark. "My dad didn't know, either. You have to believe me."

"What is happening now? Where did the sunshine go?" She looked around her as Marie continued.

"Just remember, my dad and I, we didn't know. Okay? It wasn't us."

"Wasn't you what?"

"THE BOMB!"

Ann woke, her heart racing, safe in the bed in her room. A bolt of lightning caught her attention. The crash of thunder came a second later. She jolted, all remnants of comfort fading. She ran to turn on the light, then the TV. She checked the clock. Three am. No wonder she'd had a nightmare. She caught her breath at a knock on her door. This was how horror movies began. She slowly crept toward it. Seeing it was Seth, it was opened and shut again quickly in relief.

"You have excellent timing." She hugged him with one shoulder. "I just woke up from a nightmare."

"A nightmare? More of a night message, but I guess if you don't remember it, what good did it do, right?"

She tilted her head at him. "Huh?"

"What's on TV?" He took the remote from her and switched until something interesting came on. "We used to watch this as kids."

"Yeah, but it sucks now." The cartoon showed a unicorn and griffin arguing over treasure, but they were beaten by a leprechaun that launched over the rainbow…

"Well…" he said, "it used to be awesome. How about once more, for old times' sake."

"Fine." They ate snacks and watched as the leprechaun buried his treasure beyond the rainbow, but right next to a dragon's cave.

Day 10

Tyrus woke as he always did, early in the morning at 0600. He didn't deviate from his normal routine, and one hundred sit ups and push-ups later, he grabbed a protein bar and headed outside, where he would run.

He knocked on Joy's door three times, the question. Two knocks, the answer. Joy was awake and didn't need anything. He nodded and began to walk to the stairs, only to bump into another resident.

He felt it instantly, a feeling that long lay dormant, something he hadn't felt in years, not since… It crept along his skin, fire recognizing its twin. He reached out to touch her shoulders as she lost her balance, and upon his touch, liquid lava flowed over him, goosebumps rising. He could tell she felt it as well. They stood there for three long breaths in unison.

Her eyes grew wide and she backed away. "Watch it."

He recovered quickly, saying only, "Sorry, Miss." His head down, he walked away, the feeling fading only after they were far apart. He smiled to himself. Of course, there would be one of *them* in the group. That must be Ann, Joy's friend. As he grabbed his headphones from his pocket, he knew better than to force a meeting with one of her kind. They tended toward stubbornness and great strength of character. He put his headphones in his ears, increasing the volume, then began his run.

Ann shut her door firmly, standing against it to steady her legs and her heart, both of which refused to cooperate with her. That man…what was it about him that…crept lava along her skin like a caress? The feeling, strange and unwelcome, faded shortly, and she sighed with relief.

Is this what attraction feels like? She'd never given much thought to that aspect of her life. While other girls were crushing hard for a boy, she merely wanted to survive the day. Her childhood issues weren't something she wished to discuss or share with someone else, so she kept her distance. Sure, she'd felt biological impulses before, but this…was different. This was something she couldn't ignore.

"What's wrong?" Seth had spent the night, curled up on the other bed. "Something happen?"

The image of red hair and turquoise eyes wouldn't fade. Calming herself, she asked, "you think they'd send agents here?"

He was up quickly, looking out the window. "What happened?"

She shook her head. "I don't know, but I think we should be very, *very* careful."

"I have to go check on the guys. You stay here, pack. We leave at four pm."

"That's a bit late for check out."

"That's when we leave. Ready or not. I'll see ya later." He left abruptly, walking into the room he shared, to the two others snoring soundly. Noting how early it was, he lay back down to nap. They had time yet.

Ann couldn't calm herself. She paced back and forth in her room, nervous. She tried to meditate, recall a beach, or pleasant experience, but it didn't work. Finally, she jumped into the shower, letting the cold water clear her head. No yelling, no complaining. Alone, she could relax and breathe, in a way she couldn't at her fosters. Thinking of a rainstorm, she allowed her mind to drift. Before long she was asleep, the water falling softly over her.

She woke suddenly, unsure what had cast her out of her dreamworld. She'd been flying, seeing places she'd never been. It was peaceful and she wanted to return, but she knew better than to keep the shower running.

She dried off and got dressed, walking to the beds. She looked at the time. It was an hour before checkout. She turned to pack the little she had quickly, just to be certain she was ready on time, but try as she could, the memory of flowing lava followed her.

Seth left after a short conversation with Connor and Julius about packing. His turn for a snack run, and the way they'd been eating, he should get a lot. His gut didn't tell them where they were going, only that it wouldn't be safe to stay here any longer. He felt strange sensations as he walked forward, as if change were coming that he may not be prepared for. He paused a moment, second guessing himself before shoving the doubt aside. Whistling a happy tune, he shut his hotel door and walked forward.

He was so into the song and the change that it wasn't until arms pulled at him that he realized something *was* wrong. The dark surrounded him, the door was closed behind him, before he could utter a word.

Ann finished packing hastily and walked to the boy's room. When the door shut, she asked, "where's Seth?"

"He just left to get snacks like, two seconds ago."

She tilted her head. "Why didn't I see him?"

Connor, suddenly alert, looked out the window. "Huh. That's odd. Wait here. I'm going to go look for him."

He strode out without looking back, walking to the convenience store. Ann marveled at how controlled he could be, as he started a slow jog, trying to look normal. She knew how fast both Connor and Julius could be after their run in the city. They could run circles around her if they wanted. *It must be hard for him to pretend to be normal.* Then again, it was hard for her too, in other ways. She looked at the charred remains of the building she'd burnt down and felt guilty. She watched until Connor walked out, running back. This time he didn't care if his pace was slow enough, and that furrowed her brow.

She opened the door for him and he motioned for her to shut it quickly. Julius came out of the bathroom. "Something is wrong. I can smell your fear."

Connor looked at the both of them and said, "I couldn't find Seth. He isn't in the store."

Silence followed for a moment. Julius tilted his head strangely. Ann was sure he was listening to the area around him. He looked at her seriously. "I can't hear him. You think he got sidetracked?"

Connor shook his head. "Without a portal back here to tell us what's up? No. Not his style."

Ann said what they were thinking. "You think the system suits got him?"

"No," shaking his head, Julius continued. "Then I'd have heard the struggle."

The two boys shared a look, then shrugged at her. She sighed. "Let's give him some time. Maybe he'll return. We have a half hour before checking out, anyway. Sit and wait?"

They did so, but with each minute, the tension grew. They jumped when they heard tires squeal into the parking lot, and Connor moved to the window, watching.

Tyrus heard the squeal of tires outside. He looked out the window to see Ryan exit the SUV, a stern look on his face. Whoever was after these newbies was on it. They must have secured her apartment. A moment later, Wills exited too. She looked irate.

He shook his head. He half expected this. He'd been around too long to assume any plan would work flawlessly. He hoped that Wills would still be willing to help, even though her plan had been destroyed. He needed her.

Seth would have shouted but his gut calmed him. After a moment of his eyes adjusting to the low light, a familiar face greeted him, angular features paired with bright blue eyes.

"Joy!" He wrapped his arms around her and pulled her close. "I'm so glad you're alive and awake."

She hugged him back, longer than expected. "I'm so glad I can finally see you again."

"What are you talking about?"

"I'll explain. Everything. I promise. For now, we need to stay here. For about a half hour before…"

"Before we check out?"

She gave him a look, then smiled. "Exactly."

"Ann will want to know you're okay."

"She…will have to wait."

"Why?"

"I can't explain without making it worse. Please understand. If we reveal me now, then she won't meet Tyrus again, at least not properly."

"Who is…"

She sighed and switched on the TV. The same cartoon was playing from last night. "He's the dragon." She sat down on the bed, motioning for him to sit beside her. This was crazy, but his gut was telling him to trust her. She knew more about this than he did.

It was a quarter to four, and there was no sign of Seth. Their bags were packed and they sat around the room, concerned. In only a short time, they'd come to depend on him, more than they realized. His sudden loss was crippling.

Connor paced back and forth. "Where the hell is he?"

Ann whispered, "*Should we check out or wait another hour?*"

"We can't leave without him." Connor's pacing increased. Ann could tell it was making Julius nervous. A low growl, barely audible, escaped his lips.

"What if someone got to him?" Julius shook his leg, unable to sit still. "What if we're next?"

"Won't happen unless they take me out first." Connor's voice began to change as he spoke, from human to something lower, deadlier. "And I won't go down easy."

"Calm down. We can figure this out." She backed away from him, concerned. His voice was more animal than human. He tilted his head at her words, and his eyes changed from human to…something primal. "They won't take the two of you."

She felt fear rise out of instinct, then heard a growl from the other side of the room. She looked over to see Julius in a similar state of flux. "Calm down, cat boy. You're scaring her. That doesn't help us think. We need a plan."

Ann watched them face each other, suddenly aware of how much damage they could cause. Fear filled her, her power falling away. She could only watch as they approached each other, the threat obvious between them.

Julius's hair was standing straight up, his front fangs larger than they should be. Connor's hands grew in size, strangely changing form. "Calm down, both of you." The unknown caused the panic within her to rise, and they responded by becoming more aggressive.

"See? You're terrifying her."

"This isn't your pack, wolf. You don't get to tell me to behave."

"If you can't control yourself, I'll *make* you behave."

"Don't you two see what's happening? You have to calm down."

Ignoring her, they both growled at each other, the low sound causing her muscles to clench, goosebumps growing along her arms. Whatever was going to happen would happen. She couldn't stop it now.

Julius moved between Connor and the door. "Out of my way, wolf. I'm getting Seth back."

"Not a chance. You leave, they see you like this, our cover is blown. What if they kill Seth then? Think, cat boy."

Their voices had lowered by at least an octave.

"If you don't move, I'll move you." He let out a roar.

Julius crouched, his hands changing into dark paws. "Try it, pussycat."

For a moment, they stared each other down, frozen, two predators keenly tuned into the threat the other posed. Then suddenly, Connor moved. He launched himself at Julius, who dug his claws into his sides. With a scream, Connor smashed him against the door, once, twice. On the third, they fell through, the door mere splinters.

They were propelled over the second story railing and fell below. She followed them out into the afternoon sun, worried that they'd be injured, by themselves or others. She jumped the railing and landed on the ground next to them, while they rolled, scratching and clawing at each other.

Three adults gathered below, all wearing neutral colors intended to blend in. *Definitely not friendly, fellow travelers.* They looked official, and Ann wasn't about to let them near the others. As the man she saw earlier approached them, her fear faded, replaced by rage. With no clue to Seth's whereabouts, she assumed the worst. Her anger grew quickly, and she let it flow over her. The man stopped walking forward and stood with his hands in his pockets.

She walked toward him, saying, "stay away from them."

He smiled, then, which was totally inappropriate. *He doesn't see you as a threat.* He'd learn better. "I mean it."

The smile faded. "I know." His hands came out of his pockets, and she watched him change. "But they're going to cause a scene, and we don't need that here." His body began to turn, his voice lowering, but instead of fur, his hands transformed into red, scaly claws. The fear returned, the fire faded, and she stepped away from him, her heel slipping into a hole in the concrete. She fell backward and hit the ground, as the man stepped toward her.

The two stopped fighting each other as she let out a moan of pain. She looked back at them to see they were rounding on a perceived attacker. She had a second to look at the man, his eyes still human. He sighed aloud and took a defensive stance as the two of them attacked, together.

He easily evaded them both, their inexperience causing them to make mistakes. Whoever this was, whatever they were, he was…like them. The question, then, was friend or foe? Was it possible the system suits were…different like them? Was the government actually involved in this?

Before they could round on him again, he breathed deeply, as if his chest was much larger than it should be. An image of Julius's death howl flashed in her memory, and she covered her ears. His shoulders tensed, then he let out a roar. The sound felt different than cold fear and death. This made her shake; her body wanting to move and stand still simultaneously. She heard massive glass shattering, the sound of car alarms blaring. When she opened her eyes, she saw her friends lying motionless on the ground.

The man walked toward her, grabbing her arm, pulling her up. She reacted instantly. The anger rose as she realized she was the only one left. Her nature was survival. It always had been.

No way, after the crappy childhood she'd been given, that her journey was going to end like this.

Her eyes shone with fire as the lava flowed between them again. He reacted, grabbing both her arms, taking a deep breath. He shook his head, and in his normal human voice, said, "not here." A second later, they were flying…

Ryan and Wills acted quickly, running toward the two boys, checking their pulse. Their hearts beat strong. Nodding to each other, they picked up one and carried him to Joy's open door. She had a wet cloth and some ice waiting for them. "On the bed, quickly."

They looked at Seth, who shrugged. "Do what she says, I guess."

Without time, they ran back out to drag in the other boy. So many questions, so few answers. Wills mentally took stock of the situation, a checklist of strange activity forming in her mind. She was more curious than ever to solve this biological oddity.

Her fire was gone the moment they were airborne. Her fear of heights kicked in, causing her to wrap her arms tightly around his toned body. He growled low in his throat and said, "not so tight."

"Put me down." She looked over to see…wings. Red, scaly wings.

He laughed. "Is that really what you want?"

"I mean, safely, on the ground."

"Gladly, in one moment."

The wings shifted, as he glided back to earth. Her grip loosened as he dropped her onto a rooftop, a few blocks away from the hotel, in an old, abandoned part of the city.

She took a second to remember to breathe, worried she may pass out. When she was ready, she shouted, "what the hell?!" She glared at him, her anger potent again. "What did you do to them?"

"I neutralized a threat. This is bigger than the five of you."

A voice at the back of her mind, the logical part of her, wanted to believe there was more to the story, but the image of them wouldn't fade. Her anger strengthened, of its own accord. "Are you the one who did this to us?"

He shook his head, his eyes sad. "No."

His face, his stance, they told her he was telling the truth, but her anger boiled over anyway. His early behaviors contradicted his current body language, and she couldn't afford to ponder those implications. "I don't believe you." A fireball formed in her hand, and she didn't stop it.

His shoulders slumped forward as he almost looked sad.

"Don't do this, baby bird."

His words, meant to calm her, enraged her instead. She tilted her head, her eyes changing to flame. She watched as he changed with her. She didn't know much, but she knew she was on solid ground. She knew he'd hurt the only others in the world she trusted, and she *knew* he was in trouble…

Chapter 8

Connor became aware of the softness beneath him. His eyes opened slowly, revealing one of the hotel rooms. He sat up suddenly, remembering everything. The world spun as his head, still dizzy from the shout, fought to right itself. He looked over to see Julius already awake.

Seth sat in the corner, and with him, a blonde girl. *Coma girl.* She had a name… "Joy?" She glared, a finger over her lips. He took the hint and waited silently, while outside, the real agents snapped pictures. The clock showed 3:58. In two minutes, they would leave.

When the agents had passed, Joy looked at Julius. "What did they say?"

"Two agents, FBI. Talking about us. They were going to hand in their surveillance to the Director? They were happy that the operation was over, as it's been two days. They've been here watching all of us for *two days*. We need to get out of here, *now*."

The sound of car doors slamming confirmed their decision. Joy stood, looking at the adults. "We go, now. Quickly."

Wills and Ryan were confused. "We can't leave without Tyrus and Ann."

Seth spoke up. "If we don't leave, we suffer a fate worse than death."

"What are you talking about?"

"We vote. Who wants to leave?"

The four younger adults raised their hands. "We can explain in the car, but you're outnumbered. We need to go, now."

The clock struck four, and they picked up their bags and left, the two adults with no option other than to follow. "You've got his number, right?"

Ryan nodded, opening the driver's side door. When everyone was piled inside, they left the hotel, heading toward the highway. As they left the parking lot, the sound of sirens blaring came from behind them.

Connor looked back to see police, firemen, and the unmarked FBI cars pull up. "Strange, I thought you said the FBI was already there."

"Or they just arrived." Joy laughed, but the sound was far from comforting. They drove onto the highway and Wills said, "now, explain yourselves, please."

Joy sighed with frustration. "Alright, here it is. Tyrus and Ann are going to fight. They are supposed to, so something else can happen that we need to happen for us to survive, so that something else can happen, so someone else will show up, that we need to survive. Got it?"

Wills looked back around, more befuddled than ever. "Will they be okay?"

Joy laughed, unperturbed. "They'll be *mostly* fine."

Wills looked at Ryan, who shrugged. After a few moments of silence, Seth and Joy lit up, saying, "take the next right."

Her hair was lit with red flame, her eyes shone with it. Her hands were covered in fire. She stood her ground, ready to fight. There was just one problem.

The man stood with his hands in his pockets, completely unwilling to acquiesce to her obvious anger.

"I'm not fighting you." He was so calm. How could he be calm?

"You hurt my friends. Either you fight me, or you die."

He bit his lip to keep from laughing.

Wanting him to understand she was a true threat, she asked, "who do you think took out that serial killer?"

She took a deep breath as his face grew somber and threw the flame at him, expecting it to char his skin. When his scaled hand reached out and gently absorbed her flame, her rage grew. The next fireball was double in size. Still, he deflected it.

Her strategy wasn't working. She looked at the ground below him and smiled. He took a step back, saying, "don't do it."

She took that as a challenge, her anger propelling her hands forward. She controlled the flame as it flowed from her fingertips to the ground around him, a perfect circle. Time seemed to slow as she watched the fire encircle her target, his shoulders slowly transforming into wings, but not quickly enough. He gave her an aggravated look, and after a moment, the roof collapsed, and he fell through.

She looked about desperately for the fire escape. She was three floors high and didn't want to jump down. She took three steps toward the side of the building, before the floor below her gave way and the man came crashing back through, his wings fully spread. She jumped back, landing on a solid section of the roof. She rolled and sat there, her fear overcoming her anger.

She could see it in his face. He was no longer calm. He strode toward her, presumably to "neutralize" her as well as the others. She closed her eyes tight, as if his steps themselves caused her pain. Something in her gave in, knowing she wouldn't be able to survive this on grit and willpower. She felt something open within her, like a door or seal falling away. She held out a hand and whispered, "*save me.*"

Her eyes popped open as the bird came back, swelling that same lava feeling through her from her heart out into the world. A masterpiece of flame that came forth from some unknown place inside her, it flew toward the man, whose eyes widened as it attacked him. He could see it, when others couldn't. He put his hands defensively in front of him as the bird shoved him back, so far that he flew off the building. She heard a thud and ran to the edge, seeing him on the ground, still.

She looked at him but a moment, guilt playing in her mind once again. Her eyes welled, but she didn't let them fall. He *deserved* it. She ran down the fire escape. The abandoned building was going up in flames and smoke, and the police would be on their way. She made the second story, noting the escape didn't go to the ground. She was about to jump when a dark hand held her in place. She looked behind her to see a woman staring back at her, dark features over strong bones. "This way."

She followed her temporary ally into the building as the sound of sirens grew. She heard the slamming of doors and shouting from outside. How had they gotten here so quickly? Would they catch her? Would they lock her up for murder? She envisioned them taking her away in handcuffs, off to prison, of being found guilty of the murder of not one but now two men.

She ignored the scene in her mind and followed the woman in front of her. Hearing footsteps on the stairs, they hid in a closet, not saying a word. She struggled to breathe silently, as she imagined the police opening this door, grabbing her, taking her to jail.

She could hear footsteps approach. This was it; this was how she lost her freedom. Then the woman in front of her did something she did not expect. She reached out a hand, a wall of orange flame appearing before them, completely concealing their presence. When the officer opened the door, he was greeted with it, shutting it quickly and moving on. Once he was gone, the woman passed through the flame, then stuck her head back through and said, "follow."

She did, passing through the wall of flame unscathed. She had so many questions, but now was not the time. She followed the woman down the stairs, where an officer was taping off the front of the building. Halfway down, she jumped over the railing, so she stayed hidden from the light of the door. Ann followed exactly behind her as she checked the first possible exit, an old bathroom with no window. Second door, a closet. The third door was locked.

Ann, concerned, looked behind them, worried they'd be found. When she looked back, the woman's hand was on the handle, the metal hot from her flame. She was melting the lock. That was…clever. She winked at her and opened the door, running through with style and jumping headfirst out the window. She followed, clumsily, lifting one foot over the other and jumping down.

Their escape was not complete. One look from the police at the end of the alley way and they'd be easily seen. Her heart pounding in her chest, she silently followed the woman around the corner, into a small grocery store. The woman grabbed a cart and walked toward the back with a sudden sway in her gait, as if she were meandering hastily. Ann tried to follow nonchalantly. As they reached the back of the store, without pause, the woman left the cart and walked straight into the bathroom as shouts of "police," "move," echoed behind them. The woman stomped into the bathroom and opened the window.

"Get in a stall, hide your feet. Now."

She did as instructed squatting awkwardly on top of the toilet, thankful it was clean. As she tried to quiet her breathing, she heard the police come through the door. She heard someone yell, "out the window," then the footsteps retreated. Why they didn't check the stalls was beyond her. They should have. Was this Seth's luck spilling over on her?

They left and the woman motioned her to follow moments later. They walked out of the store and strode away, casually. Vendors lined the street and she waded between them expertly, Ann trying to keep up. At the first vendor she took off her jacket in one smooth motion, leaving it on a hanger as if it belonged there, then picked up a ball cap which went onto her head. Passing another vendor, she slipped Ann a beautiful scarf and a pair of sunglasses. She did it all without the vendors noticing, and in a matter of one minute, managed to change their appearance so they wouldn't seem to fit the BOLO. Ann was impressed. After two blocks, she pulled keys from her pocket and unlocked a classy, sleek, black convertible. "Get in."

Ann paused, unsure for the first time. Why would she continue to follow her when she didn't know her, when she was safe?

"Why should I?"

The woman smiled then, and let Ann see her orange flame.

"Why is yours a different color?"

"No time to chat. Get in and I'll show you or walk away. Your choice."

Though she didn't like her options, she opened the passenger door anyway. Her curiosity won the fight. She needed to understand what had changed inside her. The woman waited for her to shut the door and pulled into traffic. It wasn't until they'd merged onto the highway that Ann breathed a sigh of relief.

Dr. Jackson stood bathed in light. Sunshine streamed into his office, panoramic windows showing an almost complete 360 view of St. Blaise beneath him. The rays reflected off of mahogany and steel, cheery among the modern industrial design. Chic and flashy, the exact image he wanted to portray. It spoke in silent support of his achievements, one way he reminded others of their status, and his own.

The situation he found himself in was not…ideal. He'd already had to double security to deal with the press. They meant well, but they only got in his way. The bus explosion…shouldn't have happened. That research had been sealed away for a reason. An image from his childhood flashed into his mind, gone a moment later. The black flames terrified him, but he didn't have the luxury of giving in to such feelings.

His phone vibrated, and looking down, a single text from a blocked number said, "Successful."

He nodded his head, relieved that at least one plan was on track.

The intercom buzzed.

"Yes, Isaiah?"

"Sir, he's here."

His lips tightened, his jaw clenched. How he handled this would be reflected in his treatment of personnel for his entire career. Too soft and everyone would be asking for special treatment he couldn't provide, but too harsh and top talent would refuse to work with him. He couldn't afford either. He took the moment to contemplate his words. "Send him in."

A small, broken man with glasses and a lab coat entered, security behind him. He shuffled in with a tear-stained face. Dr. Jackson shook hands with him, a look of sympathy on his usually stoic face.

"Director," the man began, his voice shaky, "I honestly have no clue how *any* of this happened."

Sitting back down at his desk, the director folded his hands and placed them on the table in front of him. Silence stretched between the two for a long moment, until he was sure exactly what he would say.

"Dr. Cline, let me begin by expressing my deepest sympathies for your unbearable loss. I'm so sorry this meeting is at all required."

The man blew his nose again and nodded, silently.

"I know this must be an…impossible situation for you, but there is an enormous amount of paperwork that we need to fill out. I'll help you, personally. After today, you will take a sabbatical. When I determine if and when it's time for you to return, you'll be reinstated, at full salary, plus raises and benefits."

The man nodded, tired. "You have the right to have a lawyer present. You've expressed your faith in this company by keeping this in house. Is that still the case?"

Again, the man nodded, his eyes wet. He looked down, his head in his hands.

"Very well." Reaching into his desk, he pulled out a large black binder. Opening to the first page, he continued, "please sign at the bottom of this first page, legally saying you were advised and declined your right to have representation."

This would be a long day.

Tyrus was out but a few moments before he breathed deeply, appearing to come back from the dead. He opened his eyes, a headache the least of his worries. Every bone hurt. Taking a moment, he slowly sat forward as a paramedic rushed toward him.

"Sir, please lie back down." She was young, and the worry filled her eyes. He could tell she thought he should be dead. "Please, let me look you over."

He forced a smile. "No need. I assure you, I'm fine."

He felt a bone randomly move back into place. Though it hurt, he showed no sign. She heard it, too. "I must insist. Please let me help you, sir."

"Don't call me 'sir.' I was enlisted, not an officer."

She gave him a look. "What was that, sir?"

He sighed and stood, slowly. He needed to find a quiet place to heal, without onlookers. "I refuse medical help." He shrugged off her hands and walked away, into an alley where the shadows welcomed him. He leaned against a wall, taking several deep breaths.

Then his eyes opened, his dragon's fire filling them. His scales appeared, traveling from his head down his body. As they morphed, the other bones and tissue were healed. It hurt, but it wasn't anything he hadn't already experienced. His record was six stories.

When he was healed, he sat down and thought this out. "*Ann…*" He breathed the name out, like a prayer. What were the odds? Another fire bird, stronger and faster. Smarter. It should have taken years for her to develop her psychic bird, but it'd been a matter of days. He wondered if the others could call their beasts, and what this meant. He knew the fire was manufactured. Was this a result of synthetic omega fire?

He closed his eyes, a vision of flaming hair as he was lifted off the ground by her bird. He sighed and looked away, thinking of the possible outcomes, the players involved. He knew most of those that existed, some on his side, most on their own. Survival was a difficult goal in his world. There were too many current unknowns to predict much of anything, so he walked out to the next street. A small car lot stood across the road, and he eyed a classic looking powerhouse he wouldn't mind driving. He smiled. At least he could travel in style while he tried to track her down, before someone worse than him got their clutches into her. The five victims had no idea what they'd stepped into, and very few benevolent Mythics remained. He'd have to be quick, clever, and careful if they were to have any future at all.

The black convertible veered off the highway onto a small exit. A gas station stood, still open but neglected, offering ice cream and frozen yogurt. The woman pulled in, handed her a wad of twenties and said, "go buy some yogurt while I fill up. You need to eat. Buy at least three servings."

Ann would have asked questions. She had so many, but the woman was right. She was starving. "Do you want anything?"

"Strawberry. Plain. Three servings for me, too."

"Alright." She walked inside and ordered, coming back with six canisters full of quickly liquefying but delicious coolness. Hers was piled high with fruit. The woman looked at her and smiled. "Eat it all."

She felt like she could. Suddenly ravenous, they ate in silence until each bowl was empty, the gas filling the car. The woman paid and pushed the start button, pulling away from the highway. Ann felt much better having food in her belly, though she didn't seem to be full like she normally would be.

"Where are we going?"

"How long have you been...*different*?"

"A couple weeks, I think."

"That's *it?*' She seemed shocked. "You took down…" She sighed but didn't finish the thought. "I'm taking you to a place that will help explain what…who you are now."

"You mean who *we* are?"

"Yes, who we are."

"You're like me."

"Yes. I am one of you. Open the glove box." Ann did so, slowly. "Inside is a new phone for you. Take it." She grabbed the item, noting it was brand new.

First time she'd ever owned a new phone. "Thank you."

The woman laughed. "Don't thank me. You use it to contact me, in case we get separated."

"Alright."

"Familiarize yourself with it. We've got a five-minute drive ahead of us."

"What are we?"

"The place we're going is…. a better teacher than I am. You'll know soon who you are."

Dr. Jackson shook his hand, one last time. "Mr. Cline, may I give you my deepest condolences for the loss of your daughter."

The man began to cry. The director's throat caught, before he could speak again. "Send me the receipts from her funeral service. I'd…like to reimburse you for the total cost."

"It won't bring her back."

"No. No it won't. I'd like to help anyway."

The man's eyes cleared. "If you want to help, then find the asshole who stole my daughter's life."

Dr. Jackson sat next to the grieving man, a hard hand on his shoulder. "That is my new and most important goal for this company."

"Thank you."

"Now, there's just one more paper you need to sign. This one is necessary for the police and me to do our jobs, now."

"You don't want me talking to the press."

"Yes, this is a non-disclosure agreement."

"I understand."

"I hate to ask. You should be able to speak your mind, but given the circumstances, the breech of security…"

"I understand, Director." He took the pen, signing the bottom of the document. "Is that all?"

"You are officially on leave, Mr. Cline."

The man nodded, stood and left. He took the folder and placed it behind him on the wall, taking a white one out in its place, reviewing the protocol for the next meeting, which wouldn't go as smoothly. He'd said he would figure out how this happened, at his company. And that was a promise he intended to keep. At any cost.

Chapter 9

Ann had been in this part of the city before, with Marie on summer weekends when her father took the girls to Pierside Park, a large central location with river access, fishing, and hiking trails. Her eyes watered as she thought of her friend, running through the trails with her.

"Why are we here?" She said it softly, to herself, but the woman heard her. Parking her car, she exited the vehicle.

"This is where we need to be to explain everything to you."

"I've been here, before." Ann followed her toward the hiking trails.

"Good. Then this is familiar territory, so you won't be scared."

"Should I *be* scared?"

The woman laughed. "Yes, but not because of me, or what I'm going to show you."

Confused, she followed her forward, as she started jogging down the largest path. *Great, more running.* Ann kept pace with her as the path curved, first one way then the other. As she watched, the woman sped up and she kept pace. Taking a sharp curve, they ran through the trees, on a trail she hadn't noticed before, and she knew these like the back of her hand.

After a few more confusing turns, they ended in front of a large stone structure. Ann had never seen this before, either. "This is new."

The woman chuckled again. "No, no this is very old. We just keep it well hidden."

"With what, magic?"

With a tilted head, she strode forward. "Something like that. Only people like us can see this place."

"But magic doesn't exist, does it?" Even as the words left her mouth, she doubted them, but it was what she'd been raised to believe. Magic was a fairy tale. Science was reality.

The woman looked at her. "Really? How did you chargrill that serial killer then? You pull out a flamethrower from your back pants pocket?"

Ann swallowed hard. "Are you saying we're…witches or something?"

The woman blinked. "Witches…the Halloween kind, anyway, don't exist."

"You just said…"

The woman held out her hand, and as they watched, flame erupted from it. It hit the air in front of the structure, repelled by some invisible force. The flame changed, forming a spiral, red, orange, yellow, green, blue, and purple in color, with a white and black circle.

The circle grew until it was as big as a door, its center looking like it contained both a black hole and a bright sun at the same time. The woman walked forward, disappearing through it.

Ann took a deep breath and followed, her curiosity overcoming the fear of the unknown. Darkness greeted them as the circle dissipated. "Light our path with your flame."

Ann focused, calling her flame to her hand. She suffered a moment of hesitation, unsure of the circumstances. However, she remembered who she'd killed. The serial killer, the scaly man. She needed control, and this woman could help.

She released the flame outward, and two rows lit up the very long hallway, made of old stone. "Go ahead." The woman followed her as she slowly walked forward. Strange symbols and burn marks scattered the walls.

"Turn left." She listened, and the wall was suddenly gone, replaced by a dark room. She stepped forward until the light didn't reach her anymore. Walking past Ann, the woman strode, sending three flame balls around the room, which lit up, revealing its wonder. Three circles of orange flame revealed a large open room, circular in shape, the ceiling as tall as the three-story building they'd just left.

"How does anyone keep something like this a secret?"

The woman chuckled. "Magic, of course."

"Right. What am I supposed to be seeing here?"

"This is some…ancient temple one of us built long ago. It's not the place that's important, it's the information inside it. It's kept hidden for a reason. We keep hidden for a reason."

"What are we?"

She threw one last flame to the top of the room, lighting a staircase toward some central panel with colorful artwork. "Step forward and up if you want to know."

She took her time, this strange world she now inhabited sinking in, slowly. It was as if someone took all the fairy tales she'd loved as a child, twisting them into some strange sort of nightmare, but it was real. She was here, doing this.

One step at a time, she walked up the stairs, her apprehension growing. She couldn't make out the pictures from here, and that worried her that some strange darkness may swallow her whole, as the monster under the bed would when she was young.

Looking back, the woman nodded to her. She was halfway up, and alive. She was being silly. Striding forward, she put one foot in front of the other until she reached the platform. Summoning her own flame, she could see the pictures clear as day, and she breathed in sharply.

The cartoon from her childhood. It was here, on this wall. Images of mythical creatures gathered together, in some intricate display. Cerberus, the guardian to the gates of Hades stood challenging a griffin. The dragon entangled with a bird of fire. The leprechaun bowed to a unicorn, who surrounded them both in golden light.

Names were written below each scene. She read them all, noting only one was written below the fire bird. "Pride."

"Are you "Pride?" the pieces were starting to fit.

She laughed. "That name is for my enemies. You can call me Nix. Short for Phoenix."

She faced away from the mural. "I think I understand."

"You understand what we are?"

"Yes. We're…somehow like these creatures."

"Yes. We are. You and I are…fire birds. The phoenix that rises from the ashes to become stronger."

"These are…these creatures aren't…real."

"No, they aren't, and yet…" She took a flame ball and tossed it to the roof, which erupted, showing an image of black fire, destroying everything around it. "They can exist through us, because of that fire."

She thought of Marie, of the other victims. The dark flame that made her question her sanity after the bus. "Not everyone gets to be us, though."

Nix shook her head sadly. "No, no not everyone survives omega fire."

Ann was suddenly angry. "Why did I survive when my best friend didn't?"

Nix walked slowly forward. "We don't know. The fire…randomly picks its victims, and its survivors. No one knows why one person dies and another lives."

She wiped away tears. "And it changes us into these creatures?"

"It gives us a link to one of these creatures. They exist through us. The more you use your power, the stronger that bond becomes, the more the creature becomes real."

"You're saying the bird I saw…"

"She is your phoenix."

"Why couldn't my friends see her?"

"They…don't seem to have been given the challenges that you've faced. They weren't forced to defend themselves. You are…marvelous in your ability. It took me ten years to see my fire bird."

"What does yours look like?"

Her head down, she spun away, her sympathetic tone replaced with a standard, professional voice. "Later. We need to go. I feel…another fire element nearby. Probably *him*."

"Him?"

"The one you sent flying off that building."

She thought of him falling three stories down. Relief flooded her system as she realized she may not have taken his life. "Is he one of us?"

She laughed once more. "No, he's the dragon."

"Aren't I supposed to write my name?"

"No. You wait until you're…older to choose yours. It's the nature of our kind to reinvent ourselves. Take your time choosing."

"All these names, some crossed out…"

"What about them?"

"Where are they all?"

"Most are dead. This is our only memorial. We come here to remember them."

She nodded, walking forward. "Where are we going now?"

"To my place. You have a lot to learn."

While rubbing his already weary eyes, Dr. Jackson ran over the protocol for the next meeting, which would take place shortly. While he'd been gracious with Dr. Cline, Dr. Huxley was an entirely different situation.

A news article popped up on his browser. He opened the link, reading quickly. "Mysterious Fire Engulfs Abandoned Downtown Building." He quickly read through, noting the talk of fire damage, of no victims. *Just like old times.*

With a sigh, he closed his browser as he touched his headset. "Call Nix."

The phone rang one, two, three times before she answered, saying only, "it's good."

When she hung up, he focused his attention back to the white folder. "Isaiah, is security here?"

"Yes. Should I send them in?"

"Yes."

The four security guards entered, going about their work as they had been meticulously instructed. These situations didn't occur often, but when they did, it was his job to make sure he treated the situation appropriately. The blinds were closed, cameras set around the room, secure mode activated.

Two chairs were placed in the center of the room, and one guard handed the Director a pair of gloves, which he swiftly adorned, though he felt guilty at destroying such fine leather. Resigning himself to his role, he sat, waiting patiently for his employee to enter the room.

He reached a hand out as two guards, finished with their work, stood by the door, looking intimidating. A sanitary wipe was run over his glove without a word, then the other. Everything was ready, except for Dr. Huxley, whose cries could be heard as the elevator to the floor opened. Unmoved, he sat as security forcibly walked him into the office, where they sat him down, tying his hands and feet to the other chair.

The man was distraught, tears openly streaming down his face. He gave him a few silent moments, before he stood, walking closer. The teary-eyed man reacted as if his very presence hurt, hiding his face in imagined pain.

Folding his hands in front of him, professionally, he squared off with the man in the chair.

He finally found the courage to say, "Please don't do this."

He gave him a stern look. "Dr. Huxley."

"Director."

"I'm very disappointed in you."

"I didn't have a choice." He whimpered loudly. "They took my son."

"You were hired with two PhD's and former experience in the CIA. Are you really so easily manipulated?"

"What do you mean? They took my son!" He tried unsuccessfully to remove his bonds, the anger suddenly sweeping over him. "I had no choice!"

Dr. Jackson took a deep breath in and out, then punched the man in the face. "I'm very aware of their tactics, to which you reacted as they expected."

"See? You agree with me."

"No. No I do not." He hit him again. "You see, you had a choice. You chose to betray me, instead of including me."

The man's eyes widened. "I didn't think- "

Another punch. "Exactly." He moved away and nodded to the security guards. "Start the tape."

The man cried silently in front of him, blood dripping from his nose. "You're being recorded so you cannot sue for wrongful termination. I need a confession from you, and I need it now."

The man only shook his head. "You realize the longer you are here, the guiltier you appear?"

The man nodded. "They'll kill him."

Dr. Jackson nodded. "Had you notified me, your son would already be home with you. Now, do I turn the tape off, or will you start talking?"

He just whimpered. Dr. Jackson nodded to security, who cut the feed. Flexing his hand, he punched him once, twice, three times before starting the recording again. "Dr. Huxley, why are you here?"

The man didn't answer. Dr. Jackson, his head low, sighed, thinking of the long day ahead of him.

Wills and Ryan looked at the building in front of them, to the rundown neighborhood around them. They glanced at each other, perplexed. From the back seat, Joy chirped, "What are you waiting for? Let's go inside." She seemed so excited to be here, and no one in the car understood why.

"Let me out!" She all but shoved Connor out of the way, as he moved to let her exit over his lap. Why was she so excited? He looked at Seth, who shrugged. Following, they piled out, looking at the old Victorian home in front of them.

"This is where you want to stay?"

Joy nodded, her eyes wide with anticipation. "Oh, yes. This is the one."

"There's a real hotel two blocks from here."

"Yeah…no. We're staying here. Right Seth?" She looked to him, and he nodded.

"Well, I guess that settles it. I'll go inside, see how many rooms they have."

Joy clapped her hands as Wills walked forward, slowly shaking her head.

An older woman stood inside, sweeping. She stopped upon seeing visitors, a bright smile lighting her face. "Well, hello there."

"Hi. Are you open for business? The sign says you're a bed and breakfast."

"Yes, yes I am!" She walked behind a small counter and opened a book. "How many rooms would you like?"

"How many do you have available?"

"Seven."

"We'll take them all."

Her eyes lit up at the wad of cash Wills gave her. "They're all ready. Here are the keys. So grateful you chose to stay, it's been ages since we've had any visitors."

She hid the cash in her apron, producing keys for every room. Wills walked outside and randomly handed out the keys. Joy frowned at hers. "This isn't right." Taking the keys back, she passed them out again, in the "correct" order. "There. That way these two won't fight over it." She pointed to Julius and Connor.

"We don't always fight."

Joy laughed. "Fight yourselves, fight your nature, same thing. We need you to get along for now." Without another word, she skipped inside the building, running up the stairs as the others followed behind. They missed that she'd kept two keys for herself.

"Man, and I thought your gut was weird."

Seth nodded. "Joy's always been a free spirit."

"Even before the fire?"

"Yeah, believe it or not. Still, her powers seem...stronger than mine."

"Feeling outdone by a girl?"

"No, not at all. I'm glad we've got someone like her to help. My gut tells me we'll need it." He followed Connor forward, unlocking the key to his room. From the hallway, he heard, "get some rest. We have a big night ahead."

Julius groaned, but he was ready for some sleep. His head was out as soon as he hit the pillow.

Tyrus walked the trails of the park, looking for answers more than anything else. There was a time he'd lived and worked in St. Blaise, long ago. He'd run on these trails. He remembered them like he remembered everything. With perfect clarity. Walking toward the old temple, more out of habit than anything else, he froze as he saw them exit, Ann first, followed by Nix.

He placed his hands in his pockets, hoping to appear less threatening. The last thing he needed was for the forest around them to burn. Considering their last meeting...

She saw him and froze. Nix continued walking forward, placing herself between the two of them. She glanced at both before addressing him.

"Hello, Ty."

"Nix."

Ann backed away as Nix watched her. "You know each other?"

Tyrus took a step back. "No one is here to hurt anyone."

She froze again as he moved.

Nix sighed. "Ann, this is Tyrus, Tyrus, Ann."

"We've met." Ann's eyes grew red, but Nix walked to her, placing a hand on her wrist, and the fire died. Ann looked at her in surprise. "He hurt my friends."

"Not here. This place is a sanctuary, and not now." She stepped forward again. "What do you want, Ty?"

"To figure this out."

"What's to figure out? Someone broke the rules, released synthetic Omega Flame that changed the lives of five teens forever."

"I mean, who and why."

"You always did like puzzles."

"Now is not the time for reminiscing."

She smiled wide at him. "Oh, I'm aware. You'll get your answers. You always do. Question is, will you do the right thing when you have them?" Her gaze hardened in a way Ann noticed but couldn't understand. They weren't exactly friends, or enemies, but somewhere in between.

"Nix, I only want to help these victims."

The woman looked to Ann. "You want to go with the big, bad dragon or stay here with me?"

"You."

She gave him a triumphant look. "See? She's with her own kind. Safe. I got her."

"You and I both know that three people exist with access to this technology."

Her eyes narrowed. "Watch what you say next, Tyrus."

He sighed. "So, where do we go from here?"

Nix looked past him as if someone were coming toward him, her eyes wide. As he turned to see who it was, she unleashed her flame on a large tree branch, which fell on his head. He tumbled to the ground, unmoving.

"Let's go."

Ann avoided him as they left, more confused than ever. "What was that all about?"

Nix chuckled. "I'll explain later. For now, we will continue to my place. There are worse things than dragons."

Ann shuddered at that as they walked out of the forest, afraid to ask.

Tyrus woke with a headache some moments later, alone on the trails. Cursing beautiful, deadly women, he stood and walked out of the park after having been knocked unconscious twice in one day. He should have suspected Nix's involvement, considering. The threads were there, he just hadn't put them together. Something about these five were disrupting his usual steady self. Their powers were potent. He hypothesized that the synthetic nature of the flame had something to do with their immense power. That wasn't necessarily a good outcome. So many events could end badly. Too many outcomes to predict. He didn't like that.

He got into his new used classic and held the phone to his ear, dialing. "Where are you?"

"I'm on my way."

"Did you find Ann?"

He laughed dryly. "For a moment."

Wills paused. "We need them all."

"I'm aware. For now, though, we'll have to use the four we have."

"I'm sending you the address."

"Got it." She hung up and the text came through a moment later. He smiled. A bed and breakfast. Quaint. He suspected Joy's nature before, but her whimsy nearly proved he was right. One of them was a unicorn. Their kind was precious, cheerful, but when they went bad, they went evil.

He shifted into gear and backed up, driving away, the radio loud. Somehow, they'd solve this.

Ann followed Nix into a high tech, gorgeous apartment building. Taking the elevator, Nix hit the button for the top floor. They waited in silence while the elevator music played. After the events of the day, normalcy was eerily uncomfortable for the both of them.

The elevator opened some moments later to a double door, white with golden trim. "This is my place while I'm in the city."

"Do you move around a lot?" She knew how that felt.

"For jobs. I…work internationally."

"That's awesome."

"No, no it's not."

Ann didn't understand, but she let it go, following Nix inside. She inhaled sharply at seeing the extravagance of the living room, simple, modern, clean.

"Wow."

Nix laughed dryly. "Believe me, after what I've been through, none of this really matters. It's just…for show."

"I wish I had your problems."

Nix stared her down until she felt small. "No, Ann, no you don't."

She tilted her head, a silent question, to which Nix didn't give an answer. "Down the hallway, to the right is your room. Mine's on the left. Last door. Go check it out."

Ann had so many questions, but she knew better than to ask half of them. Walking down the white corridor, she came to the last door and opened it, to a large bedroom. She smiled wide as she realized that this would be hers, that for the first time in forever, she didn't have to share with anyone. This was her space, albeit temporarily. It felt wonderful.

She took a moment to check out the closet and bathroom. Clothes of all styles and sizes were inside the large walk-in closet, as well as shoes. So. Many. Shoes. She looked for some in her size, and walked into the bathroom to change, noting the floor to ceiling mirror and large walk-in shower with beautiful tile.

She smiled again, giddy at her luck. Whoever Nix was, she was generous. She looked herself over, looked through the drawers, noting the hair product and unused makeup just sitting around. After a few moments of applying a bit of it, she walked out to the bedroom, plopped on the bed, which was like a cloud, and turned on the TV, convinced her life was finally beginning to look up.

Nix knocked on the door some moments later. *This must be what privacy feels like.* "Come in."

The older woman entered. "You settling in alright?"

"Oh, yeah."

She gave Ann a half smile. "You can have anything you want in the fridge. Don't feel like you have to stay in here. Use the living room and the kitchen as you need to. I have a job to do in the green zone."

"What's the green zone?"

Nix just stared at her. "Never mind. I'll be fine. Don't leave while I'm gone. We have a lot to discuss. Bye." Her questions, like she'd suspected, would have to wait. Nix shut the door softly and Ann increased the volume. She forgot about everything for a few moments, watching a reality show about finding love.

◆ ◆ ◆

Nix left the apartment, walking through the lobby to the valet desk, where they retrieved her car without inquiry. They were used to her being here, knew what she expected. She sighed, the routine of the job monotonous. The fire bird upstairs though, that was…interesting. She hadn't known that when taking the contract. *Another fire bird. Strange.*

She unlocked her phone, a moment of indecision overcoming her. Should she fulfill her contract and hand the girl over to her employer? She knew what would happen to her, there, what always happened to fire birds, like herself. She gripped the phone tightly, before forcing herself to dial her contact. This *had* to be just business.

One ring and he answered. "Yes."

"She's at my place."

"And the others?"

"Working on it. Only found one so far."

A pause. "We need them all."

"I'm aware, Director. You hired me because I know how to get things done. That hasn't changed. I just need more time. It's…complicated."

"Are more Mythics involved?"

"Tyrus."

"Interesting. Do you need…assistance?"

She felt a rush of panic. She knew who he would call. "No. I can do this on my own."

He hung up, and she waited for her car, thinking on the threat he'd just given her. Time was not on her side in this. Her car pulled up and she entered gracefully, two outcomes and their consequences pulling at her once more.

He stopped in front of the bed and breakfast. He found the old Victorian home strange in the neighborhood. Not many houses with that architecture still existed. It looked out of place; a huge building surrounded by small, more economic homes in the depressed area. A closed school sat across the street, the sidewalk cracking, crumbling away.

He sighed, dealing with the anxiety he always experienced, a reminder of his past. He didn't like being surrounded by so many people. He, more than most, was aware of his…capabilities, aware of his power, and with it, came the burden. Looking at Ryan on the porch, talking on the phone with his wife, he walked forward, his movements showing no hint of the constant war that raged within him.

Ryan nodded, pointing. He gave him a half smile and moved on. No way was he getting involved in that unless he had to. Ellie was a great woman, with great plans for Ryan. He entered, immediately greeted by Joy. "What took you so long?"

The hug was slightly uncomfortable for him, but natural for her. She ignored his discomfort. "No Ann?"

He lowered his head. "No Ann."

"That's okay, birds of a feather, you know." She handed him a key then walked up the grand staircase in the middle of the hallway. "Your room is the last on the right. Soundproof." A strange, innocent giggle escaped her, and he glared after her. She didn't turn back.

He sighed and followed, the sound of teens living in the building almost too much for him. A lot of noise, a lot of people. Still, he'd already committed himself to helping, so he walked calmly to his room, ignoring them as best he could.

"Don't worry, we'll grow on you!" Joy shouted it from another room and he smiled to himself. He opened his door and rolled his eyes. No wonder she'd giggled. He looked at the frilly, lacy hearts covering the entire room. The ambience of the room was clear. *Just what I need. The honeymoon suite.*

Noting that he had his own bathroom, complete with a large tub, he smiled at that. He had privacy, at least. He locked the door and sat on the bed, his head in his hands. He breathed in and out, replaying the events that had upended his life. He felt a moment of guilt, after all, though he hated being around others, the teens weren't at fault for their situation, and they clearly needed some guidance. When he'd been in their position, he would have benefited from someone…older helping him through. He didn't have that, but they did, now, with him. Determined to do better, he let go of the hermit and embraced the soldier. They needed his strength, not his doubt.

They didn't deserve this burden they'd been given, the great responsibility and dark fate that awaited them. They didn't understand it, couldn't comprehend its magnitude. He'd done this before, saved the new only to watch corruption and decay erode their will. Still, he hoped that this time, with these five, it'd be different.

He lay on the bed, wondering how the baby bird was doing. Nix would keep her safe, as long as she needed her, but she was no maternal figure, no role model. She hadn't been since…well, that was a long time ago. He focused on the future, let the guilt of the past fade. This time, he'd save the fire bird, instead of destroying it, and in doing so, maybe he could find some redemption.

Chapter 10
Day 11

Tyrus woke suddenly, still dreaming. The nightmare of war faded, replaced by…calm consciousness. This was Joy's doing.

She stood with her back to him, far away, alone in the middle of a field of flowers too big for their stems. The closer he walked toward her, the stronger the sunlight beamed on him. When he was close, she spun and smiled.

"I didn't know if you would come. We're going to have so much fun, as soon as you convince her."

"He smiled sympathetically. "Ann hates me, Joy. She threw me off a roof."

"Oh, she just doesn't know…" she looked over his shoulder, gasping. "See? Here she is."

He turned in time to see Ann throw a flame at him. He deflected it easily. "Joy, run!"

Joy skipped to her and took her hand, guiding her forward as a perplexed look overcame her features. "Seeing you gives me hope, Ann."

"Joy…dragon."

"I know what he is. You're the one that's confused."

Ann gave him a sideways look, standing as far as possible from him. He sighed. "Ann…"

He watched the emotions play on her face, saw the doubt in her eyes. He could almost hear her thoughts. If he was a monster, he wouldn't feel remorseful. A sliver of hope crept into his soul.

"There's no time for that. Just make up, so we can survive this…" She pointed forward, a new scene before them.

He heard Ann's breath catch, as did his own. Below them, St. Blaise stood burning. Everything was touched by flame, ash rising to the sky, darkening the earth. Screaming, torturous sounds rose, citizens fleeing in all directions, only to succumb to the fire.

He saw Ann looking at him, wondering at his nature. Words failed him for a moment, so he only half smiled, shrugging his shoulder in apology. Joy pivoted, stomping her foot. "You can't even talk here? If you two can't work together, then all of us will die."

She held out a hand between them, but as they reached to grab hers, they felt something slippery. Pulling back, he saw both their hands covered in blood.

Ann woke, sweat dripping down her back. Her breathing calmed, her heartbeat slowly resetting to normal. She looked around the room, unfamiliar with her surroundings. As her memory returned to her, she looked down at her hand, expecting to find blood. She wiped it on her shirt even though there was nothing there.

It was midnight, the world dark. She walked out to the kitchen, her appetite growing quickly. Nix hadn't come back from her job yet. She'd been gone all day. Grabbing the first thing she could from the fridge, a carrot, she began chomping away. One carrot wasn't going to stave off this hunger, though. She opened the freezer, removing a meal, setting it in front of the microwave.

"You don't need to use that, you know."

She jumped, startled. She looked over to see Nix leaning against the wall.

"What?"

"You can use your flame to heat your food."

"Really?"

Nix nodded. "Give me that." She took the meal from her, unwrapping it completely. Her eyes lit with orange flame. Ann could almost feel the heat from her hand. A few moments later, it was bubbling, hot and steamy. Nix showed Ann, who held out her hands, but Nix grabbed a fork and began to eat it instead.

"You can eat when you heat it up yourself." She unplugged the microwave. "The trick is to let the heat out, but not a full flame. It would benefit you to learn some control."

It didn't look hard, so Ann took out a meal from the freezer, summoning her flame, carefully. She ended up scraping the ashes out of the sink from the small kitchen fire she'd started. The second meal came out half frozen, half charcoal.

Starting to get frustrated, she sighed loudly. "Don't give up." Nix had returned to the kitchen. "Getting frustrated will only make your job harder. Stay calm, center, and focus."

She walked away again. This time, Ann called the ocean, the calm waves lapping on the shore. She could almost feel the wind on her face, smell the salt. When she was ready, she slowly released her power into her hand. The bird flew on top of her knuckles, resting there. Flapping her wings slowly, she blew hot wind onto the meal on the counter. When Ann looked up again, the meal was done. Sending a silent thank you to her friend, she ran to show Nix.

"I did it! See?"

Nix didn't look up, suddenly cold. "Great. Now eat it."

Unperturbed by her apathy, Ann did exactly that, missing the jealous look Nix sent her way. Sitting next to her, she ate happily. One little exercise had helped her more than Nix knew. She was learning control and gaining her center with it.

"What else can we do?"

Nix smiled slyly. "Anything we want."

Tyrus woke as well, sitting up quickly in bed, images flashing in his mind. He shook it to clear his confused head, coming back to the room, back to reality. He touched a hand to his heart, willing it to slow.

He stood, ignoring the pain that was always there, deep in his bones. He rubbed his eyes as he walked into the bathroom, hitting the light switch. He remembered everything. It was part of the curse of his kind, to remember, with perfect clarity, while others forgot.

He pushed her message aside, focusing on the tasks before him. He showered, letting the hot water take the pain from him, if only for a moment. When he was finished, he walked out, wearing a towel, looking for his clothes. The tattoo of a dragon on his back.

"Nice towel you got there."

He jumped, clutching the towel so it would stay in place. Glaring, he saw Joy standing in the doorway. "What do you need Joy?"

She winked at him, which only made him more uncomfortable. "Bad dream?"

He returned her inquiry with a hard stare. "You know damn well what I dreamed of. Get out, Joy."

"Hurry. We're ready when you are." She gave him a pout as she left. Walking forward, he checked the lock on the door. Yep, he'd remembered to lock it. *Damn unicorns....*

He walked out of the room a few minutes later, dressed in black and ready for the night ahead. Everyone was waiting downstairs. Wills began as she saw him enter the foyer.

"We'll need to split into teams. I have vials and some medical equipment, but I require a few additional items from the nearest drug store. Ryan will go with Seth and Julius to get those things. Here." She handed him a list. "Meet us across the street at the abandoned school. No flashlights until we need them."

"Got it." The three left, and Wills faced the remaining group. "We go to the school, find a science classroom to work. We can't do it here. We scrub it, clean it, and wait for the other team to arrive. Then, I will take some blood samples and analyze them to see if I can pinpoint what is actually occurring to you. I'd love to run tests on your DNA, but we don't have access to that equipment, so this will have to do."

Tyrus watched Joy bite her lip and hoped she would keep quiet. He followed them out, scanning the sky for drones. The still night greeted him, the only sound the chirping of crickets. No one had found them yet.

Reaching the building, he took out some tools to open the locked door. Instead of waiting, Joy simply touched the handle, and the door gave way. Skipping inside silently, she walked down the hall as Wills gave him a confused look. "Her kind can open locked doors."

"Fascinating." They followed her through the hallway. She took a sudden right, then a left and stopped, motioning to the next door. "Tada!"

Tyrus looked at her. "Aren't you going to open this?"

She folded her arms awkwardly in front of her. She opened her mouth as if she was about to speak, then abruptly closed it and frowned. "You can do this one." She then spun away, humming a tune.

Taking out his tools, he unlocked the door. Walking in, they quietly got to work. It was several minutes before the room was sanitized. They waited until the others returned. At the sound of the car, Joy disappeared from view.

Wills grabbed his arm, her eyes wide. "Unicorns can transport themselves like that."

"Where did she go?"

"To get the others."

"You heard them pull up?"

"Yeah, didn't you?"

"No." She opened a notebook, jotted something down. She was keeping close tabs on all of them, which was fine, as long as she was on their side. When they appeared, she got down to business, arranging everything she needed. "Turn on a small light. Here, so I can work."

Tyrus lifted the flashlight above her head and flicked it on. She moved his hand as if he were a lamp. "There. Now I can begin."

The teens sat at the back of the room on stools, waiting for the doctor to finish. Julius seemed agitated.

"What is it?" Connor didn't want a repeat of the fight they'd had. He still didn't understand why they'd been so quick to attack each other.

"Smell of blood. That's all. My sense of smell is overpowering lately."

"Here." Joy produced a flower from her hand. "Smell this instead."

"Do you know everything?"

"No." She looked at him with innocent confusion. "Why?"

He just chuckled and took the damn flower, its scent more comfortable than the blood that was threatening to upend his stomach. Reluctantly, he held it to his nose, feeling uncomfortable. When Connor noticed his awkwardness, he glared at him.

"What do you think they'll find?" Seth said it half to himself, half out loud.

"Ooh, a game. Okay, how about radioactivity?" Joy clapped as she said it.

"Or maybe we're all aliens?" Connor added sarcastically. "What do you think, Julius?"

"We are blades, honed by the fire to be wielded by the powerful."

Silence greeted them. It was such a profound thing to say, and not at all amusing to think about. They looked at the adults before them, then back to each other.

"We can trust them, right?" Connor adjusted his stance.

Julius shrugged, as did Seth. Joy bit her lip, then said, "we… are where we need to be."

"That doesn't exactly answer my question."

She smiled at him, bright and wide. "Don't worry. None of us will die tonight."

Julius eyed her, wondering if she actually thought that was reassuring.

Wills set freshly collected vials one through six out. She'd taken a sample of Tyrus's blood earlier. The seventh vial was hers, the control group. She performed meticulous tests, the same she'd done in the lab at the hospital, one after another.

She checked everything she knew how to with the tools she had available. She took hours, pouring over each result, recording everything in her notebook for later. She worked quietly, as Tyrus acted as her light source. He followed her silently, while Ryan sat in the corner, the look out.

When she had gathered all the info she could, she sat back, noting the night was not as dark anymore. The sun would rise within the hour.

"Well?" Tyrus looked at her.

She gave a frustrated sigh. "The abnormal results we got at the hospital don't correspond with these. Whatever changed them, it's done changing. Their blood is stable, now. This was useless to me."

She took off the latex gloves angrily, throwing them on the counter. Tyrus shut off the flashlight and leaned in, talking softly to her.

"I'm sorry you didn't find what you were looking for."

"I just don't understand. The results were all over the place at the hospital."

"Usually, it takes months for the…change to occur. In less than two weeks, these teens have done what it took me eighty days to do. Believe me, you didn't do all this for nothing."

"Really?"

"Yes. You feel the change, and you know when you're done. It was awful for me. Somehow, the nature of the synthetic fire has caused them to change faster. They're…stronger than I was, more powerful. It worries me."

"Why does their blood's stability worry you?"

"Because we…don't usually live long, happy, fulfilling lives. Most of the people I've known like me are gone." He gazed at the four of them, watching them banter. "Now we have five newly arisen powerhouses that can kick even my ass. Someone other than me is bound to notice, and to come for them."

"What will you do when that happens?"

"Hope I've prepared them well enough."

"Do you think you have?"

He laughed, sadistically. "I haven't even started."

"Well, if their abilities are growing this quickly, should you?"

He nodded. "Oh, yeah. The sooner the better." He watched Joy and Julius circle each other. She giggled while he just looked annoyed. A sad look crossed his face, and he was caught in a memory of another time, another place. With melancholy, he gave Wills a sympathetic look. "Let's get out of this place. They need to rest."

"What happened to you?"

"The same thing that happened to them, only my lesson was more sinister."

Nix waited until Ann was softly snoring and then slipped out. She had to placate her employer, make it look like she was too busy to complete the job, so she decided to focus on another contract she'd taken from the same company.

This contract was about vengeance, cold and unforgiving. She was one of three that took these kinds of jobs. Not every Mythic had her iron stomach. She walked along the street, away from her apartment, and whistled.

Two blocks, three blocks passed, then she rotated left to arrive at a broken-down apartment building. Taking out her phone, because police response time in this area wasn't great, she dialed 911.

"911, what's the nature of your emergency?"

Holding a flame up to the phone so it could be heard, she said, "get someone over here now!"

"Is that a fire? Can you tell me where you're located?"

"Oh, I don't really know," she stammered, pleased with her acting skills. "Uhm, looks like the cross streets of 22nd and Lester. An old apartment building. It's on fire! Please hurry."

"Can you stay on the line with me?"

"No, I have to go. Phone's on fire." She hung up and powered off the burn phone, wiping it clean and tossing it into the nearest trash bin, and as she walked forward, the bin lit on fire, its heat creeping up the side of the target building.

Opening the front door, she climbed the stairs quickly to the third floor. Spinning right, like the floor plan indicated, she threw a flame ball down the hall, directly under a sprinkler. It was set off almost immediately. As soon as residents started to exit, she turned to the door directly behind her and opened it with heat.

Stepping inside, she fused the lock. They couldn't get out this way now. Walking toward the living room, two men came out, carrying a little boy. Nix bowed politely, partially to disguise her surprise. The boy was moving, still alive. Though she'd prepared for it, she hadn't expected it.

"Gentlemen," she began. "I'm Pride. We have some things to discuss but first, hand over the boy."

"We didn't hurt him. Our boss wanted us to, but we didn't. We didn't!"

"Good for you. Want a cookie? You still kidnapped someone's baby. Hand him over and you might make it through this."

Grabbing the child, the shorter man spoke. "You kill us, and the kid dies too. You have to let us go."

She laughed, so hard it tilted her head back. When she looked at the men again, her normally brown eyes shone with orange fire.

"I don't have to do anything other than watch you die." The smaller man's back suddenly erupted in flame. Smoke was thick now, the fire consuming the building. As he burned, screaming, the young boy came loose and ran to Nix. Picking him up, she cradled him as if he was her own.

"Don't you worry, now, Tyler, I know your daddy. I'm taking you to your mommy."

Speaking to the other man, frozen in place despite the flames, she said, "I can shield you and save you from this mess, or you can die in the fire. What will it be?" She held out a hand, willing him to take it.

Instead, the idiot said, "neither." While he managed to use a heroic, resolved tone, his actions were misguided. Nix rolled her eyes as he rushed toward the window, breaking the glass, then diving to the ground three stories below. She strode to the window, looking down, making certain she covered the boy's face from what she may find. He was alive, barely. They'd take him to the nearest hospital. She hadn't gotten the information she needed, but she did save the kid. The director would still be pleased, but she'd only get half of the money.

Hushing the small boy, she asked him to close his eyes. Singing a lullaby, softly, she walked patiently down the stairs just as she heard the distant sound of sirens. Fire raged around them, but they walked through unperturbed, the flames opening for their mistress and her protected companion. Stepping to the back exit, she immediately walked out and to the left, away from the back of the building just as the fire trucks showed up. He had gotten lucky, for now, but once he was awake, the other half of that contract was hers. Still singing the lullaby, she rounded a corner to find her parked car, right where she put it earlier in the day. The car seat was already strapped in the back.

She placed him inside with a soft blanket and several comforting toys, then she shut her door and drove away. Pushing a button on her dash, the car said, "Please say a command."

"Call Dr. Jackson."

"Calling Gregory Jackson."

A few rings and she heard someone pick up. "Boy's alive and with me. No answers yet. I'll check the local hospital."

"I'll inform his mother. His father, unfortunately, was found dead earlier. I assume it was the mastermind behind all this. It's a good thing you found him now. Thank you, Nix." Then he hung up.

At least she made some money tonight. Besides, this was a good thing. Everyone was wondering who trashed that bus, and she was playing a small part in doing good for a change. Smiling, she hummed the lullaby as the toddler drifted off to sleep.

Dr. Jackson hung up the phone and relief flooded through him. That was one less problem he had to deal with. The child was safe. Eventually, with the right leverage, the goon would talk, and he would finally get to the bottom of this. Although he had his suspicions about who was involved, he could do nothing without solid, legal proof.

Picking up his phone, he dialed a number written on a post-it on his left. It took three rings before someone answered.

"Hello," the woman said, obviously weary from her recent tragic life. "Who is it?"

"Mrs. Huxley, this is Director Jackson. I'm the CEO of your late husband's company. Let me first say how sorry I am to learn of your husband's suicide. However, a colleague of mine is on her way to drop off something else that's very precious to you. All I ask is that you leave her out of any police descriptions. She's very shy, but effective."

He heard a knock seconds later on her door. "One moment." There was a shout on the other end, crying. She came back on the line a moment later. "Thank you! Thank you so much for finding my baby!"

He smiled. "You are most welcome. Again, sorry for your loss."

Hanging up the phone, he only felt it was the right thing to do to return her son when his company had been involved in the death of her husband. He felt guilty, although he hadn't tied the rope.

The cops ruled it a suicide, but he knew better. Someone very powerful was here, watching, waiting, anticipating his every move. He had to be better, faster, stronger, smarter. This was his company, and he'd be damned if his father's pact ended with him.

◆ ◆ ◆

Day 12

The next night, at sunset, Ryan and Wills hopped into the van and drove away. They had lives, jobs, responsibilities. He watched them depart apprehensively. They had their orders. They'd call him. They'd stay alert. They'd met the kids. This was real to them now. He'd need that in the future.

Looking back, he thought about his job now. He was no parent. Never had kids. What he did know was training marines. These teens though, they didn't volunteer for this life. They were victims of it. His job was to make them strong, capable of surviving this war.

As if on cue, Joy popped up next to him. Was this girl ever anything but happy?

"What do we do now?" she quizzically stated.

"Gather your friends. There are some things we need to discuss."

With that, he wondered how to soften the blow for them, or if he should. This shouldn't have happened. They shouldn't have to go through what he went through.

Standing in Joy's room, they collected themselves on the bed, laughing. He tried to remember if he had ever been that happy. He couldn't come up with anything.

"Okay, settle down." He waited until they chose to listen. Took a few minutes. "There's some things we need to talk through." Pulling up a desk chair, he sat facing them, hands clasped in front.

"How old do you think I am?" He could begin with that.

"Like, fifty?"

"Thirty-five!"

"Forty?"

Joy was the only one silent for a moment. When she spoke, she said, "two million, one hundred seven thousand and forty…" she paused, counting on her fingers, "…six."

"Thanks for that," he said sarcastically.

"Welcome." She smiled. She actually smiled.

Great. He gave Joy a confused look, and she shrugged her shoulders at him. Clearing his throat, he continued. "I'm almost two hundred years old."

Their jaws dropped. Except Joy's. She giggled.

"How are you not dead?" Connor asked.

He paused. "Because, like you, I was a victim of a supernatural force that has existed for almost as long as this planet we occupy."

"What, you mean the government?" Julius asked.

"No. Everyone always thinks the government did it, but this time, no. It was something else. Something greater than human greed and cruelty. Something much more random and unforgiving."

He took a deep breath and continued.

"You were victims of a powerful, lifechanging force."

"The black fire?"

"Omega Fire is what we called it. I'm no scientist, but after exposure to that, we change, or we die."

"How did it happen to you?"

"That's the thing, it found me, one day on the battlefield. It was suddenly… there. All around my unit in the middle of a battle. I was the only one…" He sighed, trying not to get lost in that distant memory. "And it changed me. Who I was. Gave me strange powers that you're all experiencing. The part that makes me mad is that research into this has been banned. You shouldn't have had to worry about this. Someone broke the rules, and the result are you, being victimized by this."

"So, what do we do?" Seth asked.

"We make you into a unit. You have to be prepared for the worst. You're different now, and that usually means danger, headaches, and trouble."

Day 13

Ann was getting into trouble. Nix was helping. The two girls were out in the town, in the middle of night, trying out her powers. Laughing, they turned onto a busy street, crowded with small shops.

"Remember, only one. Nix talked to her. "Response time is fast. We have to be able to get away. You pick."

Walking up and down the shops, looking in the windows, she had a moment of doubt. She desperately wanted to learn about her "gift" as Nix called it, but she had been raised not to steal. It was a stigma fosters carried, that they were vagabonds and thieves, untrustworthy. While some of those existed, she'd resisted the urge to become that herself. If she didn't do it though, Nix might get angry, and leave her. She cared for this adult, in a strange but strong way. She didn't want her to leave. Not now. Besides, this was a test of her power.

A jewelry store caught her attention. There had to be something in there worth taking. She'd never really had a nice necklace or a good pair of earrings before. Motioning to Nix, she called, "this one."

Nix walked over, noting that most of the jewelry was removed from the windows at night. "Challenging," she paused, thinking. "You have to bust the window, and the glass cases to get at anything good. What did you have in mind?"

"Maybe a nice pair of earrings or a necklace?"

Nix nodded. "Sure. You know what to do. I'll let you know when the police are on their way. Take a deep breath and begin."

She wasn't at all sure about this. What if she got caught? Nix said to fight your way out, never to end up in jail, but she didn't know if she had that in her again.

She forced herself to stop thinking ahead. *Focus on your power. Focus on what you want.* The flame came easily now, burning in her right hand. She summoned it, condensed it, until it was big enough to do what she wanted. Then, she released it.

The window shattered and an alarm blared. The flame was not gone. The heat from it broke the glass cases easily, and she stepped inside to see what she could get to.

She only had a few moments to choose. Surrounded by pretty baubles, she looked around wildly, not sure what to take. She glanced at a pair of diamond studs. They were princess cut, perfect and shiny. She grabbed them and spun to go. Running out the front, several lights had turned on, but Nix was nowhere to be found.

Crap. Where was she? "Nix," she called. No answer. She had to make a choice, had to do something, so she ran to the left. She could already hear sirens. How did they get here so fast? She took the first alley she came to, barely missing the cop car that turned down the street. Her adrenaline pumped through her veins. She wasn't safe though. She blasted a hole of flame through a metal gate and ran. Getting to the other side of the street, she ran across, cars swerving to avoid her. Into another alley, and she continued to run.

When she felt like she couldn't run anymore, she summoned the flame. It lit her feet, helping her cushion her steps from the harsh concrete. She was hovering over the ground, walking on the flames. Pivoting to the right, she was three blocks from Nix's apartment building. No sirens, now. When she found her, she just might kill her…

Nix, on the other hand, used this opportunity to finish a small contract, three streets over. Coming out of a rundown studio apartment, she looked at her boots. As she thought, blood spatter covered them. *Wonderful. I'll have to burn them.* These were her second favorite pair.

Taking a sanitary wipe out of her pocket, she wiped her boots down and started walking back to her car. From the building behind her, a scream erupted, followed by a woman's voice yelling, "Someone help! Please!"

Nix laughed. Another satisfied customer, another useless news report, another payday. Hearing the sirens two streets over, her little phoenix-in-training was creating a grand distraction for her. If she learned something in the process, great. Nix walked three blocks, then took out her keys. She stepped into her car and drove home.

◆ ◆ ◆

Ann was waiting, calming her breath. Seeing her car pull up, she nonchalantly walked over to Nix, approaching just as she handed her keys to the valet. Nix aimed a wide, genuine smile at her, but she knew better than to discuss it publicly, so she smiled back. It looked just as genuine, but inside she was seething.

They walked in silence to the elevator. Once getting in, Nix hit the button for her floor. She sighed aloud, the only sign of agitation she was willing to show. She knew her eyes were showing the anger for her, the red flame reflecting off the metal around them. Her hands felt warm, but no flame came. She was learning control.

Nix spoke but kept facing forward. "I knew you could do it. Whatever you found, keep it in your pocket for now. It's yours, and yours alone. You owe me nothing." The doors opened, and they walked in.

"I thought you were my look-out tonight." She somehow managed to keep the rage down. "What happened?"

Nix looked at her then. "Did you survive?"

"Well, yes, but-"

"If you survived, then I did my job. I know you're young, but in this world, you can really only depend on one person. Yourself. Anyone else can betray you."

She gave her a look. "Are you going to betray me?"

Nix smiled at her. "No, but you've entered a harsh world where your only goal is to survive, at any cost. I can't guarantee that there won't be a day where my needs and yours clash. You need to be prepared, question everything, everyone, or I'm not helping you, I'm hurting you."

She walked to her room and slammed the door. She understood Nix, but she didn't have to agree. There were people in this world who would never betray her. Letting her mind drift, she wondered how her friends were faring. Joy was awake, somewhere, alone, the boys, who knows. She was sure Seth was fine, but the other two....

Her eyes welled with tears. The image of them lying on the concrete was still hard for her. If she ever met that dragon again, she'd kill him.

Taking the earrings out of her pocket, she placed them in. Tying her hair back, she studied herself in a nearby mirror. *I look... pretty*. The square diamonds glistened in the moonlight. Without really trying, her fire bird appeared in the mirror, landing on her shoulder. She smiled at it before she shooed the bird away, getting ready for bed.

Nix watched from the next room. She kept it locked, so Ann couldn't enter. Around her, several surveillance cameras captured images from across St. Blaise, the lobby in the apartment, the park, and several other important areas. Three laptop computers sat on a table in the middle of the room. Several burn cells were sitting next to the laptops. A gun cabinet stood just inside the door, with a fingerprint lock. Only Nix could open it. It was high tech, her base of operations while she was here.

She couldn't think about that right now though. Jealousy welled inside of Nix. It had taken her years to be able to summon her psychic powers. This girl, she just…did it. It wasn't fair. Nothing about this was fair. A moment came when she thought of taking the bird from the girl. It wouldn't be easy. They were connected, but it could be done.

A single tear slid down her cheek. Surely, she hadn't become that much of a monster, as what she debated was the same as stealing candy from little children. Surely, she wouldn't stoop to that level. This girl was all she had. The contract, that was delayed. She could keep her safe, keep the bird safe. Maybe this was what she was really meant to do. Keep her safe.

Shaking her head, her sensible nature overcame her heart. *She's just a job. You just lectured her about looking out for number one. You should be doing that. If you can take her phoenix, you should.* Frustrated, unable to come to a decision, Nix left the room, the door locking automatically behind her. Going down the hall, she paused briefly by her door. One thing was certain. This teenager had no clue how valuable she was, and who would kill to control her.

The Director sat in his chair, his tablet screen in front of him. His hand covered his mouth, his jaw clenched. He was not a happy man. In fact, he was very upset.

In front of him, on the screen, was Nix's apartment. He made a habit of trusting no one, and it looked like he couldn't trust her either. Though this saddened him, he'd expected as much.

He knew something was amiss when Nix couldn't deliver the girl to him. She kept stalling for time, giving reason after reason she wasn't pursuing the other four. He wasn't used to being swindled, and her betrayal cut deep. He'd protected her. Saved her from the dragon. Picked her up, given her everything she had when she had nothing left.

There was the girl, the next phoenix, sitting in bed, getting ready to sleep. Nix was also in her room. Touching the screen, he zoomed in. His broken bird. He paused the image, touched her face, committing her to memory. Then, he touched his earpiece, saying, "call Levi." If she couldn't do what needed to be done, he had to.

He looked up at the moon. *If I have to summon the Kraken I will.* Waiting for his friend to answer, he stared up at the waning satellite.

Miles away, the same moon lit the shore of a beach, the gentle waves the only sound. Seagulls fluttered away from the shore as the sounds of humans approached. A group of teens ran to the shore. Building a fire, they opened a cooler and took out some beers. They weren't old enough to drink, but that's why they came to the beach.

Laughing, two teens walked to the water's edge, downing their beer and removing their clothes. Diving into the water, they splashed each other and began making out.

Their friends at the fire didn't notice when they stopped splashing. They were too busy getting drunk, having fun, blowing off steam. If they'd been paying attention, they would have seen the man rise from the ocean, as if he didn't have to breathe. They would have seen the ocean itself bow to him, flow around him, as he moved onto the beach. They didn't notice anything until the waves had collected them, washed over them so suddenly that they didn't have a chance to scream.

The man stopped at the cooler, the fire exhausted. The witnesses gone, he thought it a shame to waste the alcohol. He picked the cooler up and headed to their car, whistling some country sounding tune. This would be great fun. The wind picked up, blowing his long platinum hair to the side. As it caught the moonlight, shades of blue, green and purple reflected back.

Chapter 11
Day 14

Dr. Jackson stretched, leaning backward in his office chair. The unfolding crisis within his company deserved his full attention. He'd been putting in long days, longer nights just to come to terms with the betrayal in his company. Now, he alone was responsible for maintaining his father's empire.

Four of the five Mythics were in the city, but unaccounted for. That…worried him. They were unpredictable, their powers uncontained. That meant trouble for every genetics institute that was researching the Omega Fire phenomenon. They needed to be found, their threat neutralized, somehow. He'd called the second operative for this purpose. Maybe the current contract load on Nix was…just too much for her.

Opening his tablet once more, he sipped straight whiskey with two stones. He leafed through the archive, opening a document that was recently added. He'd sent ahead for all the records he could, anything in lore or print that could tell him more than he already knew. Omega Fire was back, by his own company's hand, and he intended to understand it.

The first occurrence of this enigma. The first written account. The black flame was attributed to witches, a work of Satan. The flame was sudden, overwhelming. It left only one survivor. This incident happened in a rural area. Not much collateral damage, this time.

He skimmed the archive, finding a picture with a familiar face. The Red Dragon's image displayed, the same age he appeared now. He'd met Tyrus in the past, as a child, a teen. The man was a dragon in every sense of the word. Smart, prone to long periods of solitude, and powerful.

The black and white image of him was more…naive than the tortured man he knew. Looking at a picture of the aftermath of Tyrus's rebirth, he saw a black figure in the distance, a trick of the camera. Something clicked in his brain, a thought hoping for coalescence. What was he missing here?

Early cameras were imperfect, prone to glitches like this. Still, if he assumed…

"Isaiah," he said over intercom.

"Yes, Director?"

"Get me every known picture of Omega Flame. I need visuals. I'll send you a link to the archive. Call in favors if you have to. Use the incidentals fund. Have Dr. Matheson help you. He's the head of that department anyway. Notify me directly of any progress."

"Right away."

He downed the whiskey in one swig, placing a hand over his mouth in quiet contemplation. What if this…wasn't a glitch?

He tapped his earpiece. "Call Levi." It rang three times before he answered, silently. "Progress?"

"Location B. Surveillance. You sure you want me to stay back? I'd enjoy the…exercise, sparring with the dragon."

"While I would enjoy that video, no. We need information. Their types, their personalities, their current capabilities. All these will help us apprehend them appropriately."

"Understood." He was not hiding his disappointment, though.

"Report on Location A?"

"Set up like you asked. I'm on the floor below. I'll be watching everything Nix does."

"Excellent."

"May I inquire why it's important for her to finish this…specific contract?"

A pause. "Loyalty is always important. I hope for her sake, she stays that way, and I trust you'll be able to handle this professionally, given all facts?"

"I see no reason I can't complete this quickly."

"Excellent to hear. The first payment should clear within the hour."

The Director hung up, and he went back to watching, calmly, with a patience matching his age. His eyes swam with blue water, the ocean always a moment away. He felt his Mythic pull beneath the surface, the leviathan within restless. He wanted a fight, and one way or another, the universe would provide. He just had to wait. Water can wear down any stone.

His mind on the task at hand, he watched Tyrus teach the teens the same moves Levi had taught him. Watched the new Mythics fall, get back up. Watched their reaction to the adjustment in discipline so few displayed lately. For newly changed younglings, they were…incredibly adaptive and competent.

As he watched two sparring, his mind alerted him of some change. The teens stood alone now. Tyrus had vanished. A slow, sadistic smile crossed his lips as he turned around and greeted his former protégé.

"Hello, Fire Dragon."

"Water." Tyrus placed his hands purposefully in his pockets. Better not to appear a threat before he had to. His former mentor's smile gave him no comfort. "What are you doing here, Levi?"

"Someone broke the pact." He motioned toward the teens.

"And I bet you know who." He stared Levi down, looking for a sign of deception.

Levi's smile changed to a frown. "Fifty years of peace, gone. I didn't have a hand in this."

Tyrus nodded. "Yes, but I also remember you being an infamous liar."

Levi gave a menacing laugh before bowing. "You honor me. While it's true I'm better than you," he shook his head, "this isn't on me."

"Yeah, but of the existing three, you're the most…successful. Who is your employer in this, Levi? What was the contract?"

Levi looked for a moment as if he would reveal that very detail. Tyrus knew he was changeable, like fluid. "Unfortunately, they pay me for discretion, as well. You're training them…well. I see you didn't use some of the more…lethal techniques I taught you. Why is that?"

Tyrus, suddenly angry, let his arms turn to scales. "Not every Mythic needs to be a killer."

"No, no they do not…" he gave Tyrus sad eyes. "We both know what happens when a Mythic loses a fight."

Tyrus gave no sign that he was affected by the other man's words. "Exactly my point. Back off."

Levi walked toward him, slowly, while Tyrus stood, unmoving. He wouldn't be intimidated. Levi pulled him in with a firm hand on his elbow, and whispered, "*in this time of peace, you may have forgotten your nature, but your Mythic never will.*" Fire and water suddenly clashed, framing them both before the water enveloped Levi and he vanished from view.

Tyrus sighed, relieved as he watched the teens practice basic combat skills. Levi appeared to keep his word, for now. *This time will be different. What better fate to end my existence than the struggle for peace?*

Ann sauntered into the apartment, a smile slowly spreading on her face. Nix sat on the couch, but she locked eyes, then she began to chuckle.

"Alright, put the spoils on the table."

Proudly, she walked forward, and produced the night's valuables. First a wallet, then a necklace, then several more expensive looking baubles. Nix looked them over. "You're improving. Take the necklace, leave the rest. It will match those earrings you stole."

She did so, walking quietly back to her room to store them in her very own safe. Not even Nix knew Ann's combination. Upon returning, she plopped down on the couch. She still had too much energy to rest.

"What was it like for you?"

A confused look crossed her mentor's face. "What was *what* like?"

"The day you changed?"

Nix set the remote down and faced her. "Why do you want to know?"

"Is it…always so…"

"Graphic?"

"Yes."

"It is."

"Were you the only survivor?"

"Yes, but my brother was there. We lived on a farm, gifted to our family after the abolishment of slavery from a benevolent friend. We had been there for generations, and it's where my brother and I grew up. I was…nine? Ten? It's been so long."

She rubbed her eyes. "We were running through the woods. The fire was sudden. Just…surrounding me. I blacked out and woke to my brother shaking me. Somehow, he'd avoided the fire. He…never got over that day, not like I did. He dedicated his life to 'fixing' me."

"Changing you back?"

"Yes."

"Is that possible?"

Nix sighed. "Not really. They made some progress in ability suppression, but no. I was never the same again. In spite of his 'work.'"

"Do you still speak to him?"

"He passed away five years ago."

"I'm sorry. What of?"

"Old age."

Ann looked Nix up and down. "You don't look old."

Nix chuckled. "I look amazing for my age, yes."

"How old are you?"

"Old enough…" Nix looked at her, changing the subject. "Did you eat today?"

"With all that excitement…"

"You need the calories. Get some cake from the fridge before you combust. You know you can't leave yourself vulnerable like that."

She stood, walking slowly away. She knew she'd forgotten something, and now she felt shaky. Her bird could fuel her, but the energy needed to be replenished at a higher rate. She needed to consume double the number of calories as a normal person to keep her body in balance. She'd relied on her bird all day, forgetting to stop and eat.

"The chocolate?"

"Yeah. Grab me some too."

Ann walked back with two pieces and sat. "Can we talk now?"

Nix ate silently for a moment before answering. "So, talk. You get three questions before I have to leave."

She thought them over carefully before she asked. "When do I get to learn more?"

Nix gave her a look that silenced the fire. "When I think you're ready."

She took her time, again. "Are you working tonight?"

She nodded. "That's two. One more."

"Why can you see my bird, but I can't see yours?"

She thought that an innocent enough question, but the change in Nix's face showed anything but. She watched as her mentor's face filled with anger, then sadness, then determination. "Someday I can tell you why, but as I am working, tonight is not the time. Finish your cake, watch some TV, do what you want as long as you-"

"Stay in the apartment. I get it."

"I'm locking the security system on my way out. I'll be back before dawn if everything goes well. Try to sleep."

She stood without another word, wiping a tear away, so slyly that Ann almost didn't see it. Another three questions for tomorrow, she supposed, while many more played inside her mind. The door was locked, the system beeping. The room was secure, and she was stuck until morning. Used to the routine, the rules now, she walked slowly to her room, getting ready for bed, her firebird in tow.

◆ ◆ ◆

Nix got the call in the elevator. She answered quickly. "Nix."

"Progress?"

"I got great video of the girl in action. Make sure you use the infrared filter so you can see her Mythic. I'll upload it to you."

"So, she is one of you."

"Yes. Definitely."

"And the others?"

She paused. "Tyrus is blocking me. I haven't gotten close enough yet."

"I have an…operative on standby, should you need me to eliminate him."

"No, I just need the time to do this right. No bloodshed, no evidence."

"Fine. You have a week." The line went dead.

She'd just bought herself her last extension. Her conflict continued. Each day, Ann grew closer to her. She'd never met another phoenix. The kinship she felt toward her was…slightly unsettling, but nevertheless, it was there, and she had to come to a decision. Would she hand Ann over, or would she protect her? This was not the first time she'd had to choose a side, and when she did, her focus had to be survival. Maybe if she taught Ann well enough her decision might not matter?

Letting go of that thought, she walked out of the hotel lobby, waiting for her vehicle. Ann was incredibly capable, but there were some things, dark, twisted things, that someone so…new to this world shouldn't have to learn. Jobs she took too soon, they'd left scars on her that her student didn't need.

She thought of the times she'd been outwitted, helpless, of the benevolence she was not shown by others in their community. Her orange fire lit her eyes beneath her cap. Her head down, she walked up to the car, debating her path. One thing she knew, the world couldn't stand the burden of another broken-winged bird.

Wills was beginning her workday, as well. She walked into the large hospital lobby, greeted by faces who thought she'd taken family leave. They asked if everything was alright, and she lied flawlessly. She didn't want anyone catching on. This was too important.

She wanted to convince herself that the past few days had been a dream, a nightmare. She was so comfortable at the hospital by now that it took several moments for her to process what had happened, how her world had been turned upside down in mere days.

Then she felt guilty. That was nothing compared to what the teens had gone through. Hitting the elevator for the third floor, she rode up, sipping her coffee. In addition to her other work, she had an assignment, and she intended to complete it all.

She walked into the first room, an unconscious victim of a building caught on fire, who plunged three stories to save himself from the flames that had trapped him. A new nurse was changing his IV. "Oh, hello." She plastered a huge smile on her face. "I don't believe we've met. I'm Dr. Wills, the resident assigned to his case."

Nix thought fast. "Sorry, I'm Jean. I'm just rotating through, saw his bag happened to be low, thought I'd do my friend a favor and replace it on my way out."

"No problem. Where is Sheryll?"

"Don't know. Not here, though." Nix chuckled at the half joke and left without another word.

No handshake, okay. "Thank you for your help." Just because she was rude didn't mean Wills should be. She checked the IV bag. It was all in line with the chart. The man may never wake, but as long as he was in her care, she could make him comfortable.

"*Sleep tight,*" she whispered as she turned to leave. She looked for the nurse but there was no trace of her. *Must be a temp or a floater.* Humming a tune, she walked toward the lab. She'd asked for nightshift for this very reason, so she could use the lab to go over the data she'd collected and stolen from the hospital. She sat down to work at her station, biding her time while other doctors came in and out. When they left, she began to work.
While she worked, "Jean" waited. She saw the doctor work privately. Someone was up to no good. She debated what to do for a moment, then went with the simplest solution. She needed the thug's doctor distracted, needed her to forget to check on him. When no one was around, she shot a flame ball at the garbage can next to her and left, without looking back. The scream that soon followed brought a chuckle to her face. Alarms blared and she walked out of the emergency exit as everyone else did. No one would see her, think of her. She was just a nurse.

Tyrus stared down at his phone, almost expecting it to ring. When it did, he only felt trepidation. He didn't have the power of precognition as Joy did, but he did have a long, perfect memory. The odds of this being a good call, based on all his life experience, were slim.

"Tyrus."

"It's been destroyed, all of it." Wills sounded like she was running.

"The data?"

"Yes. Random fire in the building. Still not sure what started it, maybe someone smoking where they shouldn't be. I had to leave. The data was on the table."

He sighed. *Damn it, Nix.* "I'm sorry to hear that."

"Really? You don't sound surprised."

"I'm not."

"Why?"

He took a moment. "Because Mythics tend to pop up when you least expect them, and they do more damage than you could imagine. I'm glad you made it out safely. Data can be recreated. Human life..." *and their Mythics,* "cannot."

They talked for several moments before she was placated enough to hang up. He walked up the staircase and into his room, removing his shirt, then his socks, then the rest of his clothes. He walked into the shower and let the stream calm his aching muscles. A black eye was forming on the right. Several bruises from training made him wince. Even newbies got in a few lucky punches, once in a while.

When he didn't feel tension any longer, he walked out with a towel around his waist. He was contemplative tonight, thinking of Angela, of Amanda, of Tommy. All the Mythics he hadn't been able to save, and the weight of survival drained him. He lifted his head to the full moon and wondered how Ann was, if she would be a survivor or a casualty of this ancient war.

The moon was almost gone, darkness covering St. Blaise. Dr. Jackson sat at his desk, reviewing the pictures they'd been able to compile. Not always, but in enough of the photos the black figure stood. Until now, they'd worked under the assumption that Omega Flame was a strange, random, natural occurrence. Now, he began to question everything he knew.

Omega Fire has popped up in references from over a thousand years ago. Black flame, causing a mass amount of destruction wherever it went. He kept finding references in Lore from various myths and cultures referring to this. Putting them together, he'd been given a road map of the path Omega Flame traveled.

First solid reference other than hieroglyphics, occurred in Asia. Then India, the Middle East, followed by Africa. By the time it reached Europe, five hundred years had passed in between sightings, at least recorded ones. It never seemed to hit the exact same area twice. Like the flame chose a spot on a map and moved on.

If this was the roadmap, maybe he wasn't dealing with a natural occurrence. Maybe he was dealing with something bigger, more sinister than they could have imagined. Some ancient power, associated with godhood? Some old legend or tale based in truth? Some sage mage with untold abilities?

He went back to the photo with Tyrus. Old, worn. Who was really pulling the strings, and how could he dig around without causing too much trouble? Had he already alerted this monster? Paranoia overcame him, had him dialing Levi's number.

"Yeah."

"Bodyguard duty."

"Something happen?"

"Something is going to happen."

"Right boss. On my way."

He learned a long time ago that his brain was his biggest asset. He learned to trust his sense of logic and foresight. In a world dominated by those changed by Omega Flame, he was lucky to be a mere human standing among the cursed chosen.

◆ ◆ ◆

Nix watched as Wills left the hospital. Upset she hadn't been able to finish her off, she'd placed a bug on the girl's car. She'd be able to track her every movement. Placing her binoculars away, she hopped into her car and started the drive back to her apartment.

Singing to the radio, it was some time before she noticed lights following her. She was driving on a particularly snaky mountain road, enjoying the wind in her hair. As she turned the next corner, the lights grew closer.

Noticing them now, she didn't panic. She knew this road, even in the early hours of morning when the night was darkest. Coming to another curve, she sped up, shifted, and rounded it flawlessly, speeding up as soon as she was done. Let them get into an accident and die. She intended to live.

However, noticing the lights continuing, she took another hard curve, then floored her vehicle past the mountains toward downtown of St. Blaise. She could lose them on the highway, maybe in the city if necessary.

Lights still ceaselessly gaining, she admired the driver's skill, even if they were trying to tail or kill her. Driving over the shoulder, past three cars trying to merge, she quickly dived through three lanes of traffic and floored it through the fast lane, swerving as she did so effortlessly using the stick shift to her advantage.

The lights were gone. Smiling to herself, she continued down the highway. Taking her exit, she didn't see the car until it crashed into hers. *Stupid! They switched off their lights.* That was her last thought before a car rammed her in the intersection and blackness surrounded her vision.

She woke on the soft grass, the sun just reaching beyond the horizon. Her head hurt, her sides hurt, and her legs hurt. Before she could protest, strong hands picked her up and carried her away, opening a whirlpool portal and leaving the scene. She fell unconscious again before she could protest. *Anyone but him…*

Day 15

Waking again, some hours later, she was in a small motel room, bandages covering her arm, her left knee, her forehead and her stomach. Lifting herself up carefully, she strained to keep herself conscious. The world spun as her head moved, but other than that, she didn't feel the darkness again.

"You're lucky."

"This is lucky?" Her voice was hoarse.

"If you were a regular human, you'd be dead right now. The two guys chasing you didn't make it."

"Really? What was the cause of death? Drowning?"

Levi laughed. The sound brought back mixed memories, both innocent and demented. Her skin bristled with emotion. "Nothing so obvious. I've gotten much better at my work."

A shiver ran down her spine. Even with all she'd done, all the contracts and lives taken, she had some semblance of respect for life. Levi, however, was as changeable as his element. He felt no remorse. Knowing that, she could never trust him.

"What's broken?"

"Nothing, but your ribs were bruised, your head concussed. You took a pretty good beating."

"Why am I here?"

"What, you think I was going to let the hospital treat you? They don't understand your needs like I do, Nix."

"My *what*?"

"Your needs. What your body can do, what it can heal on its own. They'd pump you full of drugs and slow you down. I just let you be, let your body heal."

"How caring of you."

"You're lucky because I was on my way to a contract and I happened to feel you in the rain."

"Great, so you're a stalker now?"

She looked at him, and a slow smile crossed his lips. It was an intimate smile, far too knowing. "Don't look at me like that."

"There was a time you loved me, Nix."

"There was a time you destroyed me, Levi."

Sighing, he stood. "If it'd been anyone else in that car, even your precious Ann, I wouldn't have bothered. Like it or not, I'm on your side now, Nix."

Rage welled up inside of her. "You still don't get it."

His eyes grew strangely sad. "I never will, and I'll never stop loving you." He dissolved into a puddle of water on the floor, gone.

Nix sat up slowly and called her employer.

"Dr. Jackson."

"I need a car."

"Levi already told me. One is waiting out front. Be more careful next time, Nix."

"I hear you."

"I'm serious. This is bigger than I last thought. When I have more info-"

The call was dropped. *Weird.* He paid for the best cell service money could buy. That frightened her, made her wonder who or what was listening in on them.

Setting the phone down, she slowly put on her new clothes, courtesy of Levi, and walked outside to see a shiny black limo waiting for her. The driver opened the door and she slowly slipped inside, wincing as she did so. The thing that scared her the most was lying to her young protégé. She wouldn't understand. Giving the driver her address, she looked out the window into the rain. It used to comfort her as a child, but after what Levi said, she just felt like she was constantly being watched. A shiver ran down her spine again. Then she winced. She *was* hurt badly.

Ann paced back and forth in the apartment, wondering why Nix wasn't back yet. She'd been gone a long time, over twelve hours. She tried to calm herself, tell herself that it'd be alright. She wasn't used to this life, after all. Maybe this was normal? Failing, seeing no comfort, she began pacing again.

She didn't realize how fast she was breathing until she heard the familiar ding of the elevator and released a long, slow breath. Dark patches swam in front of her vision, threatening to consume her, but she stayed where she was. Nix walked in slowly, her arm and head bandaged.

She stared at her for a moment. She didn't say a word, just sat down on the couch, and powered on the TV. Ann swallowed hard, wondering what she should do.

"Ice cream." Nix said it so softly she didn't understand her.

"What?" She asked.

"Ice cream. It would help. The chocolate, I think."

She ran to the freezer and took out the gallon, finding a spoon and delivering them to Nix, who opened the lid and slowly began to enjoy.

"This is," Nix started. "This is unfortunate. However, it doesn't have to be a terrible thing. I'm alive. I'm fine. A contract didn't quite go as planned. What you can learn from this, though, is that you can heal yourself from most injuries with your flame. Not that one."

She pointed to the scar on her arm. "That happened before you were completely changed by Omega Flame. We can't heal old scars. Me, though, I can heal myself as soon as I've had enough food. So really, this isn't a bad thing. This is a hard lesson. Do you understand?"

"Yes, I do. Did you at least kick their ass first?"

Nix laughed. Then she winced. "Food first, then after I've healed, I'll tell you the story."

"That works." She plopped her feet on the coffee table and silently watched TV. When Nix was done with the ice cream, Ann brought her Chinese. When she was done with that, she brought her more. This continued until almost everything in the fridge had been consumed.

All that remained was a cake. She brought it out to her mentor who said, "no, no. I don't think I can look at any more chocolate for a month. You eat it though. I have work for you to do today."

She complied. Nix lifted her body, standing in the windows facing the morning sun. It shone bright in the sky now, an hour before noon. Letting the sunlight surround her, she called her flame. She watched from the couch as Nix's orange burn surrounded her, starting at her feet and traveling to the top of her hair. Orange light, flickering, lit up her features, in a way that showed her just how much power this woman held within her.

Standing, drawn in, she moved around to the side, where she could see Nix's face. Gasping, she saw the orange light burning in her eyes. It was so intense. The light grew brighter and brighter, until all at once, Nix crossed her arms in front of her and the light vanished.

Panting, shivering, Nix said, "Shower."

She was confused. *Where did the pretty light go?*

"*Ann! Shower*!"

Drawn out of the spell, she ran to Nix's bathroom and turned her water on. Nix slowly walked down the hallway, still shaking, sweating. "Cold. Make it cold."

She adjusted it to cool. Nix walked in and without getting undressed, stepped into the spray. Steam came off her in waves. It filled the whole apartment with fog, starting in the bathroom and quickly running through Nix's bedroom all the way out to the sun in the living room. She shut the door, giving her privacy.

She went out to the living room and seeing the fog, powered on the fans in the kitchen. Several minutes later, the fog receded, and she could sit and watch TV. It was some moments before Nix emerged from her room, wearing new clothes and completely healed.

"Wow." She was amazed. "That's so awesome."

Nix gave her a sideways glance. "Is it? I almost died doing that. Had you not been here to start that shower, I'd be a pile of dust right now."

"I…don't understand." She was confused.

"I know. You won't until you've ascended. Trust me, for all the power we have, a price is paid double."

Sitting on the couch, she looked to her. "Now, I owe you a story about last night."

"Yeah, what happened to you?"

Nix smiled smoothly, no trace of deceit on her face, and did the hardest thing she'd have to do that day. She lied.

Chapter 12

"What happened?" She sat on the couch with a glass of iced tea. Nix sat next to her.

"I was following up on a contract. I can't say much about it, but I'll tell you what I can. I was tailing someone in my car. Long story short, I survived, but my car did not."

"Ouch. I liked your car."

"It's just a vehicle. The important thing is that I'm still standing. It looked a lot worse than it felt. I'm just glad that I was able to get back here in one piece."

"How's the other guy?"

"Dead. Burned."

"Sucks for him."

'Just goes to show that you never stop being careful. You never forget the basics. That's why it's so important to be in the now, be present. You never know when something I've taught you will save your life."

She felt pride in her teacher, not just for what she had endured the night before, but her emphasis on Ann, instead of herself. Practically beaming, she said, "what are we doing today?"

Nix laughed. "Well, first, groceries. I need to restock the fridge. I also need a new car. After that, we'll see. Want to help me pick out a new convertible?"

Ann's eyes lit up. "Oh, yes."

Nix chuckled. "Alright. First stop, auto lot. Next stop, groceries."

◆ ◆ ◆

Levi watched them leave, knew where they were going. He wasn't going to gain much more than he had, so he created a portal, and stepped through to an overgrown grass field outside of the bed and breakfast. He waited. Ten minutes, fifteen, no one came out. *No training, today. Wonder why?*

◆ ◆ ◆

Tyrus had taken the kids to Pierside Park. They were young, they needed time to de-stress. It wasn't just kind of him to do this, it was essential as they started to define their new normal.

Connor and Seth threw a football in the field. Julius was distracted by all the smells and sounds. He was still learning to control his beast. Joy was true to her name, doing whatever she wanted, currently on a jungle gym. She was so small in stature that the equipment sized for kids still was accessible to her.

He walked further away, just watching his charges. His phone rang, and he answered, noting it was Ryan.

Connor tossed the ball to Seth who caught it, barely. He had better accuracy now. His eyesight was just amazing. His friend rotated, about to throw it back, when he stopped cold, his merriment fading.

Connor had enough time to turn around before a punch landed directly in his face. Thrown to the ground, he looked toward his assailant and saw his brother. Connor stood just in time to stop Julius from hurting his only blood family left.

"Chill man! It's my brother." Julius took a minute to calm down, but he was able to. *Progress.*

Looking back, he noted the rage and relief on his older sibling's face. Placing his hands carefully in his pockets, he had no clue what to say or do. No one had come in contact with their family since the bus ride to St. Blaise. What were they supposed to do?

Seth left, running to Tyrus, who was on the phone. Julius returned to observing the environment. Connor stood facing his brother.

"I..." his voice broke. "I've been looking *everywhere* for you."

Connor looked at the ground, not sure what to do or say.

"I took time off from work. I drove here. I called the cops. Where the hell have you been?"

Connor looked up, ready to explain. His brother punched him again.

"Don't you dare! Don't you dare…" His brother sat next to him and hugged him tightly. "Don't you *dare…*"

Connor hugged him back, unsure of what to do. His feelings since the accident had changed. It wasn't that he didn't love his brother, but his family had grown, his responsibilities had grown. He'd tried calling a couple times but got no answer. Probably because his brother didn't answer the phone for strange numbers.

"I tried calling…" Connor said it softly, carefully. "I tried."

His brother just continued to hug him. After several moments, with Tyrus there and the others with him, his brother let go. Everyone in the park was watching them, fascinated.

Tyrus stepped up. "This isn't something you should have to do here. Let's take a walk."

"Who the hell are you?" His brother's eyes were red and puffy from crying.

"Someone that wants to help." Reaching down, he held out a hand. Connor's brother took it, standing. "Let's go to the parking lot. Less eyes."

Walking quietly, they felt the stares. People didn't start to look away until they were out of view. The only one who wasn't somber was Joy, who skipped along the path in front of the men humming something about an "urchin queen."

Coming to the parking lot, they stopped. Tyrus spun and looked at Connor. "Tell him everything."

"Really?"

"He'll either understand, or he won't. It's his choice. He's your blood. He has a right to know."

"What the hell are you talking about?"

Connor faced Damien, took a deep breath, and started at the beginning. To his brother's credit, he listened without judgement until the end. Rocking back and forth on his feet, he was silent some moments before he began to speak.

"So, either this amazing thing happened, or this is some weird brainwashing cult."

Everyone laughed at that, but his brother was serious. "I mean, what am I supposed to think? I know you're no liar, but this sounds utterly ridiculous."

Tyrus stepped in. "You're already more open-minded than most people. Not everyone can wrap their head around this. Connor, go with your brother. Go home. Come back in a couple of days. Take some time, help him understand. The more allies we have, the better off we are."

"Here I thought you were going to tell me that we were a super-secret society, that we couldn't tell anyone who we were."

Tyrus looked down, thinking briefly of the loved ones who were no longer with him. "Family is precious. One day, you'll be grateful for a brother like that."

Connor nodded. "Already am." He held out a fist, his brother did the same. "Let's go home."

The two left together. Joy waited until they'd gone and looked at Tyrus, whose sad expression touched her soul, making her wonder who he'd lost. Of course, she then answered the question without having to ask. "What if they take him?"

"Are they *going* to take him?"

She thought for a moment, tilting her head to both sides. "Nah."

He laughed. "Then why did you ask?"

Joy shrugged. "Small chances don't mean it won't happen." Looking up to the sky, she saw storm clouds rolling in. "See? Twenty percent chance of rain, it's raining."

He grabbed his keys out of his pocket. Unlocking their new rental, they stepped in. "Time to go."

"Who was that?" Ellie asked from the kitchen.

"Tyrus. He says 'hello.'" Ryan sat down behind her on a bar stool in their kitchen. She spun and handed him a plate of eggs. "Thank you."

"You should invite that man over for dinner. I miss him."

"Yep."

"Also, the baby is coming any day, so keep your phone on you."

"Will do."

"My mom wants to be in the room with us, so you'll have to deal with that."

"Mmhmmm."

"Are you listening to me?" A threat loomed in her voice.

He loved this woman dearly. He hated her hormones. "Yes, Dear."

"Good. Here's your lunch. See you after work." She kissed his cheek, and he walked out the front door. Noting the tail that had been placed on him for the past two days, he walked to his car and headed to the police station, like always.

Tyrus had prepared for this. He knew it was there. He'd investigate.

"No reason to alarm them," he had told Ryan. "Continue living your life."

So, he would. The cop in him was patient. He'd be able to do this. He had to, for the sake of his family. He loved Tyrus. They'd been through hell together in the war. If it'd been anyone else, Ryan would curse that person for endangering his family, his brother-in-arms.

Wills had a tail as well. The same person sat outside the hospital every day, drinking a coffee for as long as her shift lasted. She'd love to know who it was and let them know there was help for their addiction. It made her uneasy, and she was not as patient as Ryan. As she entered the hospital, she made sure she walked in and out with groups of people. She was never alone. She texted Tyrus on the phone he gave her periodically. She felt like a spy with two phones.

Her comatose patient was still out as of last night. The fire had been doused, investigated, but no one thought she was involved. She narrowly got away. Upset that her research was lost, she walked into the elevator. One of the other residents turned to her.

"We're going out for drinks tonight. Wanna come?"

Wills smiled at the person asking, not recalling her name. "No thanks. I've got early shifts all this week."

She had to change her schedule after last night. If she wasn't on the roster, odds are, no one would ask her about the fire. She'd quietly changed the schedule, no one the wiser. One more thing that made her feel she was living the spy life.

The elevator stopped at her floor, and she exited, precisely in the direction of the comatose patient. He was right around the corner after all. Coffee in hand, she whistled, walking quickly to the room. She checked his vitals, adjusting his meds. *Still unconscious.* That was unfortunate. Finished with her work, she spun to leave, missing the small flick of his fingers on his right hand.

They parked in the grocery lot, walking into the store. She'd ended up choosing a black-on-black convertible of the same make and model, but this was brand new. Had heated seats and everything. It could even self-park.

Ann wondered how loaded her mentor really was, that she could just buy something so brand new and shiny so quickly. Didn't have to wait for insurance, nothing. Admiring her life, she spun and walked into the store with Nix.

"Grab a cart. I'll be in the frozen food aisle with the pizza." She laughed. If they were anyone else, they'd have heart disease by now. Spinning, she ran into an older man who had just walked inside.

"I'm so sorry," she said. He lifted his head, and her eyes grew wide. She stood face to face with Mr. Cline, Marie's father. "Oh, hi Mr. Cline."

He took a moment to study her face. "Hi, Ann. This is a wonderful surprise. How have you been, sweetie?" He encircled her in his arms, hugging her fiercely. She hugged back, tears falling freely from her eyes.

"I'm fine. How are you holding up?"

He pulled back, eyes wet from new tears. "Day by day. I… haven't returned to work yet, but hopefully soon…" His voice drifted off and he looked away for a moment.

"It's good to see you. Why are you in St. Blaise?"

Uhm. Her mind was blank. "Day trip. We're heading to the park."

"Stopping for some snacks, huh?"

"Yeah, snacks." She worried her hands in front of her. This man was the closest thing she had ever had to a father. Marie's dad had been the one positive male role model she'd encountered in her brief life.

"Well, don't let me keep you but I would like to give you my cell and a twenty to help you buy more. In case anything happens, you need anything, you call." He took out a piece of paper and fumbled for a pen. Finding one, he jotted his number down and handed her the paper with the bill. "Don't hesitate to use it. You have fun on your trip, now."

She spun away, then looked back. "Thank you. I miss her so much."

He wiped a tear away from his cheek. "Me too, kiddo. Me too."

Grabbing a shopping cart, she walked away, tucking the number into her pocket. With her new life, the constant change, she'd almost forgotten that there were normal people in her life that still cared. She wouldn't forget that again, and she'd keep the twenty to remind her to stay in touch.

Tyrus sat the three teens down outside the bed and breakfast, handing them a phone. "Call home. You never know where this life will take you, but there is no reason for your parents to worry."

Seth took the phone first. "I've been calling once a day anyway." Dialing, he waited for his parents' answering machine. He knew they both worked during the day, so calling and leaving messages was what he'd been doing. Easier. No questions.

"Mom, Dad, it's me- "

Someone picked the phone up. "Hello? Seth? Is that you?"

"Yeah, mom, it's me." *Crap.*

"Seth, what is going on. One day you just… leave? Without a word? Days before graduation?"

"I've been calling…"

"Young man, explain yourself."

"I got a job offer in St. Blaise. I already had enough credits to graduate, anyway. They can't not let me just because I wasn't there to walk. There wasn't much school left either. This job, it's really great. Once I can afford a place, I'll have you come out."

"Where are you working? Where are you living?"

"Mom, I'm fine, I really am, but I have to go. I'm on break, and it ends in less than a minute. I love you so much. Sorry. Bye."

He hung up as his mom was asking him to wait. He felt bad, but his friends needed him more. Handing the phone to Joy, he looked at Tyrus.

"Calling every day, huh?"

He shrugged. "I didn't say they answered."

Tyrus laughed. "Look, if you tell your mom you've got a job, you better find one when things settle down."

He nodded. "I'll figure it out. I'm sure the right thing will come along at the right time."

"For you, yeah. You're lucky. You'll be set."

Joy bounced away, talking to her parents. She'd just reached 18 a week ago. Technically, until she reached majority age, she'd been a runaway, and he'd been harboring one. He could have been charged with kidnapping. This mess was nothing to ignore.

Joy on the other hand, had no problems. Tyrus suspected the use of powers. Unicorns were nothing to mess with.

"Yeah, no, remember, I was home this morning. You saw me." The person on the other line was suddenly calm, though Tyrus couldn't make it out.

"I'll be staying at Ann's tonight. You're fine with it, right? I'll see you in the morning. Love you!" She ended the call. It was Julius's turn.

Tyrus looked to Joy. "What did I tell you about using your powers on the people you love?"

Joy's face grew serious, for once. "Listen, it's better than if I didn't call every day. You'd be in jail if I didn't call." Her face lit up. "Want me to stop calling and see where that goes?"

"No, I think I'm ok with not going to jail this week. Maybe next month."

She shrugged and walked away. She saw things about the world others couldn't. Noting that Julius had called, he spun to him, but they were speaking in Spanish. Tyrus was the only one that could understand the conversation.

"Estoy bien, Mamá. No te preocupes."

"Voy a estar preocupada asta que regreses a casa."

"Ya Soy un hombre, encontre trabajo en St. Blaise. Tengo un cuarto con amigos de trabajo. A estado bien."

He walked away, and Tyrus had a hard time understanding his mother's half of the conversation. He understood anger when he heard it, though. Julius continued to walk away, rounding the corner of the house. He obviously wanted some privacy.

Looking back at the other two, he felt better. "I'm glad you're taking those ties seriously. Your birth family, though you're different than them now, they keep your humanity alive. Keep you human. Hang on to them for as long as they'll let you."

Julius came back, red-faced. "She'll be okay." Handing the phone back to Tyrus, he sat on the ground with the other two, looking up at their mentor.

"Listen, I guess it's time to stop ignoring the real world." Tyrus placed his phone in his pocket. "There's some things you should know."

Nix waited until she was back in the car before she brought it up. Turning the key in the ignition, she sat for a moment, looking at Ann who was gazing out the window. After a few silent seconds, she spoke.

"What's wrong?"

She faced her, tears in her eyes. "My best friend died on the bus. The accident. She died. I saw her dad. He lives here."

Nix placed a hand on her shoulder. "I guess it's time for the code."

"What code?" She asked.

Tyrus addressed the three. "The code is a set of rules that have been passed down from generation to generation. We have no clue who started the code, and it always changes, but it's the rules we live by."

"Like what?" Joy asked.

"Rule 1," Nix said. "Innocents are blind. This means that anyone who isn't like us doesn't need to know what we are. This keeps us safe. Except family. Family is everything."

◆ ◆ ◆

"Rule number two," Tyrus said, "Only at death's door do we knock."

"What does that mean?" Joy asked.

"Only use your powers in situations where you would die if you didn't."

Nix backed up the car, and the girls drove out of the lot. "Rule number three," she said, "Stone and water."

She repeated this one. "Stone and water?"

Nix nodded, turning right onto the nearest street. "The world is stone. It doesn't change. You are water. You do nothing but change."

"Why is that a rule?"

"It reminds you that the world does not change with you. It takes water years to wear down stone."

"This next one is important, kids. Number four." He took a deep breath and said, "three coins in the fountain."

Julius laughed. "Okay, so we should all make wishes?"

Tyrus looked at him. "The three coins are three sides to every conflict. A fountain moves these coins, as people move. Your job is to determine which coin is you, which is your enemy, and which coin is hidden. It reminds us to look for hidden motives in people. This is key to survival."

"Number five," Nix continued. "Pure then powerful. We save innocents first. We save Mythics second. This rule has come and gone. We reinstated it. I believe in it completely."

"But you take contracts and hurt people."

Nix eyed her when she reached a stop light. "I have never, in my life, killed someone who didn't absolutely deserve it."

She nodded. "Anything else?"

"Even my enemy is family." Tyrus paused. "For example, though you would defend yourself from an attacker, you would not allow someone to catch that incident on tape. Any Mythic, whether you know them or not, is your responsibility. We all work together to achieve secrecy."

Nix paused. This was a hard one for her to talk about. "Hands, not swords."

"Number seven?"

"Yes. Number seven. Hands, not swords."

"I'm guessing that means no killing."

"Yes, Ann. You should never kill another Mythic, unless they're intent on killing you. Remember, though, there are worse things than death."

She swallowed hard. She didn't like thinking about that.

"Number eight. Light the candles." Tyrus stood and placed his hands together, his fingers making fists, but his thumbs touching. "Do this."

The teens didn't know what they were doing, but they complied. "What does this mean?"

"Look at your thumbs. What shape does your hand make?"

She looked. "It kind of looks like a lopsided heart."

"Yes. This is what we do to remember. Once a year, we return to the mural I showed you, and we remember the fallen."

She nodded.

Nix continued. "Rule number nine, no word save the mural."

She tried but didn't have a clue what that meant. "Huh?"

"No written words will be kept of us, in any journal or story save the memorial which is hidden and houses a list of our names. This also implies more than words. No proof of our existence, no videos, no police reports." Tyrus spun and sighed. This next one, he'd personally failed at. Then he said softly, "rule number ten."

Nix hesitated as well. "Family comes first."

She nodded. "That's easy to remember, at least."

Nix laughed. "By family, they mean two things. Your blood relatives, and all Mythics. These are your two families. Though that might seem easy, I guarantee, it's the hardest rule for most of us to follow."

"Why?"

"When you forget that you are family, that's when people get killed, or worse."

"Did someone you love die?"

"Someday, I'll tell you the sad tale, Ann, but today is not that day." She paused a moment, and said, "repeat them for me."

She began. "No innocents shall know you. Uh, death's door knocks-"

"Only at death's door do we knock."

She repeated after Nix. "Stone and sand-"

Nix shook her head. "No…"

"Stone and water."

Nix nodded.

"Three pennies in a jar?"

Nix sighed. "Three coins in the fountain."

"Right. The pure than the powerful."

"Hey, you remembered one."

She rolled her eyes. "Uhm, what was the next one?"

Nix began. "Even my enemy…"

"Even my enemy is family."

"Next?"

"Fingers, not knives?"

"Hands, not swords."

"Same thing…" she said, under her breath.

"What?"

"Nothing. Uhm, only write on the mural."

"Close. No words but the mural. That's nine. What's last?"

"Family comes first." Connor sat on the couch with his brother. "You know it, I know it. We promised mom when she died."

"I know, I know." Connor sat, grabbing a slice of pizza from their takeout order. "I said I was sorry."

"Sorry." His brother laughed. "*Sorry*? You know how many hours of sleep I lost, trying to find you? You were gone for days!"

"I'm back now. Hell, I was never in any danger. When are you going to admit I'm an adult now?"

"Adults think things through. You didn't walk for graduation."

"I know."

"Will that affect your scholarship? You remember you're going to college, right?" The threat was obvious.

Connor forgot all about that. "We can talk to the school and the college. I only really missed the last few days. Finals were over for the seniors anyway. I only really missed two days and graduation."

"We're going first thing in the morning."

Connor looked at the TV, but he wasn't watching it. He was thinking about his other family. His brother was right. Family comes first. But what do you do when you have more than one family depending on you to protect them?

"You assess and choose the greatest kindness."

"What's that? "Joy asked.

Tyrus stopped for a moment. It had been too long since the last time he'd explained this. "The greatest kindness is the unspoken rule. We added it after… after the last group of Mythics died."

"What does it mean, though?" She asked.

Tyrus sighed. "You will be put in life-or-death situations. You will have hard choices to make. Not all of you will live forever. Most of your deaths will be at fear's hands. When in those impossible situations, people usually tell you to pick the lesser of two evils."

Nix got out of the car, Ann trailing behind. "We took this concept a step farther. After our friends were gone, we instituted another rule. This rule was unbreakable. It accounted for all the others. At the time, we meant it."

"What does it mean, though?"

"In everything you do, in every moment that you breathe, every path you take, every impossible choice, every beat of your heart, you have one job. You take the few seconds to think, and you choose the greatest kindness. If that means one of you dies so that many others live, this is the burden you must choose. Everything we do, because of who we are, we are responsible to achieve this last rule. The greatest kindness."

"Save of course, for times when, we need new earrings." Nix winked at her. "I definitely blur the lines between the rules. That jewelry store? It was insured. The owner will be reimbursed. If you've ever met anyone in insurance, you'd know, they're not innocent."

She laughed. Nix chuckled. They turned down an alley and came to an empty basketball court. Nix looked in her bag and took out a basketball. "Today, young one, we practice your aim. If you're going to be throwing fireballs, you need to know where to throw them. Need to trust yourself to be able to hit what you're aiming at. Shoot a few baskets, then we'll make it tougher."

She groaned. If she had a nemesis, they would be a star athlete. She was about as graceful as a drunken sailor. "Do I have to?"

"Want to be the next big bad?"

"Yes."

"Then start shooting."

Sighing, she followed instructions. They started just by aiming for the basket. Her arm felt like liquid a half hour later.

"Alright, let's take a break." Nix stretched her arms. She tried to follow, as much as she could with her left arm still weak. "You're shooting lefty."

"Left-handed, yeah. That's part of the reason this is so hard."

Nix nodded. "Well, maybe by the time I'm done with you, you'll be ambidextrous. At least with flame balls. Switch hands and try with your non-dominant."

She chuckled but the humor didn't make her enjoy this more.

Tyrus watched as they ran around the school property and back. He was glad they knew the code, but living it was almost impossible. He left that tidbit out. No need to scare them. Looking at the teens, seeing Joy skip running behind the boys, he wondered how long he'd be around to watch them grow. Something about this group was different. They all encountered the flame together. As far as he knew, everyone else had to go through it alone.

He did. One minute he was in the trenches, the next, the men on both sides were all dead. His friends, his brothers-in-arms as well as enemies for miles, and nothing but ash remained. He alone was left standing. To this day, he carried that burden on him. Why did he survive Omega Flame when no one else did? And how were there five survivors, all on the same bus?

Dr. Jackson had the same thought and was busy researching that very question. Yes, he knew the bus was sabotaged, but in every other written account, single survivors only. The options for this change were few. One, the human race was suddenly evolving to tolerate Omega Flame, meaning more children would survive the fire. He didn't mind that possibility. More survivors meant more data. Was it possible that the synthetic nature of the Omega Fire, that it was made by his people, responsible for multiple survivors, or was it a coincidence?

However, there were other, more sinister possibilities. Were they all put on that bus by some hidden third party, knowing their potential? Dr. Jackson didn't know of any way to determine that. Was there something in their very DNA that would show their susceptibility to the flame?

Or the third coin in the fountain. The black figure. The mysterious unknown. It was entirely possible that someone had a motive that, even with his intelligence, could completely elude him. This was the scariest possibility. The one he couldn't predict. How could he continue his empire, grow it, if his enemy was nothing but a shadow?

Chapter 13
Day 16

The two fire birds sat in the apartment, gorging on pizza while watching TV. Nix flipped to the news, remarking, "you definitely look at events differently now. A fire isn't just a *fire* anymore, huh?"

A laugh escaped Ann. "Yeah, in my head, there's a group of evil fire elements just…wreaking havoc on the entire world. And dragons…everywhere."

"You'll eventually be able to tell the difference. Your gut will help you just…know. You'll be able to tell the normal fires from the Mythic ones. Who's after you, who's just a conspiracy nut. You'll stop seeing people where there are only shadows."

Increasing the volume, Ann's mirth faded quickly. On the screen were her fosters. "We are so distraught after hearing some survivors have contacted their families. Yet, we have no word from our beloved Ann."

Handkerchief in hand, she played the grieving mother well. There were even tears. The hand on her shoulder from her husband seemed reassuring and sincere. Then again, the cameras were on. "I just know that she's out there, I know it. As a foster, we try our best to help these troubled kids, but sometimes it isn't enough."

"It must be so hard for you, knowing she's gone." The reporter was either naïve or craving the ratings. She couldn't really think someone intelligent would buy this crap.

"It is. Oh, we've been so terrified since she left." Ann chuckled at her short haircut, courtesy of her flame, no doubt. That brought back her smile. "Listen, Ann, if you're out there, please come home to your family. We love you, Sweetie."

They faced the camera, their acting skills on full display. It then panned to the sympathetic reporter. "I'm sure many of our hearts are grieving with this family. So many have lost their loved ones in the awful explosion two weeks ago. It would be a shame for this family to lose another.

"Our website has set up a fundraiser for the families of this tragedy. You can donate online or in person. We've added the Millers to the list. Each family has listed supplies they need, though many only want enough to bury their loved ones in peace. Please donate at…"

She stopped listening and snorted. Nix muted the TV. "You're *their* Ann?"

When she looked at Nix, she was overcome with emotion. She almost cried. "I was *never* theirs." Her skin burned with her anger. "They were more like keepers than parents. They just…were all about the money. It makes me upset that people will donate, thinking they're helping, when in reality none of the money they get will go to their foster kids."

Nix focused on her. "Do you need to talk about it?"

Ann sighed. "In a therapist's office, maybe. Not now, I want to move on, you know? I want to grow and become…stronger, better. I want to leave their small life and the small box they tried to push me into, move on to something better, which I feel like I already have. You're more family to me than they ever were."

Nix nodded. "I had a friend one time tell me they don't get even, they get ahead. Wisest words I've ever heard. You just let me know what you need and I'm your girl."

Ann smiled. "I need a different life."

Nix nodded, showing she understood her. Ann stood, placing the rest of her pizza in the trash. She walked away, shutting the door of her bedroom. She fell asleep, dreaming of a better family, and burning hair.

Nix slipped away after she was sure she was out. She didn't want her waking up, didn't want her to know what she was doing. The rage burned within Nix, and she couldn't do much about her past, her life, but she could help Ann now. She stepped into her vehicle and began the long drive, the road ahead dark, the woman behind the wheel fearless. She listened to some inspiring music, humming along as if she wasn't going exactly where she was headed.

Three hours later, she walked up to the small house and rang the doorbell. No one answered, at first, so she tried again. This time, there was movement. After a third ring, a lethargic woman answered after yelling at everyone in the house. *Pleasant.*

"Who are you?" She yawned and rubbed her eyes. "Do you know what damn time it is?"

Nix smiled and tilted her head. "Call me Pride. I'm aware of the late hour." She handed a briefcase to the woman, who only frowned at her.

"What the hell is that?"

"More than *you* deserve." She let the words drip with venom.

"That doesn't answer my question." The woman seemed nervous now.

Perfect.

"It's money."

She tilted her head. "For what?" The nerves vanished, replaced by curiosity and greed. Ann's assertion was right on the…well, money.

Nix gave a fake, but deadly smile. "To leave Ann the *hell* alone."

"You've seen the brat? Where is she?" The woman looked around as if she would materialize out of thin air.

Nix leaned in, set the briefcase down, and grabbed the woman's shirt, pulling her close.

"Listen, you miserable hag, she is mine now. I'm her *real* family."

"No way you two are blood. None!"

"Blood doesn't make a family. Proximity and control do not make a family. Family is something rare that a selfish twit like you wouldn't be worthy of. You come near her, go on TV with your pathetic bullshit, tell the cops, anything," her eyes lit up with flame.

She saw the fear creep into the woman's eyes. She smiled again. "…and I come back. No money, all fury. Enjoy your newfound wealth."

Nix punched the woman in the left eye and spun away. She walked quickly to her car as the woman screamed for her husband. She knew once they opened the briefcase that they'd shut their mouths. Unfortunately for their current foster children, money was really all those half-wits cared about.

Pleased with herself, she checked the time. There was still plenty of leeway to get back to her, maybe get a couple hours of rest. She powered the radio on, singing quietly along, a smile playing on her face. These were the moments she lived for, when she was absolutely certain that she'd done something moral, something right. Ann wouldn't have to worry about them, ever again. She adjusted the volume on the radio as she drove away, full on singing instead of humming. The world really was wonderful.

◆ ◆ ◆

Day 17

Joy woke before everyone else and left her room without a sound. She snuck into see Seth as he woke. Placing a finger to her lips, she sat on the edge of his bed. He smiled up at her, and she frowned back. "Not yet."

His smile faded, but he didn't have time to respond as she revealed her plan. "We need to go find Ann today. I'm tired of waiting. We should leave before the dragon wakes."

He looked at her. "My gut doesn't like this."

"Odds are as good as random. Fifty-fifty chance this works. Listen, if it doesn't, at least we can find her. If it does work, our friend comes back. We won't have another chance like this. Not for days. We need to go today."

"If you say so. I'll wake the others and meet you downstairs."

Joy made her way past the snoring dragon to the entrance, where she waited for the others. It wasn't that the dragon couldn't help, it was that in spite of her efforts in the dreamworld, she couldn't help them reconcile. They would have their work cut out for them when Ann *finally* arrived.

Connor was the first to descend. He'd return the night before, his scholarship secure. Their school allowed them to graduate, as they assumed the stress of the catastrophe made it hard for them to return. Their diplomas would be mailed this summer. He'd advocated for all of them, a feat of a leader, which made sense considering his Mythic. The speech was apparently rousing.

"How did you sleep?"

He gave her a look. "Some weird dream about the world ending. You were there."

She gave him an innocent look. "What? Really?"

He gave her a half smile and shook his head. "I slept ok, Joy."

"Good."

Julius showed up moments later, with Seth. "And now we're ready to go."

"Where to?" Seth asked.

"Let's start at Pierside Park and go from there."

Julius scratched his head. "Are we sure we want to do this? Tyrus isn't going to be pleased."

Joy looked at him. "He…doesn't know Ann like we do."

Seth tilted his head toward her. "I've got more than enough money." He pulled out a roll of twenties from his pocket and waved his hand, a shimmering portal appearing to the right. Joy walked through followed by the others.

They came out into the morning sunrise, along the trails in the park. Joy took a moment of silence before turning to Julius. "We can use your sense of smell."

He chuckled. "What…you want me to just…sniff the whole city?"

She thought for a moment, imagining the possibilities, debating whether that would work.

She glared at him. "Of course not. You know her scent. We'll take the bus until we find the trail. Then you find her."

She walked forward, hoping that she was right about this. She wrung her hands together when no one could see. If she wasn't right, it would make everything that much worse. Was she doing this out of emotion, or was this the right decision? Even a unicorn could make mistakes.

Ann woke to Nix pounding twice on her door. "We work today. Ready to leave in ten."

Used to the routine now, she was immediately up, showered, and dressed. She grabbed a banana and met Nix at the door. "Where are we going today?"

The somber look she received was unexpected. "I'm working on a new skill you'll need. Developing contacts. Recruiting eyes and ears. Knowing who you can trust, who you can't. Having those pawns in play can keep you safe or distract your enemies long enough for you to keep *yourself* safe. What you see today took years of cultivation and is mostly in code."

She pushed the button for the elevator. It opened instantly. "I don't expect you to do anything other than watch, listen. You take it in, every movement, every note, every gesture. The one thing you aren't allowed to do is interfere. You open your mouth once, and you've failed. You got it?"

She nodded her head, a little upset at the serious turn her education had taken. "Got it."

When they stepped out of the elevator on the ground floor, Ann was surprised that her teacher didn't summon her vehicle. "We aren't taking the car?"

Nix kept walking, but said, "hard target. Don't always do the same thing the same way. New valet. Don't trust him." Ann had missed that. "Besides, exercise is good for you. With all the power we're given, your physical abilities are just as important. You can't ignore your health. We walk today."

Nix rounded a corner, and they were surrounded by a row of locally owned shops, apartments and street vendors. Nix walked expertly through the maze of people that littered the area, into the coffee house on their right. She walked up to the counter, nodding to the employee. "Medium, non-fat mocha latte with extra whip, extra espresso, dash of salt."

He wrote it down and picked up a cup. “Name please?”

“Eve.”

He didn’t even eye her, he merely left and walked into the back room. A moment later the manager came out, all smiles. Ann watched Nix smile back, warm and open, but the deviation from her stoic nature was eerily unwelcome. Ann shivered.

When the drink was made, it was handed to Nix, who hadn’t paid for it, yet a receipt was given next. With a wink, the manager walked away. The two women walked out of the store silently.

“Read this.” Nix handed the receipt over. Ann skimmed it. “What does this mean?”

“First line.”

“Drunk patrol?”

“Local cops are at the bar, drinking instead of working.”

“Oh.” She looked at the next line. “Shark is fed.”

“The boss is happy.”

“If he was unhappy, what would the message say?”

Nix stopped and looked at her. “Shark smells blood.” She continued on as Ann gulped. “The last line says Nancy needs milk.”

“Someone has a job that needs my attention.” She walked into a nearby convenience store, grabbed a carton of milk and placed it on the counter. The clerk smiled at her and rang it up. As she took her change, Nix said, “how’s Nancy?”

The clerk, who must have been new, let their eyes widen before motioning to the back room. Nix shook her head at the newbie letting them know they’d slipped, then entered it without asking permission. Ann followed. A woman sat at a desk, intently focused on her tablet in front of her.

“What is it?”

Nix cleared her throat. The woman looked up, recognizing her. "I heard you needed milk. I'm your girl."

"Yes, you are. Here are the details, Eve. How are you, by the way?"

"Better than yesterday."

"Even better tomorrow, right?" Nancy laughed. "Yeah, I got something, but it'll cost more than a store purchase." Nix tossed a wad of money her way. "Good. The boss has a delicate package, needs delivery back to the original sender. You play this right, you get two contracts done. Double the pay, right?"

Nix smiled. "Always."

"It's a blind kitten. You up for handling that?" Nancy looked to Ann, who had no clue what the code was.

"Yeah, I got this." Nix stepped into her line of sight, a protective gesture. "Anything else?"

"You need the key first." She produced a slip of paper. "Across the street, two beers and a vodka."

Nix walked out silently, although she snickered once at the paper. This time, she didn't let Ann read it. The girl wondered silently what was so funny. They crossed the street, an apartment building in front of them. Nix hit the button for room 202, and a voice came on the line. "Yeah."

"Animal control."

The buzzer sounded, and they walked in, climbing the stairs to the apartment. The hallway smelled of alcohol, cigarettes and mold. Nix tapped on the correct door and a large man opened it. "Yes?"

Ann noted a thick eastern European accent but said nothing.

"Here to return a kitten."

"Center closes soon. Take it directly or the boss will get mad." He handed her a small box.

"Will do."

The door shut securely behind him and they exited the building, turning left. Ann was eager for an explanation, but she held off. She had faith her teacher would fill her in later. Instead, she committed as many details to her memory as she could.

They walked into an animal shelter a few moments later. An old, hard-faced woman sat behind the counter. "Can I help you?"

Nix walked forward. "Here to adopt."

"Cat or dog?" The woman didn't look up from her phone.

She leaned on the counter and said, "More into exotic pets. You got any…snakes?"

The woman looked up then, smiling at Nix. "Eve. Why didn't you say so?"

"Got this for you."

The woman took the box, opened it, and took a picture with her phone, but Ann couldn't see what was inside from her vantage point. So much for committing everything to memory. She frowned but stayed quiet.

"Well, that bastard won't be raping any more underage girls in the green zone." The woman shut the box and took a moment to send the pic to a mystery number. "This from Nancy?"

"Yeah."

"How's the old girl doing?"

"Fair pay, fair weather. She did mention you might need me today. Courier?"

The woman looked up, at Nix, at Ann, then back again. "Not a job for a kid."

Ann breathed in sharply, but a snap of her teacher's fingers held her tongue. "I'm taking the job."

The woman glanced at her. "You're right for it, just been a while since you took one." The woman eyed Ann slowly up and down. "Who did you say this was, Eve?"

"Eve" stepped forward, her hands flat on the counter. She leaned in toward the woman and sweetly whispered, "*I didn't.*"

The woman's eyes widened. "Right. No kid was here. Details." She took a pen and paper, wrote something down. Nix looked at it, then took it in her hands. "Good day."

Ann followed her out and they walked a while in silence. Her patience wore thin and she found herself asking, "what's the job?"

Nix gave her a half smile. "A movie."

"I'm eighteen. I can watch any movie I want."

"Yeah, but the content of this particular film isn't appropriate for adults under the age of jaded." She motioned to a park bench. "Sit there, grab a hot dog, enjoy watching the kiddos. Sun is still rising. Do whatever. I'll be back."

Ann walked forward, concerned that her teacher wasn't including her. What could be that bad? She watched Nix walk into an abandoned-looking warehouse. Her curiosity was driving her crazy, but she turned and watched little children playing anyway. Nix knew she hated hot dogs.

Nix walked inside, up the corroding staircase and knocked three times on the first door. A voice inside shouted, "password!"

"Key grip."

The door opened without another word, and Nix stepped forward, taking out her burn phone. She saw a broken, bloodied man crying on the floor in a puddle of his own fluids.

Three men stood around him. The largest stood and nodded. "Eve. Boss wants this on video. Calls it a deterrent."

She nodded, pressing record, assuming this was the rapist.

"Hey, boss. Flynn here." The man grabbed the rapist's hair and lifted his face up to the camera. Speaking to the broken man, he said, "boss takes care of his own, you sick bastard."

The others grew restless as they sat on the bus, the window slightly open so Julius could smell. They turned down a street with shops brimming on both sides in the heart of the old downtown district. He perked up. "Here."

They exited and followed him toward a coffee shop. Joy couldn't help but feel a bit excited. Maybe this would work out?

Nix shut off the phone after sending the video. As "Flynn" watched, she burnt it crispy. "No trace."

She walked away but not before she heard him whisper, "*freak*," under his breath. She didn't even let it phase her. She was used to it by now.

Having done her "good deeds" for the neighborhood that day, she walked out of the building and toward the park where Ann sat waiting. She smiled as she sorted her thoughts, how she would explain all of this. Then, her eyes caught sight of someone else interested in Ann as well. They were walking a straight path in her direction, not even bothering to hide their intent.

Her eyes lit with fire. Of course, he would try to take her. She ran forward, throwing fireballs at the would-be kidnappers. No way the local boss would use her own protégé as leverage.

Ann sat unaware of the unfolding calamity, her body relaxed, until she saw parents rushing forward to grab their children. Taking her ear buds out, she heard the screaming and turned in time to see Nix facing off with her friends.

Seth materialized next to her, and she was suddenly across the street from the scene. She glared at him and said, "what the hell do you think you're doing?"

He shrugged. "Saving…you?"

"I wasn't in danger." She looked at the scene before her. "Get me back over there, now."

Seth smiled and touched her arm again, transporting her instantly closer. "Thanks." She then promptly threw up on the very well-kept park grass. She wiped her hand with her mouth and scanned the scene.

She had little time. She watched as Nix fought the two other boys, who were physically stronger than her. Still, her mentor was holding them off, quite well, until Julius's hands turned to paws and he began clawing at her. Ann's eyes wide, she stepped toward them, shouting, "STOP!"

Calling her flame, it surrounded her teacher whose stomach had just been ripped open. The boys turned to her then, and quickly changed to their normal selves.

She sighed, trying to control the fear and relief flooding her body. "What are you doing here?"

Joy answered, kicking her feet at nothing. "We came here for you. Then she attacked us."

"Attacked? No, she was just protecting me. You need to go, now."

"We came so you could come home, with us. Where you belong. Aren't you coming?" Connor and Julius both held out a hand but knowing the blood of her mentor stained it crushed her heart. She knew her friends were trying to protect her, but she feared losing the only adult in her life who hadn't ended up abandoning her.

Ann sighed. "Not now. She needs me more than you do. Go. Before someone calls the cops or gets this on video."

Joy felt it. They had failed. Fate was shifting and they were no longer doing any good being here. She looked toward Seth who nodded. In spite of her best efforts, she had failed. The timeline would be darker now, all because she had been impatient.

"As you wish." Joy turned away, tears in her eyes. This was the ending she'd feared, but she hadn't seen all the pieces until it was too late. Going through Seth's portal, they left Ann alone. They were instantly at the entrance to the B&B, Joy softly sobbing. After a moment, her eyes widened, and she hid behind Connor. "Uh-oh."

From within the building, Tyrus bellowed, "JOY!"

Ann rushed to her teacher, the flame disappearing. "What can I do?"

Nix said, "Food, water."

Ann remembered the hot dog stand. She ran over and purchased what she could, bringing it back. "Twelve dogs and three waters."

Nix ate the hot dogs quickly, then took the water with shaky hands and poured it out. "What are you doing?"

Nix placed a bloody hand in the middle of the puddle and frustratingly said, "I need you."

Ann watched as the puddle moved, the water surrounding the bloody hand. A cold wind blew then, storm clouds overhead, rain falling. It happened so quickly that Ann knew it wasn't natural. She leaned over her teacher, trying to protect her from the rain, but a strong grip on her arms pulled her backward.

She stood, ready to face the threat, the fire in her eyes hot. A tall man in a black trench coat stood in front of Nix. Long, platinum hair trailed down his back, flowing in the wind. The look on his face stopped her, one of tenderness and compassion, totally foreign to someone so imposing.

"Levi…" The word came out of her mouth as she lost consciousness, too much blood loss. Ann was worried. If she couldn't heal herself….

"What do we do?" She shouted over the storm. Levi turned to her, his bright eyes like a storm themselves. With a small flick of his hand, a portal, like Seth's was created, out of water, instead of the shimmering light. "GO!"

Ann picked up Nix's limp body and walked forward, unafraid. Back in the apartment, she had another dilemma. How did she heal Nix?

She placed her hands on Nix's stomach and called her flame, asking her bird to heal her. She watched as the wounds were cauterized shut. *Oh, that's how.* Still, she could have internal bleeding. Panic overcame her as she wondered what more she could do.

She didn't have to wonder for long. The man, dry as a bone, stepped out of a similar portal a moment later. "How is she?"

"I…sealed the wound but she's still out."

"Good job, baby bird."

Ann narrowed her eyes at him. "Don't call me that."

Placing a hand on her forehead, he was quiet for a few moments. Nix opened her eyes with a deep breath, the pain clear on her face. "Back away."

Levi grabbed her arm before she could protest and dragged her out of the way. Nix's fire came quickly, exploding from her chest as her body raised itself off the ground. Flames licked along the lines of her form as they burnt away the dead flesh threatening their master, while new tissue was woven effortlessly to match the old. After a few moments, the light darkened and Nix was dropped to the floor, moaning.

Ann didn't hesitate this time. She stood to head to Nix's bathroom to start the shower but was stopped by Levi. "Don't bother."

"Don't you need to cool off?"

"Ann…go to your room. NOW!"

Confused, Ann glanced at the man one last time before leaving, narrowing her eyes, letting him know she was no friend. She ran to her bedroom and shut the door behind her, reclining on the bed. The events of the last several minutes rushed through her mind, causing questions to arise with it. What were they thinking, coming for her like that? If they'd been seen….

Who was this Levi guy? What was his connection to Nix? Lying on the bed, she sighed, and waited anxiously.

Levi walked toward her as soon as Ann left the room. Nix shook from the energy coursing through her. "You know what to do."

He smiled, waving his hand. Water flowed quickly from his fingertips, surrounding her entire body. She released her energy, let it go, and the fire pushed against the water, which held firm. If there was one thing she could count on, it was that Levi wouldn't let her die. She let go of the control, and let the energy pour out of her, flame meeting the watery cocoon to dance as they turned to steam.

When the fire was spent, the water gone, she opened her eyes, lying on her side. Levi smiled at her, and she smiled back briefly. Images came to her mind, of her past, her life before, the good and the bad. She shook her head to clear it and said, "Levi, the code…"

After a last look, he was gone.

Tyrus stomped out of the building. The three boys formed a protective front ahead of Joy, who hid. He sighed, allowing his anger to dissipate before he approached. He attempted to go through the boys, but they wouldn't allow it, so he walked around them. Joy ran in concert with him, so they were always opposed, the boys in between.

A giggle escaped her before he realized she was playing a game. He sighed then softly whispered, "*may I speak with you, Joy?*"

Her head momentarily popped over Seth's shoulder and she said, "Sure." The boys moved and she folded her hands behind her back and gave a bashful look. "What about?"

He stared her down for a minute before remembering her nature. This behavior was natural for her, as much as his scales were to him. You catch more unicorns with positive energy than threats. He smiled pleasantly. "Tell me about your day, Joy."

"We…failed. Spectacularly!" She waved her arms around and began to recount the events of their morning.

Levi knew what Nix meant when she reminded him of the code. It had been a long while since any Mythic was stupid enough to battle in public, and it required some clean up. In the age of wireless cameras, this was especially challenging to most, but not to him.

Noting the security cameras on the street, he started there. Personal videos uploaded to the internet, containing the keywords would automatically fail, but security cameras were a bit tricky as many businesses kept a physical copy. It was a good thing he could control water, even through indoor plumbing. His hand on the pipe leading into the nearest building, he merely followed the water in his mind's eye, until he reached the server. Cooling the water's temperature, slowing its vibration, he formed condensation above the equipment and waited for the drips to short circuit the hard drive.

When he was finished, he sat down and sighed, wondering if he should check on her. He instantly decided against it. She was a strong woman, independent and capable. As much as he was saddened by her absence, he would not intrude. Not after what he'd been manipulated into doing.

Standing, he called the Director.

"Speaking."

"I contained the situation."

"One video made it to my desk."

Crap. "And?"

"She is…as amazing as Nix was."

His throat tightened for a moment. "They tend to impress, don't they?"

"Indeed." A short pause followed. "Her abilities are…stunning, considering it's only been a matter of weeks since her change."

What to say without giving too much away…? "I noticed."

Silence again. "I'm glad you took care of the immediate area. She needs to be delivered soon, and my patience is running thin."

"May I remind the Director that with this…particular problem, things are better taken slow."

"I need no reminders of the nature of fire. Quickly. Quietly. It's what I pay you for."

The line went dead, and Levi cracked his neck, then his shoulders. Now, the hard part of his day began. Convincing someone who hated him to voluntarily give up someone they loved. Cracking his knuckles last, he gave a half smile. Difficult, but not impossible. Walking forward, he began to plot his next move.

Chapter 14

Tyrus listened to Joy until she was finished. With flair, he might add. *Did she really just use spirit fingers?* Hiding a laugh, he cleared his throat.

"Joy, what were the odds you would succeed or fail?"

She twitched her nose. "Even. Completely even! No way to tell." She said the last as if it justified her actions.

"Were the consequences worth the odds?"

That made her think for a moment. Tilting her head, she silently asked for clarification.

Placing his hands in his pockets, he said, "you were unsuccessful, something that we try to avoid by itself for obvious reasons."

She nodded vigorously. "You also caused a rift in your friendship with Ann."

Her shoulders slumped and her normal charming attitude faded. "It will be more difficult to convince both her and Nix to join us now."

Her lip quivered. Seth placed a hand on her shoulder. It stilled. "Plus, the damage of exposure. It was in a public place. Those are the big issues. Was that worth it?"

She looked down at the ground, kicking a foot, then back up at him. "What would you have done differently?"

He gave her a wide smile, which brightened her spirits. "That's exactly what I'm here for. To teach you not only to survive, but to thrive in this new world you are all a part of. Let me. Trust me. I'm not an adult that makes rules just to lord my authority over you, I'm here, fighting with you as an ally. I have a plan for all of you. It will work, if there are no other setbacks."

He walked inside quietly, aware that they were following him. Though he was seething inside, he controlled himself. He pushed away all the awful possible outcomes that could have happened and focused on moving forward. They needed training, and now, maybe that was possible.

Nix knocked on her door that evening after they'd both recovered. Sighing, she sat on the bed next to Ann and gave her a watery smile. "How are you?"

Ann smiled back, then looked down. "Peachy."

Nix snorted; the dry sarcasm not lost on her. "Right. Wonderful family outing. I knew there were other survivors, but it just didn't occur to me that they would try to find you. It should have, and I'm sorry for my part in today."

"Who did you think they were?"

"Goons of the local criminal element."

"I thought you were on good terms with them?"

"As good as anyone, but that doesn't stop them from seeking leverage."

"How so?"

"They could have used you to ensure my…loyalty, so to speak. Our kind are valuable, Ann. Many would love to have a pet phoenix."

Ann scoffed at that. "I'm a person, not a pet."

"You would be amazed at what some people think they're entitled to."

"They aren't entitled to me."

"No, and as long as you remain uncaged, you can continue to make your own choices. Your friends…I'm sorry I caused a rift. That's not how I imagined the events of the day progressing."

Ann felt a tear collect at the corner of her eye, wiping it away before it could fall. "Well, you couldn't have known."

"I'm supposed to be getting you ready to survive, not taking you from your family."

Ann felt the heat coming off Nix's body. "Why are you angry?"

"Because I seem to keep making the wrong choice, even though I have good intentions. Whether or not it was my fault, I'm sorry." Ann could tell Nix was trying to calm the fire in her eyes. Maybe a change of subject would help.

"Nix, who was that man?"

"The one who saved me?"

"You called him Levi."

Nix's face darkened. "A necessary evil. Watch yourself around water. He controls it all. Though he helped me today, he's as likely to kill you tomorrow. He is not your friend. Understood?"

"What makes him so evil?"

Nix took a moment. "His moral compass is as changeable as the water he controls."

Ann swallowed, wondering if she needed to fear the shower now.

Nix stood and walked away, leaving Ann alone. She thought of her friends, how close they'd grown in so little time. They *were* family. A few tears fell before she managed to drift off, and she let them.

Tyrus watched the four communicate as he taught them, without speaking, an invaluable skill. Basic, yes, but a step up from the haphazard looks they gave each other before. One step closer to a group with effective survival skills. They would need every trick and technique he could give them.

Joy turned to him as he felt it, a change. Another Mythic was here, and he thought he knew who it was. He signaled for them to retreat and pointed at the building. Joy tilted her head as if to ask, "Why?" He merely repeated his instructions, which were instantly followed.

Tyrus looked out at the school building in front of him, then suddenly called his dragon and flew to the top. Levi stood, waiting for him.

"Tyrus. Lots of activity today."

"What do you know, Levi?" His rage returning, he was ready for a full-on fight, and Levi could provide him with one. Still, he kept the conversation civil.

"I know your ducklings left the pond. Met a wolf they weren't prepared for. You sure you're the kind of leader they need? Maybe they'd listen to a big stick better than a soft voice." Scales shone down his arms. Levi saw them. "No need for that now, I only came to talk. Nix and Ann are fine, if you're wondering."

The scales receded. "That's good to know. Why the charity?"

"I don't do charity. I do contracts. Just, listen," he said, hesitating. "There's a lot of players invested in this, Tyrus. Things are going to heat up from here on out, and your ducklings aren't ready. Are you going to die for them?"

"Stay away from them, Levi."

"Not me. I don't have a contract on them." He sighed. "Three coins in the fountain." Then he evaporated.

Tyrus felt a headache immerging between his eyes. Turning to the bed and breakfast, he flew down and walked inside.

The teens were there, sitting in the cozy living room, sipping tea and daintily eating muffins. Joy even lifted a pinkie as she sipped. Joy looked completely relaxed, while the three male teens looked incredibly uncomfortable. *Apparently, we are having a late tea.* Tyrus smiled, sitting, and bit into a muffin. Joy presented him with tea and said, "Cream and sugar?"

He kept a laugh inside, knowing this was part of the price of having a happy "precog" on your side. "Two sugars, no cream please." He looked at the others in the room, who unanimously shrugged. Unicorns…

Dr. Jackson didn't even flinch when Levi appeared inside his office. He asked him to wait outside while he was on a conference video. Levi complied, sitting down and ordering food from Isaiah, who happily took his order, obviously flirting with the dark, broody dreamboat. Sitting in his desk chair, he pushed a red button on the bottom of the desk.

The doors locked, lasers scanned the room, sensors were activated. A panel opened on his desk and scanned his face, while he placed a thumbprint into another slot. A few seconds later, a mechanical voice said, "Room sweep complete. Secure mode active."

Standing, walking to the center of the room, he pressed a button on the side table. The middle of the room split apart, revealing a staircase to a lower level. Walking down, he entered a room filled with screens and computers. No one was around. Turning two screens on, he said, "Europe, Asia."

A few minutes later two hidden figures appeared, their faces in shadow. Voice processors disguised their accent, leaving them anonymous. However, Jackson had met both in person before. This was just the safest way to communicate.

"Are you both ready to start the monthly briefing?"

"Europe is go."

"Asia is go."

"North America is go."

"First order of business," Asia began. "How is the situation unfolding there? Have you discovered the source of the Omega Flame?"

Dr. Jackson cleared his throat. "I have not, however, I've recovered as much data as possible. It is clear that it was sabotage."

"No one remains alive?" Europe asked.

"One thread remains. A goon, in a coma, at the local hospital. If he wakes, I'll be able to have an agent question him. I don't know how helpful he will be, as he is just a hired thug."

"This is most disappointing," Asia stated. "We will have to decide what course of action to take now. It may not be favorable to you, Dr. Jackson."

"I accept full responsibility for my part in this. However, I would like to note that the art of sabotage is not generally inflicted on the self."

"What are you daring to imply?" Europe inquired.

"Nothing at this time, except to say that the two most powerful, most capable companies are in the room with me, and the two who stand to benefit the most are before me."

"Well, I never…"

"Do not make the mistake of assuming my location is equivalent to my value or intelligence. I'm not some 'dumb' American you can wrap around your finger any time you please. I know quite well of what you are each capable."

Europe went blank. Asia remained on the line. "I do not know if it is youth or foolishness that would force you to tempt your fate, but may I remind you that you are only there, working as you are, as a debt the two of us owe to your dear departed father. I would walk softly if I were you. Europe is powerful."

"Powerful enough to cross oceans?" He hoped his implied meaning was clear.

"Powerful enough to bank the stars. I must go. Europe is on the other line. For what it's worth, I believe you." Signing off, the screen went blank. Turning away, Dr. Jackson walked up the stairs, smiling. Playing the two powers against each other would buy him time to finish the plan.

Walking up the stairs, he closed the stairwell and said, "Secure mode, shutdown." Instantly, the windows opened and the doors unlocked. Opening the double doors himself, he gestured for Levi to enter. They both had data to review, a plan to concoct and a bird to capture. It would be a long day.

Tyrus continued with the basics by having the teens run. Though they were magical beings, physical fitness could still save their lives. They were running around the school yard, joy even doing cartwheels. Was that girl ever *not* happy?

"Mr. Tyrus, sir. Would you like some iced tea?"

The owner of the bed and breakfast handed him a glass while he hid his annoyance at the unwelcome title, and he wondered if you could overdose on tea. Still, it was cold on a hot day. "Thanks."

"Having your nieces and nephews run? Good. They need exercise. How long is this trip? Their parents joining you soon?"

"No, they're too busy working. The whole point was to take the kids away from the parents. You know how it gets. Kids in the summertime, school's out, parents still have to work. But Uncle Tyrus, he's got vacation coming, so sure, I can help out." He made sure to emphasize the sarcasm a little for show.

"So good of you. Most people wouldn't take the time to help their extended family. Listen, rent is due soon. Will you be staying another week?"

Tyrus took his wallet out, watching as Connor and Julius bumped into each other. *Great! The second stupid fight of the day.* "Here. This should cover the next couple of days. After that, home they go."

Walking away, she added, "been a pleasure. Wish you the best." Tyrus stood and ran to the teens, ready to break up the fight. The owner watched for a moment, before walking back into the house.

Turning to the kitchen, she picked up her rotary phone and placed her glasses on her nose. Dialing slowly, she waited to hear a voice answer. "Yes?"

"They're leaving in two days. I thought you'd want to know. Listen, do you think you could swing a little more money my way, since they stayed so long and all?"

The voice was disguised. "Of course. Check your mailbox in the morning. You'll find more than enough compensation inside."

Hanging up, the old woman walked to the fridge and began preparing dinner. Guilt ate at her a bit, but she had to remind herself that unlike those kiddos out there, she was alone in this world. She needed that money. People didn't come to the neighborhood like they used to, with all the crime lately, and she was no spring chicken. This money would help her last at least another year on bills without any clients.

Had to look out for number one. Still, that didn't mean she couldn't feed them well. Looking through the fridge, she decided that an apple pie would be the right penance for her. She'd bake them a delicious pie.

Humming to herself, she got out the ingredients and began to roll the dough on the counter. It wasn't long before two of the boys entered, and without speaking, walked straight to their respective rooms, shutting the doors. *Good. Send them to their rooms if they fight.* She respected that.

On another TV screen, in another darkened room similar to Jackson's, a dark figure watched several monitors. They were watching for something very specific. Any hint of a threat.

On one screen, a lab, the other, a line of people. They stood there for miles, tens of thousands lined up down a road, waiting to be processed. If any of the other powers found out about this very important side project, this facility would be shut down. Secrecy was its lifeblood.

Turning to the lab, the figure hit a button on the screen. Their voice disguised, said, "break it down for me, Professor."

The startled man in the lab looked toward the camera lens. With a thick accent, he said, "yes, well, we have completed the chip. The first test subject results should be coming through to your computer now. Can you see it?"

Looking at the data, the figure was pleased. "Excellent. When can we begin mass production?"

"A few more hours, to correct the errors, and we will be online, ready to begin."

"Continue your good work. It will benefit all mankind."

The man in the lab continued, his back to the camera. As the figure turned to watch the other monitor, they suddenly saw a large chuck of people start to riot against their fate. Unsatisfied, the figure hit another button. "General, the lambs grow restless. Please deal with your flock."

On the screen below, several military style vehicles pulled up, throwing tear gas and opening fire. The figure was pleased at the quick response.

Realizing the risk, backing away, several thoughts came quickly. One, this was not for the good of mankind. This was business. Two, the most lucrative resource was people. Three, they were starving anyway. Under this new system, they wouldn't even know they're hungry. In a world where overpopulation was draining resources far too quickly, intervention had to happen. It was better to be the one profiting off of it than the one with the chip in your brain. Survival of the fittest, and no one was more fit than them.

Ann woke hours later and walked out to the living room. She saw Nix sitting on the couch. Nix turned to her, and noting the scrunched nose on her face, said, "I know you hate it, but…"

"News is on?"

"Yeah. We have to watch it. Remember, try to tell the difference between a real threat and just smoke."

"Got it."

Turning the channel, though, there was no doubt in Nix's mind over which this segment was. Turning the volume up, they listened to the report.

Dr. Jackson sat at his desk, watching TV. Noting it was time for the news, he switched over. What he saw made his blood run cold.

Tyrus came inside, followed by Joy and Seth who got off on good behavior. Sitting in the living room, he turned on the News.

"We are here, risking our very lives to bring you this story." A woman with a thick accent stood before him, on her camera phone. "Please, you have to help South America. We are in Columbia in La Tatacoa. They are everywhere. They took us from our homes, our families. Behind me, you see the destruction they cause. We don't know who is killing us, but they are killing us. Someone help. Please!"

Turning off the camera, the news anchors returned. "We are reporting on a developing situation in South America. This video was released, just minutes ago from an unknown location. We are suspecting, given the remote location, that this woman took great pains to find an internet tower and to get the word out about this crisis. Indeed, she may have risked her very life. All news channels are tuning in now to alert you on this breaking story."

Flipping to another station, Tyrus watched. "It appears to have come from somewhere in South America. We are hearing reports that the president himself plans on making a speech regarding this incident later tonight. Please stay tuned."

He flipped again to another news station. "It's a conspiracy! The government is trying to distract you!" He rolled his eyes.

Turning the TV off, Tyrus sat, torn. There had been a time that he would have willingly boarded a plane to defend those people. If it was big enough for the news channels to report on it, it was big enough to involve a Mythic. Some strove to save their humanity, but others strove to wipe it out. He was worried that whoever was killing people, whatever was going on, had "Mythic" written all over it. Grabbing a leather jacket, he walked out, the teens safe in their rooms and started his car, heading toward the closest airport.

Nix turned the station off. She too, was torn. This could have been her redemption, but there was no way Ann was ready. No way she could leave her, was there?

The phone rang. Answering, she said, "what, Dr. Jackson?"

"I need you to go. I'll pay double. You'll be back in two days."

Pausing a moment, Nix looked at Ann's face. The girl was crying, worried over these people she didn't even know. How could Nix not help? "Fine. What time?"

"The driver is already there. If this has to do with the business, it's up to us to make sure the pact is enforced. I'm also sending Levi. Call in Tyrus."

Trying to stay calm, she said, "that won't be necessary."

"Yes, it will." He hung up. Nix turned to Ann and said, "I have to take care of this. I'm going to Columbia. You're going to stay in this apartment. Got it? Eat what you want, but no leaving. I'll be gone for 48 hours."

"That isn't very long. How are you going to deal with this so quickly?"

Nix smiled. "You are so young. Business, Ann. This is about money, and business. Stay put."

Nix walked out the door, turning on the security system as she left. Ann couldn't really leave even if she wanted to. Besides, Nix was helping people. This was a good thing. Once the elevator shut, she dialed his number. He picked up immediately.

"On it. I'll meet you at the airport."

"Our current conflict won't be a problem, will it?"

He sighed. "No." The phone went dead. Nyx hadn't been lying about the code. When it was necessary, they could put their emotions aside and do what was right.

Levi waited in the lobby. Barely glancing at him, she strode past, ignoring him as much as possible.

Walking with her, he waited until they were in the car to say, "Just like old times, huh, Nix?"

A shiver overcoming her, she turned to face him. Getting very close, enough to kiss him she said, "I'm here for the contract. You touch me, I steam your ass. Got it?"

Laughing, he relaxed in the vehicle as they headed toward the airport. "To think I even packed a bag for you. I am so unappreciated."

Sighing, Nix turned to him. "Let's talk business. What do we know?"

"As much as the media. Not enough. That's why we're going. We aren't expected to fix it, just remove our footprint before the American government decides to be a hero. Which they will."

"So, we get in, get out and take any evidence of mythic participation with us. Anything else?"

"No one would be doing this without a reason, a motive. Greg seems to think it's tech related. He wants us, if possible, to scout for a lab, secure any tech we find and report it to him."

"Why does he think tech? He involved?"

"No, he's not the third coin. He's the real hero. You should be proud of him."

Turning, Nix said nothing, just sat back and waited to meet Tyrus at the airport.

Day 18

They flew on a private jet to a hidden location. From there, a unit of paid mercenaries took them to a spot a mile out. The morning sun shone brightly by the time they arrived. Nothing could be done until dark, so they waited, watching the line of people moving in and out of the facility. No planes flew overhead, and very few security measures were in place. Whoever this was, they didn't think they could be gotten to. Or they were no longer there.

"Watch the line of people leaving."

She used her binoculars to zoom in on them. She noted that though they struggled to go in, they very obediently came out. Boarding a bus, they were taken away. Unable to help them now, still, they noted the behavior. Turning back, they continued to wait in silence.

A few hours later, with the sun high in the sky, they noticed a guard with a prisoner walking toward them. Hiding, they hoped their camouflage worked. The man was begging for his life. The guard told him to shut up. Placing the man on his knees, the guard fired his weapon.

The man fell to the ground.

Nix looked away, but Levi and Tyrus stared. Turning, the guard left him there, apparently to rot in the sun.

"I wonder why he was killed." Nix turned to Tyrus.

He shrugged. "Best guess, whatever is making them so obedient and mechanical didn't work on this one."

"I'll check the body." Levi didn't do well in dry environments. His voice was gruff, his movements difficult, using more energy in the desert heat. Still, he was able to become liquid, to flow along the hot earth giving off only steam until he reached the man's body, delving in to discover any anomalous information.

Creeping back in water form, he quickly returned to his human self. "We need to get out of here. Now."

"We barely did anything."

Reaching out his arm, a bloody microchip sat in his hand. "It was inside his brain."

"What?" Tyrus took the chip, noting the emblem sketched into the metal. It seemed somehow familiar.

"It's broken, but that's where it was. Why he was killed. We need to get this back to Dr. Jackson so his tech guy can analyze it. Now. Call the team."

"What about the victims?" Nix didn't like leaving without at least attempting to shut this down.

Tyrus and Levi shared a look, causing anger to fill her eyes. "Speak. Now."

"If...they're being controlled, the key to saving them, safely, without loss of life would be to bring this back to Dr. Jackson and have his lab examine it. Approaching now may cause massive loss of life we don't intend." Tyrus gave her a sympathetic look.

Levi chimed in. "We don't know if they put in a kill switch. While this is defective, it may still be better to examine and reevaluate instead of risk loss of life."

Nix was frustrated but calmed her fire. "Where are we meeting the extraction team?"

"We'll meet them a mile over. We can walk that far. Let's go." Without waiting for a reply, he started moving through the brush. Nix followed, then Tyrus. She noted their efforts to keep her in the middle of both of them and rolled her eyes. The chivalry was sentimental, but she wasn't incompetent.

Walking slowly through the brush, they paused each time a new busload of people left the facility. No screams, no pleas for help. It was like they didn't have minds of their own anymore. It scared her. If they could turn normal people into slaves, what would happen to a Mythic?

Arriving at the rendezvous point, they hopped into the vehicles and drove away. Their plane left the runway just before a very official military aircraft landed, loaded with U.S. soldiers ready to bring the freedom.

When in safe airspace, Levi called Dr. Jackson. Tyrus sat alone at the back of the plane, making mental notes and researching the internet. Nix sat next to Levi, ready for the call. It took a few moments for him to answer. "Is it done?"

"Yeah. Got the package. Bringing it directly to you."

"That was faster than expected."

"It wasn't what we thought. When you hear about it, you're going to crawl out of your skin. Whoever is behind this is a twisted person."

"We shouldn't talk over the phone. A driver will bring you directly to my office." The line went dead. Turning to Nix, he said, "how are you?"

She laughed, surprised that he took the second to ask. "I'm *fine*." She paused, wondering if she should say what she wanted to say. Ann was making her soft. Her humanity was starting to surface. "It is nice to know the three of us can still work together."

Turning, he smiled, open and honest, his creepiness gone. "Really."

"Let me rephrase that, as I'll still kill you if you touch me." Placing a hand to her forehead, she continued. "It's comforting to know that all three of us are still upholding the code and caring for innocents. I appreciate the cooperation on this mission."

"I care about you *too*, Nix." His gaze was intense, burning through her.

She lowered her voice, afraid Tyrus would hear. "You lost that chance with me a long time ago, Levi. Let it be."

Signaling to the stewardess, he asked for a glass of bourbon. Sipping it silently, he waited a long time before he decided what he would do next. After a few moments, he reached up to remove the hood from her jacket.

She backed away, saying as she did so, "what are you doing?"

Taking her hand, he said, "I'm so sorry. Nix, you know I am. You are the reason I even have any good will left in me."

Taking her hand back, she said, "you have to understand, I lost more that day than you will ever lose, even in death. Levi, what the two of you took from me… I will never trust you again."

Turning to the window, she looked out, ignoring him. She didn't see a tear run down his guilty face.

Levi downed the whole glass of bourbon. "Nix, believe me, if nothing else, I'll die before I let anyone hurt you."

Slowly turning to face him, she said, "you're the reason I *can* be hurt."

Walking away, knowing he'd tried, he ordered another drink and downed it. He couldn't get drunk, however, tonight he needed the sting of the alcohol. For old times' sake.

The figure turned off the screen and smashed their fist to the ground. How the video got through was beyond them. Watching the Americans approach the facility, they waited patiently for what would happen next. On the screen, as the soldiers approached, a slow smile spread, showing white teeth reflected on the screen. A few moments later, the entire facility blew, soldiers flying everywhere.

Noting that at least they had no evidence, the figure pushed a button on the bottom of the panel. "Professor, how are you?"

"Fine, here in one piece."

"How many subjects did you manage to acquire?"

"Ten thousand."

"That's fantastic. Thank you for working under such difficult circumstances. I assure you in the future, I will not interrupt your research."

"Thank you."

"Were any chips defective?"

"A rate of 10,000 to one. Only one. It was amazing."

"What happened to the subject?"

"The mercenaries you hired had him… terminated."

"Did you verify?"

"No, but on the off chance that the person is alive, the chip, though it didn't work, will still send a Wi-Fi signal to you directly through the computer program I installed for you. You'll see it if it's in range, as you can see all the other active and working chips. This is so exciting. I'm so ready to change lives."

"Thank you, Professor. Continue the good work." Discontinuing the conversation, the figure logged on to a local computer and entered their password. A moment later, they threw a glass against the wall. There, on the screen was a little blimp of a data chip in North America, near Colorado.

Picking up their phone, the figure called someone. "Yes."

"I need you to take out Jackson Genetics."

"That…will be difficult."

"See it done, or I'll come for you. NOW!"

The line went dead. The figure sat back, continuing to seethe. That twerp wouldn't stop the process now. They were too close. Too close.

Chapter 15
Day 26

Tyrus smiled at the teens before him. *What a difference a week makes when they commit.* They were not quite soldiers, but they had their own way of solving problems. They were a unit. He was proud. For a second, his mind drifted, back to another time, another place.

He shook his head to clear it. *Not now. Right now, I have to test these kids, see what they can do.* He stood and gathered his things.

"I'm leaving, for a while." The looks he got made him chuckle. They were caring kids. "I'll be back in a day or two."

"What are we going to do? No way we're finished with our training." Connor folded his hands in front of him.

Joy's face went from sad to happy in an instant. "It's a game."

Seth spoke up. "We are going for a walk around this part of the city today."

Julius shook his head. "Why?"

Tyrus spoke up. "You have to see what you're made of. Just remember the things I taught you. Stay away from the cameras, don't talk to cops, and help people. Try not to use your powers any more than you have to, or you know what can happen…"

Joy said, "boom!"

Tyrus nodded. "You're still learning, but you also need to take care of each other, take care of yourselves. So, I'm going to do some searching for Ann. You're going to help people."
Joy's face went sad again. "The odds aren't any better than when I tried."

He nodded. "Well, I know I cautioned you. Told you not to act impulsively, and I won't either. You need me to leave to become what you need to be. Right?"

She nodded, suddenly happy again. "We'll get you a cupcake. Bye!"

As he walked away, he thought it through. *Nix.* He thought of her, and his guilt came to the surface. She was the only other fire bird alive that he knew of. Nix had her and wouldn't give her up without a fight. He was hoping the recent truce would allow them to converse civilly, for her to see Ann belonged with her friends. Hopefully, they could once again put the complicated past they had behind them and focus on the future.

Ann wasn't allowed to leave the apartment today. Nix had more "business" to deal with, and though she said she trusted Ann, she did make a good point about this world being larger than Ann thought it was. She implied that Ann might not be ready to handle the unknown. While Nix was out, the security system for the apartment was on lockdown. She couldn't leave even if she wanted to.

Slightly frustrated, but seeing the bigger picture, Ann gorged on some ice cream in the freezer. Nix always kept the food well stocked. She explained that the energy they used for their power meant that they had to eat more calories than an average woman. She suggested 3000 calories on days that Ann used her powers, and a diet of 2500 calories on days she did not. Ann was fine with that, *cause ice cream.*

Sitting down on the huge white sectional, she found the remote and turned on the news. It was another habit from Nix. She said it was always good to keep an ear to the ground, and News stations might catch a piece or two of what she needed to know. Still, it was boring. As she watched, she was sarcastically thrilled to see that someone had broken the world record for largest cupcake. Ann shook her head. Even she couldn't eat that…

Nix stood at the entrance to the only hospital in the city. Wearing nurses' scrubs, she walked straight into the building, waving at the receptionist.

"Got to run Cindy. Love the sweater." Learning names was easy when people were so friendly. Sliding into an elevator full of people, she rode it to the fourth floor. Today was the day she would get her answers, placate the director. He was awake.

As the elevator doors opened, a group of doctors stood waiting.

"So, Wills," one of the doctor's said, "can I get your number or something? I mean, we've been working together for weeks now…"

The woman walked away, ignoring him completely.

Smart woman. Turning down a hallway, she arrived at his room. Opening the door, slowly, she surveyed the room around her. Monitors were beeping, humming away. The man lay on the hospital bed, attached to machines with plastic tubes. The doctor had forgotten to close her email account. Apparently, the orchids she ordered were delivered in a red vase. The frivolous things people were into…

Nix walked up to him and noted that his skin was slightly wrong. Checking his pulse, she suddenly scoured the room, checking his vitals. Her hands slid up his arms, first his left, then his right. Finding a small pinhole, unattached to wires, she cursed silently.

She immediately turned and walked out. Now they had a nurse on camera. *Dammit!* As she turned the corner to the elevator, the familiar long buzz of death, the man flatlining, echoed behind her. Joining a group of lawyers on their way down, she kept her breathing even. She slipped out the back way as sirens approached. Her fire burned her clothes off her, leaving a T-shirt and jean shorts. If they were focused on her curvy body, they wouldn't focus on her face.

Walking around to the front, timing her stride, she managed to avoid the incoming police as they checked in at the reception desk. Taking the revolving door, she exited the hospital without looking back. Crossing the street, she unlocked her car door and drove away.

It wasn't until she was on the highway that she began to hit the wheel in frustration. Screaming at the top of her lungs over the sound of the music, she quickly composed herself. Because of her skill, the fire did not rise, except a small flame burning in her eyes.

Dialing his number, she took a deep breath.

"Yes, Nix."

"Director, I couldn't get the info."

Silence for a moment. "Why not?" She could tell his patience was wearing thin.

"Director, he'd been poisoned before I even got there. I don't know who this is, but they're very connected. He'd just woken up. My contact never wastes time."

Silence again. "I understand, Nix. Was your escape clean?"

"They'll catch a nurse on camera, bulkier than me, but won't be able to make me."

"Good. I'll give you half of the monies for attempting to carry out my will. I've had some…other issues with this as well. I'm very aware that this wasn't your fault. Good day."

He hung up, and Nix breathed a sigh of relief. One thing was strange though. Why was he being so pleasant? He should have at least been angry. Something else was going on, and her instincts told her it wasn't good.

Miles away, a reporter on live TV didn't enjoy her day much, either. It was the first time she'd be reporting from the scene. Her dark hair pulled back, red suit on, she was ready to sparkle and shine. *But a gigantic cupcake?*

They were going live in minutes, and she took a moment to wish that something more exciting would happen. Anything would work. A bank robbery, a car crash, anything. Then she felt guilty for wishing disaster on others. *You just need to get through this and be the best you.* Turning toward the camera, she performed a sound check, asked the camera man if he was ready, and waited to begin.

Joy walked along the sidewalk. Across the street was a camera crew, setting up for a segment. She looked at the shop behind them. *Oooh, cupcakes!* Joy liked all things sweet lately. She appeared alone, but the street was covered. Seth said this was it. This is where it would happen. His gut told him so. Joy could go either way…

Suddenly, as a change in the wind, she perked up. Someone had made a wish close by, and the universe was listening. Ready to react, she walked down an alley. Moving some trash cans, she placed them in peculiar angles, and looked at the dumpster. It was on the wrong side. Closing her eyes, she envisioned the hunk of metal on the right side of the street, not the left.

Opening her eyes, she picked up a twisted piece of metal, and walked back out. Her part was done, for now.

◆ ◆ ◆

Seth could feel it too. A change in fate had occurred, and they were on the wrong side of the street. Running across the busy road, it was as if he knew exactly the moment to cross to avoid the vehicles, as if they moved out of the way for him. Connor and Julius followed, albeit more clumsily.

Across the street was a news crew. That was unfortunate, but he felt an emergent need to be standing outside the jewelry store. Looking in the window, he motioned to Connor and Julius to go inside and check it out.

Connor crinkled his nose but obeyed. Julius was a few steps behind him. Walking into the jewelry store, he pretended to be looking at watches, then moved to the rings. A sales attendant approached him.

"We have rings in all sizes for both sexes. What can I help you find today?" She gave him a huge smile. He froze for a minute.

Julius stepped in. "We were looking for a…ring."

The attendant turned to him and said, "oh, we love customers of all creeds here. Let me show you some matching men's sets."

Connor turned and gave him a look. This was not going well.

Julius stammered to reply, "Uh, no. We aren't…together. It's for his sister…" this was harder than he thought. "Bertha."

Connor fought the urge to roll his eyes. "Well, you're the one getting married to her, so come here, guy!" He motioned to Julius and brought him to the counter. "I'm just gonna look around."

Connor left him to deal with the attendant. Searching, he tried to see if anyone suspicious caught his attention. Right now, only one other customer was in the store. She was an older lady trying to return a necklace. Didn't think she'd be much of a threat.

He was looking at random jewelry when someone burst into the store, guns in their hands, face masks covering their features. *Here we go.* He raced to protect the old woman while Julius leapt at the robbers.

Seth had already called the police, telling them there was a robbery in progress. He hung up the phone as two shady characters with a duffle bag approached the store. Walking quickly across the street, knowing Tyrus was going to kill him, his gut told him that he had to notify the reporter. Something about this was important enough to break the rules. He had to get it filmed. Waiting several seconds to the left of the camera man, he watched the store. When the time was right, he shouted, "look! Across the street! Someone's robbing that store!"

Turning instantly away from the camera, as if he knew where it would be, he walked away to the left. His job was done.

The reporter's eyes drifted to the store, where a window had just broken. One of the customers inside came flying out. She turned to the camera and began. "It looks like we have some breaking news, bigger than even the world's largest cupcake. Across the street from my location is a robbery in progress. Our camera man will try to capture as much of the scene as he can. It looks like one of the customers, a Hispanic boy, was just tossed out of a window behind me…"

Her day had just gotten a lot better.

Connor saw Julius "exit" the building. He also saw the men realize their mistake. They must have known the layout of the building, because they ran through a door in the back. Close on their heels, Connor followed them up a stairway and onto the roof. They were quick and had guns. Even he was susceptible to a bullet hole in his chest. Hiding behind the door, they shot rounds at him while they jumped down.

He heard their screams as they hit the pavement. "You were supposed to move the dumpster!"

"I did!"

Looking down, Connor saw one man lying on the ground, holding his knee. The other stood and ran to the left down the alley. His luck wasn't any better. No matter which way he went, he had to move a trash can to keep from tripping. Connor watched as he finally made it to the end of the alley, only to be struck in the chest by a metal bar.

Joy shouted, "STAY," and walked off. Seconds later, the police arrived. Connor turned to the other side of the alley, jumped down, and placed an arm around Joy. This day just kept getting better and better.

The teens met up at a park two streets over. No cops stopped to question them, and they were fairly sure that the reporter didn't have them on camera, other than Julius, who would appear as a random victim. In that way, they hadn't broken at least *one* of Tyrus's rules.

Joy was playing, swinging away like a little kid. Connor sat on a bench underneath a shady tree. Julius arrived a few moments later with his hand on his side. Seth was the last. He had stopped to get a first aid kit.

"I figured you might need this." Opening it, he began to dress Julius's wound. It wasn't deep, but he was bleeding. When he was done, he turned to Connor. "Let's get home."

With that, they left, the boys in front, Joy skipping along to catch up.

Ann saw the whole thing on TV. Her breath caught in her throat. She just knew. She knew it was her friends the reporter was talking about. Several anonymous good Samaritans had moved the dumpster from its usual spot. They'd saved the life of Edith, the older customer in the shop. They distracted the robbers so the employees could hit the alarm, and they managed to do it all with only one of them being caught on film. Julius, alive, ok and thriving. A tear stained her cheek. Her people were becoming heroes and saving lives.

She wondered for a moment if this was really the best place to be, not that she could go anywhere. The lessons that Nix had taught her over the past week were helpful. She knew how to spot and avoid cameras, how to blend into crowds. She knew the average. typical police response times for the various parts of St. Blaise. She knew the layout of the whole city from Nix making her study maps, memorize landmarks. She knew how to read blueprints, how to plant a bug on someone, and how to pickpocket.

Still, none of it was very above board. Nix always said the same thing, though. "This is not a dream world. This is hell, and you have to fight fire with fire."

Those words echoed in Ann's head, but she couldn't help missing her friends. In the short time between the accident and now, they'd become her family. Her family s*aved* people.

Throwing the remote on the couch, she stood and walked to her room. She'd tell Nix tonight that she was ready to rejoin her friends. They'd talk, she'd let Nix give her a burn cell, just in case, and she'd go home to her people. It was time.

Nix watched from afar as the teens finished their escapade. She still kept tabs, in case she could collect on her contract. No way would she approach with the dragon around. Frustrated, she hid in an alley as sirens blared down the street. *Not today…*

Turning, she shook her head. What was he thinking, letting kids roam on their own? If the wrong person got wind of this, the teens would be in deep trouble.

She turned down the next street over, then she sensed him. A feeling of dread crept up her spine. Blending into a crowd of women, she walked into the first store she found.

Tyrus watched Nix from across the street. *So, she was still keeping tabs on them.* That meant Ann was likely at the penthouse. Though it narrowed down his search, it didn't make it easier.

As he watched Nix, she suddenly blended in with a crowd of women and walked into a grocery store. Her body language was tight, rigid. What did she sense?

"*We meet again,*" a deep, familiar voice behind him whispered.

"Levi," Tyrus said, "what can I help you with now?" He didn't even turn to face him.

"Business. The Director would like to speak to you."

Tyrus sighed. "The Director can kiss my ass."

"Hey, now," the gruff, southern voice began, "no need to make this violent. Not with so much for you to lose. This is a courtesy call, nothing more."

That meant either Nix or the teens, or both, were still on the Director's radar. "Just a chat, huh?"

"Just a chat. Come on."

Tyrus turned away from Nix and cursed his bad luck. Joy had told him. He should have listened.

Ann heard Nix enter the apartment. She had a bag packed, but she kept it in the closet, out of sight. She didn't want her mentor to think less of her, so she had to approach this conversation the right way.

Nix sat on the couch with another tub of ice cream. The TV was off, and she looked exhausted. Ann sat on the other side of the white sectional and took a deep breath to speak.

"I know," Nix stated before she could start. The woman turned her golden-brown gaze toward Ann. Sadness permeated her features, making her appear much older. "I know what you're going to ask. Before you do, there's something I need to share with you."

"Are you going to finally enlighten me on Levi?"

Nix sighed. "Would you accept it if I told you now was not the time to talk about it?"

Ann took a moment. "I would try, but I believe it is the time. The exact, perfect time."

Nix looked forward as she recalled the memory. "You five are unique, but you are not the first. You know that because you know me. Tyrus, Levi and I were part of the last rise of what we call, Mythics. People with the abilities and powers we have."

"How does a friend become an enemy?"

"Apparently for us, all it took was subterfuge, lies and money."

"How so?"

"When we were younger, we belonged to the same group. We fought bad guys and saved people, we learned the code and most abided by it. For a long time, I'm talking a decade, we were able to maintain that. We had a bit of fame, enough that some writer made a cartoon of us, but we lived away from the world and tried our best to hide who we were. It wasn't perfect, but it worked.

"People change, though. We embrace change. It is our nature. Not every Mythic is so lucky. Our group split into two camps. Those that needed the money, needed mercenary work to put food on the table, to better themselves. They felt the rules were unfair, that they benefitted only those who already had enough. Tyrus was the leader of the opposing group, who felt a victim shouldn't be charged for lifesaving measures against odds that were essentially insurmountable. He refused to allow anyone to take any coin. He also outlawed contract kills.

"Levi was in the first group. I floated back and forth between the two. Looking back, I can see where the influence began, where the darkness took hold. Outside influences, Mythics older than us, who feared us, our building power. They used money as an incentive to divide the group, and to destroy us from inside."

"That's…very devious."

She sighed. "Yes. Yes, it was, but at the time, I couldn't see past my own perception. We became divided, then our interests began to conflict, and we became enemies. Quite quickly. We'd been a group for a decade, and it took them only a matter of months to destroy us.

"The first casualty was our unicorn, then our leprechaun. The ones that lacked physical power but had strong psychic abilities to keep us alive. I don't know who struck the final blows against them, but I wish I did. The next were our heavy hitters. Similar to your friends, Connor and Julius. Powerful physically, but vulnerable to both elemental and psychic attack.

"We were the last three standing." A tear ran down her cheek. "Levi on one side, me in the middle, and Tyrus on the other."

"Well, you're all still standing, right?"

Nix wiped a tear away. "Sort of."

"What do you mean?"

Nix bit her lip, a nervous habit that didn't fit with her calm exterior. "They convinced Levi and Tyrus that I was the mastermind."

"And they believed them?" Ann was suddenly enraged, her flame dancing in her eyes. She felt the bird fluff up its feathers.

"After all the grief, all the damage, I'm honestly not surprised."

"But friends don't do that to each other."

Nix placed a hand on hers. "I wish I could tell you that's the way the world works. Sometimes it does, but…very often it's easy to find yourself opposed to the ones you love. Friends on opposing sides of an issue, big or small. It takes an incredibly strong-willed person to not give in to frustration and anger at times like that, and I was not strong enough."

"You're the strongest willed person I know."

"Exactly. And I failed."

"How?"

"They cornered me and my flame reacted. I, too, was suffering from extreme grief, and my phoenix was tired of the pain. She…came out easily, too easily and overwhelmed me. I transformed, but instead of keeping my…mind, I became her. It's an experience that is hard to explain. She was in control, and she wanted to fight. A phoenix is at her core a survival expert, but she is limited as all Mythics are. Without the person in control, she began to randomly attack everything she viewed as a threat, Levi and Tyrus included.

"Their Mythics were strained as mine was. They'd suffered, just as I had, and they changed too. Imagine a fully transformed phoenix attempting to fend off both a fire and a water dragon. It was…long, hard and bloody. At the end of it," her voice broke, "they had won, but they couldn't kill me too. So instead," she paused for a long while before she continued, "they ripped her from me. A skill long forgotten that wasn't in their knowledge base. They had to have been told how. They ripped her from me and since then, I've had the physical abilities of a phoenix, but I can't call her. I'm cut off from her, if she's even alive without me.

"Without your fire bird, you can't rise from the ashes like a phoenix should. We run the risk, every time we use our power, of spontaneous combustion. If you can't control your flame, you die, but as long as you have your phoenix, you will ascend. You will come back. Stronger than ever. They took that from me. The people I trusted with my life, my secrets, stole her from me. So, before you go back to your friends, you have to ask yourself if it's really your home. I thought it was mine, and it almost killed me."

Ann wiped away tears from her own eyes. "I'm so sorry."

"As am I. I cannot forgive them, and I will caution you to be very, very careful with them, but I can't allow my hate to cloud issues either. They have their uses, but they will choose ideals over you."

"Are my friends in danger?"

She sighed. "Yes, but not from them."

"Who then?"

Nix smiled and stood. "That is what all three of us still have in common. We want to know who is responsible for the first controlled use of synthetic Omega Fire, and we want answers. And where there is common ground, there is hope. Your friends will be fine until that is no longer the issue.

"Now, how about we eat. Something."

"We don't have much left."

"Order take out from that Thai place, then order groceries."

"Your tab?"

"Of course. I'm going to lie down until the food arrives. I'm exhausted, and as you can imagine, telling that story is…draining to say the least."

Ann took out her cell phone and called the restaurant, where she ordered five dinners. One extra. Then she called the front desk.

"Good evening, Nix."

"Ah, no, it's…Ann."

"I see. What can I do for you Ann?"

"We…need groceries."

"One of everything?"

"Yes."

"On her tab?"

"Yes."

"There's a significant fee for that amount of groceries."

"I'm aware. On her tab."

"Of course. We will be quick. Have a pleasant evening."

Ann hung up and knew the bill would be astronomical, but she also knew it was very necessary. One thing about her type, they weren't cheap dinner guests. She stared at her bag, debating internally for a moment, before shutting the door. It would remain packed away, but she didn't feel she was ready to leave. Not yet.

She walked by Nix's room and heard soft sobbing. It was so unlike her to cry. She must have felt a very deep connection with her firebird. On cue, hers landed on her shoulder, it's head on hers. She had only known her bird for a short while, and it was already a part of her. She couldn't imagine losing her, especially like that. If she had the chance, the dragon and the leviathan would pay. Dearly. With fire in her eyes, she walked into the kitchen, looking for food. She was "hangry."

Dr. Jackson watched on video as Levi escorted his old friend inside the office building. *Tyrus hasn't aged a day in years. Must be nice.*

Taking the Whiskey out of his desk, he set three glasses next to it. He pulled out chilled stones and placed two in each glass. Raising it to his lips, he sipped and waited for the inevitable knock on his door.

When it came, he instructed his security with a flick of his wrist to open it. The two men came in together, both tall, but in many ways, opposite. He thought back on all he knew about them, and all he could do if they'd just accepted his offer of employment. *Not now.*

"Gentlemen," he began, "can I offer you some whiskey?"

Levi grabbed a glass, pouring exactly one shot of whiskey. Tyrus sat down, ignoring the request.

"Come now, Ty, surely you must be thirsty for your favorite drink. It's even your brand."

Tyrus sat back in the chair and gave him a blank stare. "My name is Tyrus, and I don't drink anymore."

Levi laughed. "Why? You can't get drunk." He sat next to Tyrus and playfully punched him on the shoulder. "Am I right?"

Tyrus didn't see the point in false comradery. "Just say what you have to say, Director."

Dr. Jackson took a few moments to compose himself. Before he spoke, he came in front of his desk and sat down opposite Tyrus. He folded his hands in front of him, and said, "we have a problem."

Tyrus laughed. "*You* have a few problems, one of them being me. What makes you think I'm going to let you start this research back up again? What makes you think I'm going to help you at all?

Dr. Jackson looked him straight in the eye, and in an unwavering voice said, "because it *wasn't* me."

The four teens waited for Tyrus to get back. He was a bit late, but nothing to be concerned about. They sat in Seth's room, a cabin scene, complete with a small fireplace and throw blankets, eating take-out pizza.

"Joy, you rock," Connor said, "I mean I can't believe someone so nice can so brutally knock out a guy with a pipe." He busted up laughing, placing a hand on Julius' shoulder. "Man, sorry about the window."

"It was fun until I hit the glass." They laughed again.

Seth perked up. "Tyrus is here."

Joy did too. "He's not happy."

They were suddenly silent. They could hear footsteps carefully, defeatedly coming up the stairs. Tyrus stopped at the entrance to their room and began.

"We have a problem. Make sure you get some rest tonight, because tomorrow, we're getting Ann."

Joy clapped her hands together. "Yay! My bestie!"

Seth looked at her. "I thought *I* was your best friend?"

"Yeah, yeah, you too." She got up and left the room, saying, "night."

The boys followed Tyrus to their rooms, and he turned into his honeymoon suite. They reserved the rooms for Wills and Ryan, in case they had to come back, but after tomorrow, it wouldn't matter. The group of Mythics would be on the run, cut off from their friends. Ann wouldn't come quietly. *Doesn't matter. Doing the right thing is seldom popular and never easy.*

After what he learned tonight, he couldn't help but feel guilty that he'd let this slip by. He was usually good with detecting deception, but in this instance, he'd let his guard down, and someone had used that to their advantage. He had to save these kids, all of them, from a very real, very near threat. Preparing himself, he lay down, letting the dark come.

> She was in the meadow with Joy. The overly large, too colorful flowers had become familiar to her. They were dancing, laughing, playing. The sun was bright on her face, birds chirping happily in rhythm. She could feel the wind, the grass between her toes, the strength of her friend's grip upon her hands.
>
> Joy looked away and waved to someone behind them. Ann rounded and saw the dragon. He strode toward them. She thought briefly that

she should be afraid of something, but it faded as he approached.

Ann turned to Joy. "You know, you DO have to look out for yourself, Ann." Joy held her hand gently. "Things aren't what they appear to be. Take Tyrus for instance," she motioned at him, "he's not a bad guy."

Ann touched his face. He turned toward her but didn't speak. "Is he really here with us?"

Joy giggled, "no. no," she waved her hands about, "he's asleep but he's dreaming about the past. I couldn't wake him from it, couldn't bring him here."

Ann turned to Joy. "Are you okay?"

Joy nodded. "Yes, we are. We're here with Tyrus, the Dragon, and tomorrow, we're coming to take you somewhere safe. You're in danger, Ann."

Ann couldn't help but feel safe, here. "What are you talking about?"

"The leviathan," she began, "he is…complicated. Do you hear me? You need to leave. Either way, you end up the same place, but if you stay…"

Ann saw Nix in front of her suddenly, surrounded by water, struggling to breathe. She locked eyes with Joy who sadly confirmed her fear. "If you stay, Nix will die."

Ann woke suddenly, the dream fading, feelings of safety and warmth lingering. As she remembered the warning, her breath sped up, sweat formed on her brow and she started to panic.

She had to warn Nix. Getting up, she put a robe around her waist and opened her door slowly. The door to Nix's room was ajar, the light on. She crept closer down the hall and heard voices coming from the couch.

"I was sent here to make sure you complete your contract." Levi had another glass of whiskey. He was sitting on the couch with Nix, who laughed.

"Dear friend," she began, "what makes you think I have any intentions other than filling a multimillion-dollar contract?"

Levi placed his glass down on her coffee table. "It isn't me who is getting nervous. It's your nephew."

Nix sighed. "He always was an impatient boy."

"He wants me to make sure the girl gets delivered tomorrow."

Nix thought about turning her over to the business. Her face went blank. *Over my dead body.* Out loud she replied, "of course. And the others?"

"You have one more week. After that, he's no longer paying me as an enforcer. He's paying me as an assassin."

"So, this is, what? A courtesy call? The bell tolls for me?"

Levi suddenly grabbed Nix in his arms, and kissed her deeply, passionately. Nix thought back on all they had been through. Pictures of them together came to her mind unbidden. Though she hated this man's actions, the person he was compelled her, made her feel alive. She leaned into the kiss, her body relaxing under his.

"Has the bell ever *stopped* tolling?"

"No." She was breathless. "No, I suppose not."

Levi looked down at the woman in his arms. Guilt welled inside of him. "Finish the contract Nix, or it won't be a bell you have to worry about, it'll be me, and we both know you're no match for me now."

With that Levi turned to leave. Ann was very lucky that he didn't see her. She crept back to her room silently, quickly, hoping her mentor didn't notice.

Nix sat on the couch, thinking fast. She had to get the girl out. They'd bonded. There was no way she was going to lose her. The girl was too soft. She wouldn't survive a week in that torture chamber.

She knew what her nephew would do. He'd try to reverse the process. That was their big goal now. Reverse the genetic modification and bring them back to their former selves. Except he was a misguided fool. She didn't need needles poking her, she needed to be safe.

Nix thought for a long while on the couch. She debated what to do, where to go. Levi knew most of her hideouts, but there were a few new ones he wasn't aware of. She could take Ann. They could be on the next plane out of here, to the desert, where he had no power. Maybe Arizona…

Her plan decided, she turned to wake the girl. If she was going to keep her safe, she had to go now.

She knocked quietly on Ann's door. There was no reply. "Ann?" Nothing. "Ann, open up. We need to talk."

After a moment of continued silence, Nix opened her door. She searched the girl's room. There was no window in here, no way for her to leave, but yet, Ann was not there. Tense, nervous now, she checked the bath. Nothing. She turned and walked into her room. An open window greeted her, the screen shoved out. Walking to the window, she peered out, down to the street hundreds of feet below, then over to the next building. On the rooftop, Ann stared back at her for a moment, surrounded in flame, before she turned and began to walk away.

Nix was powerful, but for flying, you needed your fire bird. There was no way she could follow. "Ann! You don't know what you're doing! Ann! Please! Come back! I'll keep you safe!"

As the girl continued to walk away, Nix gave up, and yelled one last thing. "Don't let him catch you! Be smart! Be brave!"

Ann hesitated after that last statement, but she didn't see any way around this. A tear forming in her vision, she continued forward without a word, the dream's warning loud in her mind. Walking toward the next rooftop, she wiped away tears that were streaming down her cheeks. *Another hard life lesson learned. Sometimes you have to hurt people to save them.*

She climbed down to the street and found a bench to occupy while she decided what to do. The rain began, and she remembered her warning about Levi and water. Her bird was instantly above her, shielding her from the droplets that would alert him of her presence outside the protection of the apartment.

"At least I always have you."

The bird made a sound, almost like a purr and heat rose from its body, making sure its counterpart was warm and comforted. Ann crossed her hands and placed her elbows on her knees, looking down. If Levi was coming for her, if others were in danger, how would she save them and save herself? Grateful for the warmth, she was glad no one was around on the deserted street. With the light next to her, they'd be able to tell she was bone dry while the rain fell on everything around her.

Chapter 16

Tyrus stood in the elevator, practically sweating. He hated elevators. To him, they were giant metal coffins. Still, he wasn't climbing the stairs up multiple floors. He paced back and forth and thought about what he was going to say. He didn't exactly know how this conversation would unfold. He just had to focus on finding out what he needed, then leave.

The doors chimed, stating he reached his intended floor. They opened to Nix, standing, facing him in a robe, a glass of red wine in her hand. Her tear-stained eyes didn't match the expression on her face. He placed his hand at his side and nodded.

"Hello, lover," she said, seductively…

Ann didn't exactly know where to go. She had some cash, one bag of clothes, and some stolen goods she could pawn, but really, what was she going to do? Without other options, she intended to find her friends. Something had been drawing her back to them, and perhaps, they would be strong enough together to handle Levi.

A few minutes after ordering a rideshare from her phone, she stepped inside the vehicle. She had the map of the city in her head, and she knew she could backtrack from the scene on TV.

"Where to?"

"The world's largest cupcake please."

He grunted. "Tourists."

Ann congratulated herself on not rolling her eyes. She sat back and enjoyed the city lights. She mentally noted the landmarks. She worried she may be putting her friends in danger, but on the other hand, she couldn't do this alone. Could she? Holding back frustrating tears, she sat in silence.

Joy stood outside the bakery, arguing with Seth. Connor and Julius stood to the side, trying to stay out of it.

"We need to go. Something doesn't feel right." Seth's stomach was jumping from stress. Something very bad was going to happen here, soon.

Joy stomped her foot on the ground and pouted. "Ann is coming. HERE." She pointed at the building with the huge fake cupcake on its roof. "We stay here."

"We can't help Ann if we're taken or dead."

Joy refused to listen. "If we leave, something worse will happen to Ann."

Seth sighed. They'd been over this. Giving in, he turned to the other two. "Sweep the area, please."

Connor walked left, Julius went right. They checked the street in both directions, like Tyrus showed them, noting any threats. Joy hummed a tune in front of the store, her eyes facing left down the street. "She'll be here any minute. You'll see."

Seth searched the area around the store. He checked the alley on both sides and walked across the street to see what he could on the roof of the two-story building.

Headlights appeared in the distance. Down the street, Connor signaled with a flashlight. Julius responded and started to head back. Seth stayed across the street, just in case. Joy bounced up and down and said, "Yay!"

The rideshare came closer. It passed Connor. In a few minutes, they might be reunited with their friend.

Suddenly, as they watched, a man…appeared in front of the car, as if he formed from the rain itself. The driver swerved to avoid him and crashed into an electrical utility pole. It wasn't going very fast, so the pole stayed upright. The man began walking forward, toward the driver, who exited the vehicle and started raving at the crazy individual.

Everyone started running toward the scene at once. As they watched, helpless, the man waved his hand, and before their eyes, screaming, the driver liquified in front of them. Fear did not pause them, but inside, they were scared. Who was this demon to kill so casually, so brutally?

Ann exited the other side, and seeing the driver liquify, made a split-second decision. She saw her friends approaching her, and she saw him, the Leviathan, staring at her. She'd just witnessed him kill and was suddenly filled with the urge to protect her friends who weren't prepared enough to take him on. The story Nix told her was still fresh. Watching her face, he smiled, slowly, purposefully, and reached his hand toward Joy.

The rage came easily now. Her friends were scattered along the street, but she was right next to him. Summoning all her power, with the help of her fire bird, a dome of flame lit up around her, encircling her and the sea monster. He dropped his hand, pleasant surprise filling his face. She stood, her hands outstretched, the fire in her eyes burning brightly, her power filling her completely. She made no move to destroy him, as that would be disastrous, but no way was he hurting those she loved.

"You're powerful, I'll give you that. A matter of weeks and you're controlling your flame very well. Do you know how long it's been since I've had the presence of a living phoenix? Intoxicating." His eyes glazed over a little as if he were drawn to her power.

"I know exactly how long it's been." Ann might be strong, but she was struggling to keep her friends out. If he tried to fight her, she wouldn't be able to save them.

"You remind me of her. Your spirit, your fire. She taught you well."

"Nix told me a lot of monster stories. You were there."

He chuckled. "Yes, yes there were times that I did terrible things. Dark, terrible things." He stopped, looking at the flame around him. "Tonight, however, is not a night I intend to do something terrible, at least, to you. I'm merely here to collect you. Come and I let your friends go."

"Swear it!" It came out strange, as if a power she didn't normally possess cried out, as if her phoenix were speaking through her. A strange mix of high and low pitch with a hint of roughness. Was this her voice?

His smile faded. "I swear it." As she watched, a bit confused, he knelt in front of her formally. Her bird was pleased, placated by the show of respect. She believed he could be trusted, at least in this.

Collecting the energy from the flame, she shoved it outward. It flew through the air and forced her friends in opposing directions. Though he was being truthful, she wasn't risking her friends' lives. She didn't let the energy dissipate until they were each two blocks away.

He chuckled again. "Impressive. Let's go." He held out his hand.

Ann hesitated for a long moment.

"Don't make me regret my kindness. You know how powerful I am."

Her bird urged her on. They'd made a deal. Taking his hand, she watched as water suddenly rose from the sewer around them. It formed a whirlpool in the air to their right. "Hold on," he said softly, as they stepped through the portal.

Tyrus sat on the couch in Nix's living room. So far, she'd been civil and pleasant. He didn't know if it was genuine or calculated, but he had to be here.

Nix came back with a wine glass full of juice for him. "I know you don't drink, so here." She handed it to him and sat down.

"Thanks," he said, thinking. He didn't know how to start this conversation. He hadn't seen her socially for a very long time.

Nix, however, was completely confident. "So, how are the teenies doing?"

He laughed. "They're…competent."

Nix snorted with derision. "They're babies. Babies in a world that requires soldiers."

"They're adults, eighteen and more capable than you would think."

"If you say so," she stated dryly, raising the wine glass to her lips. "How is Ann?"

Now Tyrus was confused. "She…isn't here with you?"

Nix turned to him. "No, she left after Levi played me the fool." She threw the wine glass at the wall. It shattered. Standing, she paced back and forth. "For a second, I thought that kiss was real. But it wasn't, it was just him, manipulating the situation. She must have been listening."

"Wait," he quizzed her, "you kissed Levi? You were with him too?"

Nix half smiled at him. "Jealous?"

He took a deep breath in and continued, "listen, if she isn't with me and she isn't with you, she's with…"

Nix's eyes got wide. "He played all of us."

Tyrus stood. "Can we call a truce for now?"

Nix was already running to change. "Yeah, fine. Let me get dressed and we'll go."

Joy stood slowly, dusting off her clothes. She was a bit perturbed. So, Seth was right this time. She wasn't going to point it out.

Searching, using her aura to guide her, she used the very earth to locate her friends. The first she sensed was Julius, two blocks south. He was unconscious, but luckily, he was touching earth, connected with nature. Joy called her aura to the grass, and it grew around him, reaching his stomach and head where his injuries were. Then, it began to glow, pure sunshine spreading over him. The grass gave way, and he woke, standing and running back to the scene.

The next was Seth, who was alive and well, already running toward her. *Lucky duck…* Connor was the last. She couldn't locate him at first. There was no earth where he was. She postulated that he must be in a completely man-made surface. She'd have to get the boys to find him.

Skipping back to the accident site, she whistled a merry tune. Ann was fine but scared. They'd find Tyrus and the wounded phoenix and save Ann from the Loch Ness Monster. Things were on the correct path with the least amount of loss.

Ann had a moment of disorientation before she adjusted. When her vision was clear again, she was standing in an office. St. Blaise was lit up in the night sky below her. It was beautiful. She wondered who this office belonged to.

"Take a seat. He's coming from his apartment, a few floors up." The monster turned to leave. Before exiting another portal, he said, "don't think about running. If you do, it'll just be one of your friends here instead of you."

She didn't answer. She only sat, believing him, waiting for this mystery man to arrive. Looking around, she saw that on the table in front of her, was a tablet. She picked it up, turned it on and started browsing through its contents.

Tyrus and Nix drove from her apartment in the downtown district on the highway toward the skyscrapers of the business district. Well, he was hanging on for dear life, she was…racing. He didn't remember her being so aggressive behind the wheel. She also learned to drive a stick. That was a change.

"You shouldn't have wasted time on me." Nix was slightly angry with him. "Those kids…you should have been with them. He wouldn't be so bold if you were there."

Tyrus swallowed, hard. "You overestimate my importance."

"Things really haven't changed. You're still downplaying yours."

"Listen Nix, about that day-"

"No." She was firm and insistent. "No, you don't get to explain yourself. You know what you did, you know why it was wrong, and I don't have to forgive you." Shifting into a higher gear, she raced down the highway.

For a moment, he was silent, then he said, "*Levi?*"

She looked at him, scowling. "Oh, get over it."

"Eyes on the road!" He grabbed the door handle, worried that this was how he would die.

They found Connor, limping toward them. Joy rushed up to him and hugged him tightly. "You're okay!"

Connor, wincing, said, "I was. I'm not now."

Letting go of him, she inspected his wound, touching his leg in areas he wasn't entirely comfortable with. "Watch the hands!"

Joy narrowed her eyes at him but didn't respond. Julius gently patted his back and Seth placed his arm over his shoulders, supporting his weight. A second later, Joy kneeled in front of him, ripping the pants of his left leg to the ankle.

"I need an adult," he said to Seth, exhaustedly. Seth chuckled, which made him chuckle, which hurt. He winced again.

Joy placed hands on each side of his thigh, surrounding a broken bone. As the boys watched, sunlight surrounded her. It grew brighter and brighter until it engulfed her. Seth could see inside the stores; the light was so bright. The light continued to grow until it also enveloped Connor. For several moments, they were blinded by the sunlight, but just as suddenly as it came, it was gone, a soft glow fading around them both.

Connor didn't feel any more pain. "Thanks, Joy." Taking his arm back, they formed a circle and began to discuss what happened.

Ann placed the tablet back down. There was no way that he just left it out, without wanting her to see it. There wasn't even a password. She wondered why someone would give this information away for free. He had a reason for showing this to her, and she was suspicious.

The doors opened a second later and the lights turned on. She stood and turned behind her, to see a medium skinned man with light eyes staring back at her. He reminded her of Nix, in that he was gorgeous. Though she kept a still expression, she was overwhelmed with confusion. Her time in foster care had given her a keen sense of the intent of others. She could tell from non-verbal cues whether someone was friend or foe. Though he owned the room he walked in, there was none of the callous selfishness or the degrading hostility that existed in her foster parents. Was this man really her enemy?

"Hello, Ms. Ann Cecilia Smith. My name is Dr. Gregory Jackson." Stepping down, he extended his hand. She didn't take it. "Now, now, I've been trying to get in touch with you since the accident. Let's be civil." She took his hand and shook it more harshly than he anticipated, letting the tiniest bit of warmth register. His eyes widened a bit, but he said nothing. *Good.*

"I'm sure you're curious as to why I brought you here." Taking off his suit jacket, he opened a bottle of whiskey and poured himself a glass. Two stones were dropped into it. "First of all, my condolences on the…accident. I don't know if you're aware, but Marie's father, Dr. Cline, is a lead researcher here."

Her anger flared at the mention of her friend. He knew who was responsible for the lives taken that day. "You know nothing about her." Venom dripped from her words, a clear warning for him to tread carefully.

"Indeed, I do not."

A hint of sympathy? *Strange.* Still, she kept her face free of emotion, neutral.

Taking an empty glass, he set it down on the table in front of Ann. "Now, I know you're underage, but I do have water and orange juice if you would like a refreshment."

Ann thought about her calorie content. She had used a lot of energy. She was tired and thirsty. "Just give me the jug of OJ."

He chuckled, knowingly and complied. He waited, sipping from his glass in the chair across from her until she was done. She chugged the whole bottle of orange juice down in what was record time for her.

Breathing heavily, she looked at him. "Thank you," she said dryly.

He set his glass down. "Now, if we could talk?"

"About what? The files you left unprotected for me to read? My connection to Marie? About my symptoms? About the fire and its *origin*?" The last question was brave, even for her, but she couldn't help herself. Her flame lit her eyes. She needed him to know she was a threat.

He gave a watery, apologetic smile, his face transformed from the executive suit to a sympathetic man. It bewildered her.

"About the awful event that changed your life."

Ann swallowed hard, not exactly sure where this would go.

Tyrus and Nix pulled up to the street and stopped the car near the accident. Getting out, they rushed to the group of teens. Luckily, they were unharmed, but it was only a matter of time before sirens would be upon them. Reaching the group, they slowed, eventually stopping.

"Where is Ann?" Nix asked. "Don't tell me you let him take her."

Joy looked crushed. "We were too far away. She shoved us. With her fire. Then she let him take her."

Nix punched Tyrus in the arm. "What was that for?"

"This is on you!" Nix started to pace back and forth, angrily, her flame on display.

He rubbed his shoulder. She still packed a punch. "Julius, can you locate the trail?"

He nodded. "Just waiting for you two. Joy and Seth were insistent."

Tyrus turned to Seth. "you'll have to go with him. Open the portal in the exact spot they opened theirs. If you focus enough, it should lead you to where she is."

"Been a while since my life was this… exciting," Nix said, while the boys opened the portal. Julius stood outside the shimmering fold in reality for a moment, sensing her, rather than smelling her. Seeing the trail, he touched Seth's shoulder, and entered.

Joy and Connor followed next. Tyrus turned to Nix. "Ready to see the family again?"

"You're sure she's there?"

"Where else would Levi take her?"

"Oh, I don't know, a cabin in the woods?"

Tyrus laughed, then stopped. Levi had always been troubled, and there was an even chance that side of him would emerge. Taking her hand, they stepped through the portal. It closed behind them, just as sirens lit the street.

Instantly, they were in front of a large building. Plastered across the front in bright neon were the words, "Jackson Genetics." Nix and Tyrus knew this building. It had stood for a long time. Terrible things had happened to them in there, including the death of other Mythic friends. This would not be easy.

"We need a plan," they both told the teens at the same time.

Chapter 17
Day 27

"This will be your apartment for your stay at our building. I keep a few on hand for visiting guests." He unlocked the door, and Ann stepped inside.

"Wow," she said, "you know how to treat your 'guests.'"

"Despite what you might have heard, I am no monster. If you require anything, food, groceries, new towels, dial the operator on the phone here or in the bedroom. A menu is available for your convenience."

"That's sweet of you," she stated sarcastically.

He sighed. "You know the stipulations, of course? No leaving the apartment unescorted."

"Yeah, yeah, I'm a 'guest' and you care about my 'safety.' I get it."

"I'm also giving you this cell," he placed it on the end table by the door. "It's a direct line to my personal number. Please call me if anyone treats you with anything less than five-star service."

She glared at him. "Fine," she said dryly.

He nodded and turned to leave.

"So how long will I be a 'guest' here?"

He looked back, saying, "as long as it takes to find your friends, and fix this mess." He left without another word. The security system locked the doors behind him. She was in a cage. No way she was just a guest here.

She gazed at the contemporary architecture, curvy walls, bright colors, artwork hanging which looked like originals, not prints. Looking at the walls, with floor to ceiling windows, she could see the entire city from this view. *It must be right below his office.* She recognized the landmarks. Like the princess in the tower, she was stuck, waiting for rescue. Except she wasn't relying on the knight to slay the monster. She was waiting for the monsters to slay the knight.

Walking around, she couldn't help but think that her cage was quite gilded. It was bigger than Nix's apartment by double. The open area in the middle served as a kitchen, dining and living area. The grey couch was soft and comfortable. TV and fireplace in the center. Integrated voice-controlled system. Nice. Walking to the left through the dining/kitchen area, she caught her breath.

On the left side was a lounge, with a pool table, a computer desk, and through a glass wall, was a closed balcony with a private pool. *Nice!* Walking to the right was a large master bedroom, complete with a four-poster bed, and another small closed in balcony with a hot tub. Moving right again she saw the bathroom, gorgeous marble floor and countertops, juxtaposed to the contemporary look of the rest of the apartment. This was lavish, rich, with gold plated accents and a private closet.

This was the last room to inspect. Clothes for both genders in various sizes and styles, finely tailored, hung in a large walk-in closet complete with an island countertop in the middle. Shoes of all styles and colors lined the back wall. Next to the shoes, were priceless jewelry, watches, ties and purses. Looking at the extravagance, this was indeed an apartment for an honored guest. *The best cage ever*, she rolled her eyes sarcastically. She reconciled herself to being alone, again. A lone diva on stage surrounded by cameras, waiting for the final, tragic act to begin.

Day 28

Across the street, in a lavish hotel, Connor sat watching the office complex through binoculars. He was looking for any sign of Ann. He couldn't help but feel like a failure. This was the second time one of his people was taken away. She should be with them, not being subjected to clandestine research.

Seth walked out of the bedroom, freshly showered, rubbing a towel over his hair. "I told you, she's fine," he said. "Nothing to worry about right now."

Connor snorted. "Right." Seth, though intuitive, didn't know everything.

"If we just lay low for a while and keep from getting ourselves caught, an opportunity will present itself and we can take full advantage of it. If they see you watching them, they'll know where we are. Remember what Tyrus said-"

"Invisibility is the key to survival. I know, I remember, but I can't help it. Knowing where she is and not being able to help is just not in my nature to accept."

Seth picked up his key card. "Well, I'm going to the meeting. Do what you want."

Connor put the binoculars down and followed Seth out of the room they shared. These hotel rooms beat out the bed and breakfast hands down. He was sharing with Seth, with Julius and Tyrus next door on the right, and Nix and Joy directly across the hall.

Seth knocked on the girls' door. "Coming," Joy chimed. Opening the door, she continued, "come in, come in. Isn't this great?" She took both his hands and danced him into the apartment. Was she always so cheery?

The others were already there, sitting in various positions around the room. Tyrus stood looking out the window, Nix by the door. Joy bounced on the closest bed, disturbing Julius who sat on its other side. Connor took a seat in the desk chair. Seth relaxed on the other queen.

Nix began, "so, we are settled in, now, but remember, keep room service low. My credit isn't infinite, but I am happy to help. Ann is a great girl. Very talented. We can't let her stay over there for long."

"I agree," Tyrus said, "however patience is key here. If the Director learns that you are all here, he'll send someone to retrieve you. We don't want that. I've been thinking of ways to enter the building and get Ann back, but it's not going to be easy.

"We have to deal with some pretty tight security. Cameras, infrared, lockdown protocols, network security. In addition to the tech, there's a large in-person force and thousands of employees that will alert the Director the instant they see us.

"To top that off, we have no clue where Ann is. What floor or what conditions she's being held under. To that end, we need more info before we proceed. Also, there's a secondary task. Mythic genetics research, while there's no official government policy, has been banned by all parties involved. This company, for whatever reason, did not follow or agree to abide by the ban. This sends the message that this research is valid, prompting other companies to create more victims like you.

"This is not something we want. Nix and I have talked about it. We need to take out their lab. This is bigger than a rescue. We have to send a message to these people so they know not to screw with innocent lives.

"As long as they have Ann, they know we won't risk an attack, but the instant she's gone, they're vulnerable. We have to mount a rescue and destroy the lab at the same time."

The teens were silent for a moment. Joy was the first to react. "He-he. Popcorn." She shook her head, the others confused.

Connor nodded. "This is secret agent stuff. We don't have any training for this. How are we going to pull this off?"

Tyrus motioned to Nix. "You're getting a crash course in 'spy school' from Nix for the next few days. She's one of the best. She'll tell you what you need to do, what you need to know. If you listen, we win this, so do your very best. Ann is counting on us."

Day 35

"You're sure she hasn't checked in?" Dr. Jackson sat in his chair at his desk, reading the latest reports from his head of security.

"No, sir. It's been over a week since Nix has entered her apartment."

The Director sighed. This meant that she was somewhere else, probably close by. He had her favorite pet, after all.

"Place undercover agents at all hotels nearby, starting with the one across the street. Couples, families, no singles. Pay them through the acting agency. Tell them it's modern theatre. Equip them with the cams. We need info. I'm not letting my aunt ruin this."

"Yes, sir."

"Dismissed."

The agent walked out of the office, shutting the door behind him. Dr. Jackson looked at his schedule, noting the next appointment was with the head of research. Dr. Matheson was a brilliant man, if an uncaring one. His need to advance science outweighed his debt to humanity. He'd been asking for the last several days to begin "research" on Ann. Dr. Jackson had declined.

Today, he was proposing a compromise of some sort, to advance the science of mythic genetics and keep their guest comfortable. Dr. Jackson was curious what he had come up with. As the director, it was his job to make sure all aspects of the company ran smoothly, including research, however, he would not further violate the pact he'd been entrusted with from his father. He had integrity, after all.

He had fifteen minutes before his meeting began. Sitting at his desk, he brought up the videos of Ann's apartment on his tablet. Watching her, he studied her movement, gestures, anything to give him clues he needed. She didn't use her power to escape, hadn't tried to find a hole in security, nothing. She'd given him absolutely no data about her ability. He did, however, have insight into teen fashion sense, music tastes, and a host of other completely non-relevant data. The sound of a song featuring an infant marine predator came to mind, stuck on repeat in his head.

Sighing, he turned the feed off and rubbed his eyes. This long, tedious process was draining. He ached for simpler days. The bus crash had changed his whole career, his empire, into a nightmare.

An idea suddenly occurred to him. "Isaiah, push my meeting back to four and send the head of security back up here."

If he couldn't get the info from Ann, maybe going back to that crash and reviewing everything from top to bottom would reveal something he could use. All it would take was the right data, the right leverage.

Suddenly very happy, he added, "get me sushi for lunch."

"Yes, sir," Isaiah responded. Dr. Jackson sat back, placing his arms above his head, looking toward the brilliant blue sky. His luck would change, eventually. He'd find a plan and save the business.

Ann was so bored. She'd worn all the clothes, though they always returned freshly laundered after she sent them down the shoot. She'd used all the bath products, worn all the jewelry, swam and played pool by herself. Watched the TV, searched online with the limited and restrictive access they allowed her.

She'd eaten the entire menu, called for everything she could think of. Had an in-room massage. She'd blasted music so loud she couldn't stand it and danced the night away. She'd done literally everything she could think of inside the apartment. After a week of relative isolation, she was so bored!

Picking up the phone, she dialed the operator. "VIP service desk. How can I make your day more pleasant?" The woman on the other end always sounded so happy.

"Yes, this is Ann," she began.

"Good afternoon, Ann. Did you sleep well? Need some fresh pillows?"

Ann paused, "sure, but I was wondering if it'd be possible for me to have another person to talk to. In the apartment. Someone to hang out with. I'm so bored, and I've followed all the rules set for me. I'm kind of going crazy here."

"I'm so sorry to hear that," the operator said, sounding genuinely concerned. "We pride ourselves on fulfilling our VIP guests' every need. May I place you on hold for a moment?"

"Yes."

"I'll be right back Ann."

A beep and the sound of Motown music filled the phone. Something about their love overcoming stuff. It wasn't Ann's favorite. She was on hold for several minutes, then the operator came back.

"Thank you for holding, Ann. I've spoken with Dr. Jackson. He said that he'd be willing to consent to providing you with companionship, male or female, as long as you also agree to see one of our scientists, in your apartment, once a day to answer some questions they have regarding the accident. Is this acceptable to you?"

She sighed. Of course, she wouldn't get anything for free. "That's fine, provided they don't poke me with needles."

"It's okay, Ann, Dr. Jackson assured me that your wellbeing is his first priority. As far as companionship, were you looking for a male or female?"

"Female."

"Thank you. Do you have a racial preference?"

"Uh, no." What a strange question.

"How about hair or eye color?"

"Umm, no?" She was starting to feel uncomfortable.

"And what is the nature of the interaction you wish to have?"

Ann paused, then said, "huh?"

"...Will this be a visit in which intimacy is involved?"

Ann's eyes grew wide. "Oh, God no! I just want someone to talk to and maybe play pool with."

"I understand perfectly. I'll make all the arrangements for you. Is there anything else I can do for you, Ann?"

"Connect me to the kitchen please."

"Right away."

Ann placed her head in her hands. What was this company into?

"In addition, this less invasive method would allow us to collect DNA samples and use those instead of blood, to research this phenomenon."

Dr. Jackson nodded. "I will not allow any access to Ann that involves her leaving the apartment. She is a victim of someone's vendetta. She deserves our respect, our help and our utmost efforts to rehabilitate her to a normal life."

The head of research, a short man with very thick glasses, sat across from the Director, practically sweating bullets. His hair was half gone and white from the stress of his job. It was not easy dealing with all the regulations put on his research. Sometimes he wished he could just take politics out and deal only with the science.

"Yes, as is the goal of this research, per your request Director. However, I would like to add that the rehabilitation would go faster with more data…"

"I'm aware of the limitations involved in humanistic and ethical research. I'm also aware of your personal feelings. I wish to support you, however, if you can't be a team player…"

Gulping, he stammered, "N-no, sir. I am a t-team player. I j-just wished to reaffirm our goal."

"That's what I like to hear." Standing, Dr. Jackson moved away from him and looked out the window. "Is there anything else you need?"

"I'd like several more assistants hired as the last batch were fired after the investigation into the accident. I'm running with half my normal staff.

"I've called some friends in the field and come up with a list of what I believe are susceptible, highly qualified candidates to help with our goals. I'd ask that you approve this list, pending background checks. Standard pay and benefits we offer are far superior to what they make in public health, so I don't anticipate any rejections."

"Where is the list?" Turning back, Dr. Jackson glanced over the names. "No red flags popped up?"

"Only one, but I placed her on the list *because* of the red flag. A Dr. Rebecca Wills? She's a resident at the nearby hospital.

She was the one who was directly responsible for the teens' care after the attack. I believe that this personal relationship can be used as a plus, instead of a negative."

Dr. Jackson thought about the risks versus the benefits. "As long as she passes security measures, you may include her. Send this list and make the offers. They should be ready to report in two days."

"Thank you, sir." The Head of Research stood and began to walk out.

"Don't think that I don't still wonder about your part in that unfortunate event, Dr. Matheson."

The Head froze, and slowly faced him. "Sir, I followed all the protocols, and warned you of the security breach. I'm not responsible-"

"See, that's where you're right and wrong." With his eyes locked, Dr. Jackson walked slowly to the man before him, standing directly in front of him, too close for comfort. "I'm responsible because this is my building, and you're responsible because your department has threatened the livelihood of everyone we employ. If a breach happens again, Dr. Matheson, you will bear the FULL responsibility, professionally and publicly. Do you understand me?"

Dr. Matheson couldn't breathe. Sweat dripped down his neck. "Y-yes, I u-unders-stand."

"Dismissed." Dr. Jackson gave the man his back and he walked out.

Dr. Matheson waved at Isaiah as he passed. Taking the elevator to his floor, he entered his private quarters, which consisted of a one-bedroom apartment. It had a secure entrance to and from the lab. This is where he spent most of his life since signing on to Jackson Genetics ten years ago. Times had changed, the rules had changed, but he was still standing where others had fallen.

Taking a deep, calming breath, he grabbed a bag of tea and placed a cup in the nearby microwave. Tapping his fingers on the top, he patiently waited for the water to boil and placed the tea bag inside.

He'd waited over a month to have a chance to meet the girl. To him, she was a test subject now. The advancements they might make far outweighed her value. Though he understood his restrictions, part of his brain, the part that got excited about science, didn't agree. This subject should be in the lab, at his beck and call, twenty-four hours a day if he saw fit. So much data could be obtained, like the effects of sleep deprivation on powers or lack of nutrition. He had a whole chart of hypotheses that he wanted to test. Ten years ago, he could have. Now, his hands were tied.

He forwarded the list to the head of security. *Let's get these naïve scientists in here to run labs. I have more important things to do.*

Chapter 18
Day 36

Dr. Matheson looked at his two new assistants. They were both very bright and very beautiful. He was an important man and didn't feel it was wrong to surround himself with someone pleasant to look at.

"Let's see what we have here, "he began, looking down at the tablet screen. "Dr. Rebecca Wills, you'll be my new personal assistant. I'll expect you to keep daily logs of your work and progress as well as attend to my…every need." He winked at her.

She threw up in her mouth a little. "As you wish boss." She pasted a huge smile on her face.

Straight teeth. Beautiful. "As for you Ms. Karla Valencia, you'll be our expert, our public face. When there is a press conference, you'll be responsible for representing this company. You should look stunning at all times, even while not at this site. Take pride in your work and your company and say nothing without written approval from the Director or myself. Understood?"

"Yes, sir," Karla said, slightly nervous. "I'll do my best."

"Great. Ms. Wills, this is your desk. I'll be emailing your orders today shortly. Ms. Valencia, after you." She started to walk down the hall, where he had a wonderful view. "Turn left ahead." She did. "Here's your workspace. You'll have your own orders by the end of the hour from Ms. Wills."

Walking back to his office, he noted that Wills stood with the proper respect as he passed. She'd have a hard time being a glorified secretary. She would barely be researching anything. Glad that he was who he was, Dr. Matheson sauntered back to his office, completely unaware that Wills had already planted a bug inside it.

Going to the window, she pretended to adjust the shades.

Tyrus saw the cue. He'd said three times slow, one fast. That was it. She was in and the locator was planted. Turning back to Nix, he nodded. She walked out of his room. Looking through the binoculars, he waited.

Nix walked across the street, straight toward the building. "Just like old times," she mumbled as she entered.

As soon as she was inside, security alarms started blaring. *They upgraded. They must have facial recognition now.* Placing her hands behind her head, she kneeled on the floor, while security yelled around her, pointing tasers in her direction. As long as she complied, she'd get what she needed. *Silly rent-a-cops.* She bit her tongue as they pulled her up, shoved her along. *With a flick of my wrist, I could burn you all.* Still, maintaining the ruse, she acted like a helpless woman, for the time being.

Watching from his office, Dr. Jackson couldn't believe her nerve. *Why come here?* No way she could take on this whole building alone. "Isaiah, we have a guest in the building. Direct my aunt to my office immediately. Make sure she isn't harmed."

No way he was going to miss the chance to deal with her himself, since she came willingly here. *Oh, how the mighty have fallen.* His usual in front of him, he took a sip from the chilled glass.

Nix walked in moments later, tears staining her cheeks. Before he could speak, she summoned flame to her hand and shoved it at him, pinning him against the wall. While it didn't burn, it held him fast. He admired her restraint.

"Auntie Shayla, how are you?" he asked.

"Don't you Auntie me, young man. I demand to know where she is, now!"

"I would be happy to let you see her, if you only remove my restraints."

Releasing him, Nix stood, breathing heavy, looking not quite put together. *She must not be sleeping.* He briefly debated what was so special about Ann that would cause his aunt to become so disheveled. He could use that, though.

"Auntie," he began, holding his arms out to her. Sighing, Nix gave him a quick hug. "Am I still your favorite?"

Tapping his cheek, she said, "what is going on, Greg?"

Swallowing hard, he explained. "I'm trying to fix this mess we find ourselves in. I was hoping you'd help me."

"Show me where Ann is, and I'll tell you whatever you want to know."

He laughed. "The aunt I knew would never give her hand away so easily. You lost your poker face on this one."

"Listen," she said placing her arms out in front of her, "you're the head of your father's business, but Ann is just a kid. I just need to know she's okay. Can you do that for me?"

Dr. Jackson tapped his fingers on his elbow, and said, "After you, Auntie." She swiveled on her heel, walking out of his office and he followed. Seeing Ann was a small price to pay for her cooperation. If she could reach Ann, this whole thing would go much more smoothly.

In her apartment, Ann was busy shooting pool with her latest friend. They brought someone different to her today. They obviously didn't want anyone getting too close to her. Still, she was adapting and surviving in a restrictive environment. Nix would be proud.

She laughed as her current friend, Nancy the 2nd, told a silly joke. She was even starting to get bored of people. Calling her shot, she expertly placed the eight ball into its pocket. That was game.

"You're so good at this," Nancy the 2nd said, "I wish I had more time to play pool."

Like I choose to be stuck here playing pool all day. Ann stayed smiling, but inside noted the backhanded compliment. They'd all been doing that to her. Can't buy true friendship.

"Well, you know," she said, "you could always take different acting jobs, you know, ones that don't blow your career."

She was done playing nice. She was so bored of all this, that she was done with cordial, peppy and any other socially mandated fake emotion. At the shocked look on Nancy the 2nd's face, she said, "what, Honey? You think you're the only one around here with a brain? Get out."

With that, her latest friend stormed away. Apparently, whatever they were paying her was not enough to put up with unpleasantries. *What kind of actress can't take criticism?*

Ann heard the door open as her ex-friend left, but she was too busy placing her cue back in its spot to acknowledge it. What she didn't hear was the door slamming shut behind her. *That was odd.* Stretching, Ann walked forward, only to stare into the face of Dr. Jackson and Nix.

Ann swallowed, hard. *Great. Just what I need.* Her face carefully blank now, she halfheartedly said, "what do you want?"

Nix, however, was not cold or distant like Ann expected. She ran forward and embraced her tightly.

"Oh, Sweetie," Nix began, "it's so great to see you. I've been worried sick since you left."

A little over the top, but I'll go with it. Nix was up to something. Grabbing Nix's hands, she looked her mentor in the eye, like she was taught, and said, "if only I had stayed there, I might not be stuck here."

Nix carefully cupped Ann's face with both hands. She placed more pressure on the left side than the right. This was a signal. Ann knew exactly what it meant. One of the skills Nyx had given her was a secret code, between the two of them, that no one else understood. It was for use in public, in case they were being followed, watched, or tailed. A way to tell each other important information, encoded in normal, average conversation.

"I hope you can forgive me for that awful night. I can only imagine how scared you were to be out on your own in this big city."

Ann hugged Nix again, placing her hands on her elbows and waited. This time pressure on the right side. She understood and backed away.

"Can you stay for a few minutes?"

Nix eyed to the Director. "I suppose I can allow my aunt to see you, Ann. Granted she behaves herself. I'll return in an hour. Feel free to call if you need anything. Oh, and Ann, they get paid the same amount of money whether they storm out of here or not. Remember that for your next…friend."

The two women watched him walk out. Now they could really get down to business. Sitting on the sofa, Ann remembered their code and how to start.

"Would you like something to drink?" Ann asked. This in itself would answer a question.

"I'd like a whiskey sour. Do you remember how to make it?"

"One-part whiskey, two parts sour?"

"I feel like half and half today. With ice."

"I'll get that for you." Leaving, Ann walked toward the fridge, keeping her shoulders relaxed.

Nix had told her several important things already. Hand on the left, danger.

Elbow on the right, planted surveillance of some kind. That meant she must have given Ann a bug while she was hugging her. A whiskey sour was their code for an operation. It would begin tonight. If it had been a cosmopolitan, it wouldn't start for a week. Straight bourbon meant a bomb was about to go off, so find cover. Whiskey sour was good. She could work with that.

Then on to the parts. One-part whiskey meant 9 pm. Half and half was midnight. The plan would go down at midnight. With ice meant that something valuable was being extracted. Ann guessed that was her.

"So, how's your car running, lately? Have to take it into the shop for that clutch?" Ann got out the ingredients for a whiskey sour and began to pour them as Nix directed her.

The talk about Nix's car was code as well. If the car was running smoothly, that meant their escape path was the elevator. If it had to be taken into the shop, stairs. If it was totaled, the roof.

"I had to take it into the shop after you left. No big deal."

Take the stairs at midnight. She could do that.

"What was wrong?"

"Well, the clutch was fine," Nix sipped her drink and continued, "but there was a problem with the exhaust and the starter."

Nix was telling her about security in the building. The clutch was fine, meaning they had at least standard security measures like cameras and lockdown. The exhaust was a reference to facial recognition and the starter meant the building was on a secure, closed network.

Ann kept her face happy and continued. "That sucks. Did it all get fixed or is it still there?"

Nix looked at her. "All fixed." *Good. She has a plan in place to take down the security.*

"Enough about me, though," Nix said, placing the glass half empty on the coffee table. If the glass was empty, Ann didn't have a job. If it was half empty, Nix had a job for her to do. Now she only needed to find out what it was. "What have you been up to?"

"I don't know," Ann said, thinking quickly. "It's boring being stuck here. Let's see… Oh, the menu is excellent here. Do you like club sandwiches?"

This was Ann asking, is someone coming to help me?

"Nah, I don't like clubs." No help. Great. Nix adjusted her posture. Right leg over the left, left hand on her top leg. That meant that she was about to tell Ann something important. "You know what I do love though?"

Ann asked, "what?"

Nix said, "a nice steak."

Ann swallowed. She'd never tried the nice steak before. "What, like porterhouse or filet mignon?"

Nix kept her smile intact, but her voice was somehow more urgent. "I'll take the filet any day over a porterhouse."

Ann swallowed again. Nix had just told her that she should light the place up. Filet minion meant she was going to literally create havoc, go crazy, anything she had to do to get as much attention on her as she left as possible. Now she just needed to know how long to pull the ruse.

"Rare, medium, or well done?"

"I might be in the minority of people here, but I take my filet well done."

Rare was a few minutes, which Ann could have handled, but well done meant as long as it took. Ann reviewed the info she'd just received. The plan was going down tonight at midnight. She'd create a distraction, indefinitely until the security was down, then take the stairs.

"Have you noticed the nice weather lately?" Ann asked. This was how to exit the building. Nice weather meant 'go out the front.' Anything else meant the back.

"It has been nice lately. But I didn't come here to talk about the weather, Ann. How is my nephew treating you?"

Great, it was over. Ann would exit the front of the building. Turning, she began to tell Nix about her boring world.

Dr. Jackson listened to the whole thing, watching through a security cam at his desk. This confused him. His aunt, who never took an interest in small talk was suddenly all about clothes, shoes, cars and weather. Ann must be really talented to warrant this personal attention. Slightly jealous, he turned the feed off, but kept recording. He'd review it later.

"Isaiah, page security," he said. A few moments later, several agents stood in front of him. "Double the guard tonight and escort my aunt out of the building in exactly fifteen minutes. Send a message to Dr. Matheson. He can interview Ann tonight at his leisure. Give his key card access to her apartment."

"Sir, that means he'll have unrestricted access to the whole building."

If there was one person he didn't have to worry about betraying him, it was that little man. He only cared about his research. "Authorize it."

Turning, he silently dismissed his agents, and began to replay the conversation from the beginning. He was missing something, and he wasn't going anywhere until he knew what it was.

Tyrus held the binoculars to his eyes, waiting for Nix to exit. When he saw her, he noted that she suddenly removed her jacket and 'accidentally" dropped it on the ground. Their plan had worked. Powering the bug on, he could now locate Ann's apartment. He started his computer and loaded up the software Nix installed. *There she was, sitting on the fifth floor of the six-floor building, right above the Director's Office and below his apartment. Great.*

Nix walked to the left, knowing she was being followed. For now, her job was finished. She would lose her tail with her car, check into her apartment, and meet the teens back here at midnight to finish this.

Getting into her car, she tilted her mirror slightly, so it showed the bottom of her backseat. Her double, an actress looking for work, gave her the thumbs up. *Here we go. Time to lose the goons.*

Ann watched Nix exit, accompanied by two agents who patted her down before allowing her to leave. *Too late.* She debated calling for food. Talking about steak made her hungry. However, as soon as Nix left, a polite timid knock drew her attention back to the door. *What now?*

Opening it, she saw a man standing in front of her, thick glasses, crooked tie, messy hair. "Ms. Ann Cecilia Smith, born on…oh, your birthday was last week. How old are you now?"

"Eighteen," Ann stated. She'd been so busy with her crazy life that her birthday hadn't even occurred to her. "What do you want?"

"Ms. Ann, allow me to introduce myself. You'll be seeing me a lot over the next few weeks." He held out a hand. Ann took it. *Not likely.*

"My name is Dr. William Matheson. I'm the head of research here at Jackson Genetics. My job, Ms. Ann, is to study you with the ultimate goal of improving your quality of life. Hopefully, with enough time, we can find a way to reverse the effects of Omega Fire and make this right."

Ann thought about her life before all this started, a *throwaway* foster kid without roots or family. Knowing what he expected, though, she simply said, "Really? You can fix me?"

That was it. His face lit up like Christmas morning.

"Exactly. I knew you'd understand. May I come in?"

"Certainly," Ann said, stepping away from this creepy little man. He walked into her apartment and sat down. Placing his briefcase on the end table, he took out several containers. "Let's start with a urine sample."

Ann had to struggle to stay calm. "Well, if you can fix me, it's the least I can do." Taking the sample, she walked into her bedroom and closed the bathroom door. Rolling her eyes, she thought about the long day ahead of her. *Focus on your freedom.*

Dr. Jackson replayed the video several times. He was convinced that some kind of code was being sent and received, but he didn't know how to decipher it. One thing was for sure, if Nix was here, giving her information, that meant she was up to something. He highly doubted that she would fall on his side. Not after he stole Ann from her.

Picking up his earpiece, he said, "call Levi." He'd need all the help he could get tonight.

Tyrus sat with the teens, going over some public schematics of the building they would be entering that night. They were fast learners, ready to do their part. He just hoped they'd all live to see the sunrise.

"Seth, as soon as you see Ann's distraction, and the lights go out, you go in. Do you have any questions?"

Seth shook his head.

"Okay, then, repeat the order for me."

"Wills, Joy and Connor, Julius, Tyrus and Nix."

"Don't forget it. If you go out of order, we could all be dead."

Seth nodded. "I won't."

"Great. Now let's talk about you two."

He addressed Connor and Julius. "The fight you start outside is going to have to be big enough that they pull you into the building. Think you two can handle causing some mayhem?"

Julius cracked his knuckles. "This guy? He couldn't take me if he tried."

"Hope you can back up that tough talk tonight."

Tyrus chuckled. "Once you're in, go over it with me. What do you do?"

"I run. Everywhere, and get as many guards to follow me around the building as possible. When the lights go dark, I head to the lab, where Seth will get me out."

Tyrus nodded. "You're our second distraction. Just don't get shot, okay?"

Julius laughed. "I'll be good. I can run fast."

Tyrus turned to Connor. "What will you be doing?"

"Plugging the USB into the nearest company laptop."

"You remembered what I taught you?"

"Yes. I've been practicing straight for the past three days. I can do this."

"Where are you hiding the USB port?"

Connor opened his stance. "Pat me down, see if you can find it."

Tyrus stared at the younger boy. "Not into guys. I believe you."

Connor laughed. "I'll get it done. They'll never see it coming."

Lastly, Tyrus smiled at Joy. "You know what to do, right?"

"Yes," Joy serenely stated. "At 11:03 I place the nails on the road. At 11:12 I spread the glue over the back entrance by 'accident." At 11:19 I shoot gum at the electric line. At 11:21 run away from the bad men. At 11:30 I circle back to the van, taking it out of the metal storage unit we bought around the corner. At 11:55 I leave the van in front of the building and walk away. After that, I make sure Ann gets out alive. I got it, don't worry."

Tyrus was taken back. "Flawless."

"I'll grab the van," Connor said, "after Seth removes me from the building and Joy drops it off. The automatic lockdown should be in place by then, so no one will be able to exit unless we want them to."

Tyrus nodded. "Great. Timing on that is crucial. We have to be able to get Ann away quickly."

Connor nodded. "Then, I start the van and drive the block until I see Ann."

Tyrus nodded. "That just leaves the hard part to Nix and I. Good. Go get some rest. Tonight, we save your friend and avenge your classmates."

◆ ◆ ◆

10:30 pm

Ann woke to the darkness surrounding her. Looking at the clock, she thought about the horrible little man who poked and prodded her for hours today. She hoped she would never have to see him again. Stretching, she walked to her bathroom, and brushed her teeth. In an hour and a half, she'd be free.

◆ ◆ ◆

10:35 pm

Dr. Jackson sat in his office. He wasn't sure what he was missing, but it annoyed him that he was missing it. He'd been obsessed with that video all day. What were they doing? What were they planning? He was getting more and more paranoid by the minute. The one thought giving him sanity was that his aunt was in her apartment, checked in for the night, in pajamas. Suddenly, a portal appeared in his office, whirlpool of water. Levi stepped out a moment later.

"Levi," he began, "how have you been? Thanks for coming in on such short notice. Here's the situation."

Before he could sit down to explain, darkness swam before him, and he was gone.

◆ ◆ ◆

10:40 pm

Nix slipped into the rental car she parked on the side of the street. Wearing a red wig, she stood out enough to not be noticed. Her double was up in her room, eating her food and having a great night. She hoped it'd be enough to slip past the tail who had followed her home. She started the ignition and left the parking garage, noting that none of those security guards noticed.

Amateurs.

◆ ◆ ◆

10:50 pm

Wills didn't know if she'd ever get the disgusting thought of that man's hands off of her. A shower wouldn't work, even if it was bleach. Straight bleach! She had just undergone the most humiliating experience of her life.

The man looked unconscious. She'd wanted it that way. Taking the key card off his lab coat, she walked out of the office. No one was around the lab at this time of night.

She just needed to wait until the power went. Then the facial recognition would be down, and this key card with unlimited access and his passcode would be enough to get her into any section of this building as they switched the locks to battery power in the event of a power failure, save the outside doors. Turning, she noted a large man in the hallway in front of her. They locked eyes for a moment, then she twirled and walked the other way. *Levi...*

10:55 pm

The teens geared up, not speaking. Each one was very aware of the plan and what would happen if a single thing went wrong. Silently, they went about their business, mentally noting what each person had to do. Joy was the first to speak. Her voice sounded so loud in the silent room.

"It's my time. See you guys in…a couple hours, give or take."

"Break a leg," they said. Apparently, a heist was like theatre. Saying good luck could jinx it.

Suddenly serious, Joy turned and locked eyes with each of them for a moment before speaking. "Just so you know, I love you guys!" Then she was gone. The boys stared at each other, each thinking the same thing.

Connor was the only one brave to say it. "Does that mean one of us is going to die?"

Seth shook his head, but even his gut was unsure. Though they were prepared, he felt like something was going to go wrong tonight. Not wrong enough for them to die, but it was like his gut was trying to get him to see or notice something he just, couldn't.

The boys continued to pack in silence until it was their time to leave.

◆ ◆ ◆

10:56

Tyrus waited on the roof of their hotel building. Nix had asked him to do something for her, and he was about to pull it off. He wouldn't be around for the rest of the op, but a favor for a favor. That was their way. Breathing deeply, he began to mentally prepare himself for the fight of his life.

11:00 pm

Ann finished her bathroom routine and went out to the living room. Flipping on the news, she sat and watched TV as if nothing was wrong. Carefully, she kept her shoulders relaxed.

That was the first place people looked for tension. She settled in but noted the time. *One hour to go.*

11:03 pm

Joy stood in front of the parking garage behind Jackson Genetics. Whistling while she did so, she opened her backpack and grabbed the bag of nails. If these didn't blow out tires, she didn't know what would. Placing the nails on the pavement, she skipped away, unnoticed.

Success!

11:05 pm

Ann flipped over to the cartoon channel. The news was boring tonight.

11:10 pm

Wills slipped into the server room and set up her laptop. Connecting to her phone's hotspot, she logged in using her new boss's code and began to download their files to another server. As quickly as she came, she exited. Hopefully the download would complete before the fireworks tonight.

11:11 pm

Ann grabbed a bag of popcorn from the microwave. Ooh. Extra butter.

11:12

Joy smelled butter. *There it is! Now I want popcorn.* Taking the tub of industrial strength glue, she carefully opened the can and poured it on the back step of the only other exit out of the building. The door opened, and she turned to the janitor, saying, "someone dumped white paint on the step. I found it like this. Throw this away." Then she skipped off into the night.

Strange kid. Taking the can of "paint" he walked away. It was almost shift change, and it could wait until morning. His wife would kill him if he was late again.

◆ ◆ ◆

11:15

Nix was almost there. No one was following. Parking a block away, she left the car keys and ran. Her timing had to be perfect, and she had hit highway traffic driving here. She was running late.

11:16 PM

Ann choked on the extra butter. Grabbing her glass of water, she chugged and threw the popcorn down. *Stupid popcorn.*

11:19-11:21 pm

Joy was busily chewing a huge wad of gum in her mouth. She stood right outside the entrance to the building, chewing away. The head guard happened to walk outside for a smoke break. *Score!* Taking the gum out of her mouth, she screamed, "stupid rent a cop!"

His eyes on her, she flung the gum toward the electric line, which sparked, catching his suit on fire. He was lucky to be alive, but angry. Good!

Joy took a corner, waited until the count of five for him to catch up, and ran back down the alley.

As she pivoted, he faced her. She pushed her legs, running as if she had four instead of two. She was so fast! Sweet!

She jumped over the glue and rounded the next edge of the building. The head of security landed with both feet in the glue and fell face first into the concrete, unconscious. Joy came back with a stick and poked him. When she was sure he was out, she took his walkie-talkie, and started to sing pop songs to the other guards while she moved metal garbage cans around the body.

11:25 pm

Nix rounded the corner and waited until three more security guards went to search for their leader. Easy as pie. Four down, a handful to go. One advantage of the night heist was the lack of people. Rounding the corner to the alley, she expertly incapacitated them. Grabbing one of their key cards, and the smallest jacket, she walked to the back of the building, noting the unconscious guard, carefully avoiding disturbing the fort of garbage cans. She had enough experience with unicorns to know that they did everything for a reason, and nothing was truly random. She entered the back door and shut it quickly and quietly behind her.

11:28 pm

Ann found a Yoga channel. She was currently trying to hold a very difficult pose. She fell over.

◆ ◆ ◆

11:30 pm

Huffing and puffing from that run around the block, Joy jumped the fence at the storage facility and ran to the last unit in the first row. She grabbed the combination lock and pulled. It came off easily, without her having to try. Climbing into the van, she remembered that this was her first time driving. Had she told anyone that? *Oh well.* She tossed the radio behind her and started her up. How hard could it be?

◆ ◆ ◆

11:35 pm

Connor and Julius stood out front, ready to cause a ruckus. Facing each other on opposite sides of the building, they began to jog, running into each other "accidentally on purpose" in front of the building. Nix needed this distraction to get further to the lab.

Connor shoved Julius, saying, "Hey, man, watch where you're going!"

Julius, taking out his headphones, replied, "man I don't need some white boy telling me what to do! *Viva la Mexico!*"

He ran towards Connor and the two began to fight.

11:36 pm

Tyrus was ready. Taking a deep breath, he opened a bottle of water and poured it on the ground next to him. Stepping back, he shouted, "Levi! LEVI!"

The water slowly began to pool, forming the shape of a man. A few moments later, the Leviathan was standing next to him. "Hello, Ty. What do you need? Busy night, you know?"

"Cut the crap Levi! You know why I'm here."

"No talking about it, huh?"

"Don't need to waste time tonight, do we?"

Levi tilted his head. "I suppose not. Been waiting to go against you for…ages."

Tyrus laughed. "We both knew we'd end up here eventually, lets, just, get it over with."

Levi nodded, adding, "Well, I'm surprised. For years all you did was talk it out. Finally, a man of action, Tyrus?"

"And you my old friend can't seem to *stop* talking. Why is that?"

Levi stepped away from Tyrus. "Listen, as much as I would love to kick your ass, I have other obligations tonight. You're just distracting me anyway. The next time you call, I *will* destroy you." With that, Levi disintegrated, the water splashing everywhere. Tyrus stood for a moment, confused. The possible outcomes played in his head, one after another, until he found the only one that made sense. When he did, his eyes widened, his breath quickening. *No! They'd been wrong. Everything was wrong.*

Summoning his dragon, he flew away from the entire scene. They'd have to deal without him for the time being. He had a very large fish to fry.

11:40 pm

The boys struggled to continue fighting though ten security guards were trying to restrain them. Slowly, the boys allowed the guards to carry them into the building. The guard's leader said, "can't we just act like gentlemen here?" The boys listened, stopping their fight.

"Good. Now you go to the room on the right to cool down. You! The room on the left."

Julius turned to Connor, and winked, then ran through the building, the security on his tail.

Connor walked into his assigned room, shut the door and began looking for a port.

◆ ◆ ◆

11:45 pm

Nix walked to the elevators, at a quick pace. She had five minutes before Connor would shut down everything in the building. Hitting the button for up, she waited for the elevator to open. When it did, she started at the person in front of her and said, "you're not supposed to be here."

Bright lights hit her. Then she was out.

Her assailant grabbed her feet and pulled Nix into the elevator.

◆ ◆ ◆

11:50 pm

Connor finished on the laptop from safely under the desk in the room. Everything went dark. When it was safe, he ran to the front of the building, waiting for Joy.

◆ ◆ ◆

11:53 pm

Joy started the car and with a "woo," floored it, out of the storage pod and through the fence. *This was fun.* She shook her shoulders, whistling a happy tune.

By 11:55 she'd rounded the corner and pulled up in front of the building. Getting out, she ran to the front door and opened it easily, despite the lockdown in effect. Connor ran through just in time and they got into the van.

Chapter 19

…midnight…
Seth:

He stood, ready to bounce. That's what they called it when you used a portal. Looking at his watch, the time struck midnight, and he began.

In his head, he recited the order, Wills, Joy, Connor, Julius, Tyrus, and Nix. This was the order for him to bounce so that everything that happened tonight went according to plan. Creating a portal, his first stop was the lab, to Wills. Entering, he experienced a split second of disorientation before his senses realigned with their environment.

He was suddenly surrounded by medical equipment, vials, tables, all white and shiny. Turning, he expected to see Wills, ready to hand him a USB. However, no one was there to greet him. He had three minutes before the next jump, so he set a timer on his watch and waited.

When three minutes had come and gone, he shook his head. First jump and already, someone messed up. Bouncing, he hit his next target.

Joy and Connor were in the van. This one was easy. Seth said, "stop here and wait."

"Where's the drive?" Connor asked. Seth said, "she didn't show. Stop here so I can get everyone else out."

The drive was supposed to be safe in the van, but it would have to wait. People were more important than data, regardless of what Tyrus and Nix had said. Bouncing for a third time, he was able to grab Julius just before security shot tasers at the young man. Instantly, they were back in the van. "Stay here." Seth said.

Bouncing again, starting to get sick, he was on a roof, waiting for Tyrus. Again, he was nowhere to be found. Seth was starting to get aggravated. He couldn't save them in the nick of time if they weren't doing what they were supposed to do.

Seth looked at his watch. It was 12:10 pm. In two minutes, he had to go get Nix out of the building. He began to open the portal, but no one would be coming for Nix that night, because an explosion rocked the building, knocking Seth back on the roof. He had a moment to think that this wasn't part of the plan, then he hit his head, falling unconscious. Embers burned next to him.

...still midnight...

Connor:

Connor walked to the driver side of the van, noted the keys were in the ignition. He turned the key, and nothing happened. It was minutes to midnight, and they may not have an escape route. His anxiety was high. Joy entered on the passenger side.

"It's not starting."

"I just drove it."

"Well, look." He turned the key again.

"Did you try to hotwire it?"

Getting on the floor, he worked like Tyrus showed him. Nothing sparked, nothing started. "I think it's fried."

Joy twitched her nose, touching the van's dashboard.

Cooing softly, she said, "come on girl. You're our only way out of this mess. We'll replace your oil tomorrow, give you a nice bath. How's that sound?"

Connor looked at her like she was crazy, but a second later, the car started on its own. Giving her a look, Connor said, "I'm grateful you're on my side."

Joy giggled and said, "don't forget to buckle your seatbelt."

Connor was suddenly scared. "Why? Am I going to die? Are we going to crash?"

Joy giggled again. "You never know."

A shiver ran up his spine. *If Joy wasn't all sunshine and rainbows, she'd be terrifying.* Putting the van into gear, he slowly began to ease out into the road.

They drove for a block then Seth bounced in. "Stop here and wait," he said.

Connor was confused. "Where's the drive?"

Seth said, "She didn't show. Stop here so I can get everyone else out."

Connor did as he was told. Now, they waited, making sure that no one followed them. Joy whistled an ominous tune. Connor looked at her quizzically. *What was with this girl?*

Joy turned and gave a big, beautiful, toothy smile. Then, she bounced to help Ann. Connor was alone in the car only a moment. In a few minutes, Seth brought Julius back. Breathing heavily, Julius was sweaty from his run around the building. Before he could tell Seth, the boy was gone.

"Something smells wrong," he said.

"What do you mean? Here?"

"No, in the building, almost like-"

The explosion rocked the van, blasting the glass from the windows.

… three hours prior to the witching hour…

Julius:

He rounded the corner, the stairs ahead of him. One floor up, then Seth would be there. It's a good thing he loved to run, or this would be kind of hard. He had to keep stopping so the security guards would catch up. He was happily getting some interval training in, anyway.

He ran up the stairs, the guards following clumsily. *They definitely needed the exercise.* Turning, he entered the next floor, running in front of the main server room. Sniffing in, he smelled something dangerous. Seth suddenly appeared and he took his hand. Seconds later, they were in the van.

Seth left, and Julius locked eyes with Connor.

"Something smells wrong," he said.

"What do you mean? Here?"

"No in the building, almost like-"

He covered his face with his hands as the explosion rocked the van. He was right. Someone had planted a bomb in the server room, and it just went off.

...12:00 a.m....

Ann:

It was time. Great. She was ready. The lights went off, her friends had done their job. Running out of the apartment, she swirled fire everywhere. She found the stairwell and ran. Reaching the next floor down, she continued until Joy bounced in front of her.

"How did you..." she said.

Joy simply took her hand and said, "the boom is coming. Change of plans. I need to borrow your power."

Fire surrounded the girls suddenly. "I'll keep you safe, Ann. I'll keep everyone safe."

Ann looked her friend in the eye and smiled. Joy grabbed both her hands, and Ann felt a pull, like her fire was being syphoned into Joy.

A second later, a large boom rocked the building. The fire surrounded the girls who stood in a circle of Ann's power which the blast couldn't penetrate. They stayed in place as the building fell around them, as everything fell away. In slow motion, she watched the stairs below them crumble. The roof collapsed above them, yet her flame kept them perfectly safe, in place. It was a moment that lasted forever, the syphon draining all her energy. She began to feel sleepy and fought the urge. If Joy needed the help, she needed to stay awake.

Looking around her as the building fell, she saw it wasn't just her. Joy was using her flame to save everyone in the building. Even though it was dark, there were still a number of janitors, researchers and security in the building. She saw them all, suspended in time, floating slowly to the ground surrounded by her power. She stared at her friend, whose eyes were closed, a serene look on her face juxtaposed to the chaos swirling her hair in a thousand angles.

When at last the chaos was over, when the building was in pieces, which took what seemed like ages, the girls slowly floated to the ground, safe from the ash and smoke that fell, along with the others, who were placed safely onto the ground, unconscious. Walking hand in hand, they turned the block and got into the van.

Joy switched off the lights, and said, tiredly, "I have to go get Seth. I'll be back."

A few seconds passed and she returned, Seth included. She crouched on the floor of the van near him. He didn't move. "He'll be fine in a little while."

The five friends sat in the van with no windows, wondering what the hell happened in that building. Suddenly, from the burning rubble, two figures emerged from the flame. Steam followed them. A man was carrying a woman in his arms.

As they got closer, it was obvious that the woman was Nix. Unconscious, Levi was carrying her to the van. He was gentle with her, covering her head from debris.

Getting out of the car, Ann stated furiously, "what did you do?" A flame in her hand, she was ready to defend her mentor, even though she was completely exhausted.

"It wasn't me." Placing her next to Seth in the back of the van, he said, "I saved her for…old times' sake. Make sure she's okay. You should go. Tyrus isn't here, and the police are on their way."

"What are you talking about?" Connor asked.

Joy caught her breath, struggling to stay awake from the surge of her power. "Betrayed…"

Levi laughed, his back to them. "You did good kids, but you really need to learn more about this world before you start chasing down the bad guys. You have no idea what's coming."

He walked to a safe distance, then opened a portal and was gone.

Joy turned to Connor. "What are you waiting for? Drive!"

Putting the car into gear, they reached the nearby highway just as the sirens pulled up to the ruined building. At least they were safe. Connor glanced back to see Seth, Joy and Ann out cold from the event, then focused his attention on the road. It was up to the two of them to make sure they stayed hidden from the police.

…zero…. dark…. zero…
Wills:

She walked out of the server room. Turning, she got into the elevator and hit the button for the roof. However, unexpectedly, the door opened the next floor up to reveal Nix. *Shit!*

"You're not supposed to be here."

Wills smiled, then shot the taser at Nix. The other woman fell to the ground, twitching. No way she was going to let anyone stop her now.

Pulling her into the elevator, she hit the top floor. The elevator music was blissful. Thinking about a job well done, she whistled along.

When the elevator reached the roof, she exited, hitting the bottom floor. An unconscious Nix was still inside. Walking to the waiting helicopter, Wills got in, her package in hand. As soon as she cleared the building, she dialed a number on her phone.

Then, the building blew. Still whistling, she folded her hands in her lap, flying away, a twisted smile on her face.

…yeah, still…
Levi:

He waited until Wills was out of the elevator, then he appeared. The two of them had been through too much for it to end tonight. Looking at the woman who had once been the center of his life, he gently picked her up, surrounding them with water just as the building blew.

Opening a portal, through the flame, he struggled to walk away from the explosion. He'd be exhausted after this. Walking slowly forward, they exited the explosion's radius to the left of the building. Shuffling through, the van was right where it was supposed to be.

Carrying her gently to the teenagers, he couldn't help but feel sorry for them. They had no clue how well they'd been played. Setting Nix down, he answered their questions and then left. He couldn't help them do anything but stay safe tonight. He'd accepted this contract so no one else could, controlling the situation so Nix wouldn't be targeted. He'd see it through, but he wasn't doing their enemies any favors either.

Opening another whirlpool portal, he traveled to Tyrus's family land. Walking quietly through the trees, he stopped next to a very angry Director, tied to the trunk of a very large, very old pine. Taking the gag out of his mouth, he said, "let's talk."

Dr. Jackson was seething, but he nodded.

"I saved your ass for Nix. You should have never called me to deal with her. I promised her that I'd protect her, even beyond death, and I keep my word. Your building has been blown to bits, your research taken. You can choose to start over, or you can choose to use the oodles of money your dad left you to change. Either way, you won't have the power to control anything for a long time."

"I was trying to help them, you *bastard.* I was trying to right a wrong done to those kids. I wanted to *help* them, wanted to fix it. When I got word of my employees being blackmailed to set off that bomb on that bus, I took it as my personal mission to find out what was going on. You've got the wrong bad guy here."

Levi smiled slowly. "Oh, I'm well aware of who in this world has a stake in this. They contacted me too."

Dr. Jackson's eyes grew wide. "All I need is a name."

Levi shook his head. "Can't give you one. I promised, and I don't break my promises." Taking a knife from his pocket, he saw Gregory start to panic.

"What, you think I brought you here just to kill you? You're Nix's nephew. Calm down." Taking the knife, he cut the ropes binding the Director, and turned to leave.

"I will find them! I will cut them down! Whoever did this, they'll pay dearly!" Levi had no doubt that the young man would do just that in time. Still, he had a contract. Creating another whirlpool, he morphed to his intended destination.

He ended up on a helipad at the airport. In front of him stood his employer. She'd changed her hair color since last they spoke. Bright blue eyes shimmering, she smiled at him and began to speak. He was so used to her American accent that her native British one sounded strange.

"Mr. Levi, may I be the first to congratulate you on a job well done." Wills reached out to shake his hand.

"I don't shake."

She retracted it. "Straight to business then?"

"If you don't mind, I have a small island in South America I'd like to buy."

Handing him a briefcase, she began her company line, "my father and I are grateful for your continued loyalty. You fulfilled your contract marvelously. We took down our competition and my father's nemesis, Nix, is dead. I call that a great day. I assume you handled Dr. Jackson as well? I'd hate to have issues later."

"He won't be a problem anymore. Tell your father his secret is safe."

"Grand. I'll be flying back to London in the morning. Anything you'd like me to tell my father when I land?"

"Yes, there is." He got closer to Wills. He whispered in her ear so only she could hear. Her eyes wide, he stepped back. *"Don't contact me again. We're done."*

Creating a whirlpool, he left. Wills stood on the roof for a few moments before turning and walking into the airport. Charting a private jet would be suspicious, as Tyrus had contacts with airport traffic control, so she merely opened a service door and walked to her gate, taking out her boarding ticket.

She waited patiently until they called first class passengers to board. Walking through the tunnel, she smiled at the flight attendants and sat in her seat. Picking up her cell, she dialed the number.

"It's done, Papa." Then she hung up and got ready for her flight home, feeling very successful.

In the seat in front of her, a man sat quietly, his head down, a hat on his head. A flight attendant approached him, saying, "would you like a cocktail, sir?"

He shook his head and relaxed into his seat. Lifting his hat to adjust it, Tyrus settled in for the long flight to London. He was right. This was not about research, this was war. It was coming to his people. Now more than ever, they were in danger, and his job was not done. He'd follow the unsuspecting Wills back to her father's lair. He'd been looking for her father for years. He'd do the work, use his contacts abroad, and find the gorgon before he could destroy more lives. *This is not over, you bastard*, as he pretended to drift off, fake snoring and all.

Day 37

"I'm here reporting outside the rubble that was, formerly, a thriving medical business. An explosion occurred at midnight last night, leveling the building. Luckily, many employees were home with their families. Surprisingly, only two casualties have been reported. Dr. Matheson, lead researcher, has been confirmed through DNA testing along with his key card being found, burnt and mangled. Dr. Gregory Jackson has been listed as missing, and though no evidence exists, it is believed that he died in the blast as well.

"Some very strange reports have come out of this investigation. For instance, a building manager was recovered safe by a doorway somehow stuck in glue. Also, due to a flat tire, caused by large nails being placed outside the parking garage, no one could leave their shift right before the explosion. This actually *saved* many, as the parking structure somehow didn't collapse with the building. Others report being in the building, then suddenly being outside of the rubble. Clearly, the traumatic event has affected the employees' memories.

We are comfortable with calling this a terrorist attack. More on the story as it develops."

Powering down the TV, he stood in a dark room, surrounded by wealth, pleased with his daughter. She'd managed to become quite an asset to him over the years. Maybe she did have what it takes to run the company when he eventually expired.

Looking out at the London landscape, he watched as Big Ben chimed. Laughing, he said only one word. "Excellent."

Tommy watched the news broadcast too, more excited than he had been in years. Hitting himself on the head, he said,

"Stay cool," to no one in particular. When he got excited, he got hungry.

Maybe it was finally time to end this. Maybe it was time to go see Nix and Tyrus and Levi. They were his best friends. Through the fog in his muddled mind, he rocked back and forth, repeating, "It'll all be over when they kill you." He laughed as well, but his was insane, crazy, a sort of tormented giggle.

Epilogue

three months after the bus crash…

Ann stood by Marie's grave. A tear streaming down her cheek, she remembered the five stages of grief. Denial, anger, bargaining, depression and acceptance. She was still struggling with all of them. She'd wake up one day, ready to accept this loss, and by the end, she couldn't believe her best friend was gone.

It'd been a quarter of a year since the accident that claimed her best friend's life. 9- days of struggle, toil and growth. Thinking back, she could barely remember what life was like before the Omega Flame changed her world forever. Try as she might, those memories were fading.

She lovingly placed a rose on Marie's grave. Facing the other survivors, they moved on to the next. They were grieving the people they knew, and the people they didn't know well enough. Mr. Huber was next, his grave crowded already with well-wishers and decorated by former students and colleagues.

Pulling her ball cap farther down on her head, her hair in her face, she avoided as many of the grieving onlookers as she could. She expertly placed the flower on the grave and turned to go. A hand on her shoulder stopped her, but she didn't look back.

"How did you know my husband?" his wife asked. She was also a teacher. Ann had been in her art class, though she couldn't draw to save her life.

"Same ways all the other kids do. He was a wonderful man."

Walking away, she removed herself from the crowd and joined Julius at Marcos's grave.

He hid the tears in his eyes. "This sucks. You know, he had a crush on my sister." He paused a moment. "My sister. I wish I could talk to her. Let her know we're okay."

Ann touched a hand to his shoulder. "Are you still sending a portion of your money home?"

"Yeah, but who knows now…" He sighed softly. The investigation into the "terrorist" attack on Jackson Genetics was expected to conclude, possibly today. They were all nervous at what would be officially reported.

Ann walked away, allowing her friend to be singular in his grief. Sometimes, you need to be alone. Her job finished, she walked to the edge of the cemetery, followed silently by Joy and Seth. Connor was already in the limo. Apparently, this was too much for him. The leadership role in him was strong. Probably the lion in him. He felt the guilt of their deaths more strongly than anyone.

Inside the limo, Connor sat at the back. Ann moved all the way down on the right, sitting next to Nix. The others filed in, waiting until, finally, Julius joined them. Pressing the intercom, Nix said, "we're ready. You can go."

The driver pulled away from the curb, slowly heading out of the cemetery. Taking a right, they passed the news reporters that, in a few moments, would change private mourning into public entertainment. They were lucky they'd gone early, but then, Seth told them to.

Merging on to the freeway, Nix looked at the Five and began. "We need to talk about the news conference."

Everyone suddenly looked tense and uncomfortable. "Listen, I know it's not free money and rainbows but it's something you need to prepare yourselves for.

"Officer Ryan has told me that your names haven't come up, as far as his contacts know. All files on us were consumed in the fire. I don't expect them to name any of us, but the internet videos clearly show the fight between Connor and Julius. Someone was watching and cared enough to capture that.

"If it comes out on the news that they are suspects, instead of hot-headed kids, we need to be prepared for the worst. That means they don't leave the compound for the time being."

Connor and Julius both nodded.

"And no contact with family." Julius spoke softly.

Nix gave him a sympathetic look. "Exactly, for the time begin. I know it's hard on some of you, but they could be arrested for harboring fugitives, or if swat raided their home…"

Connor chimed in, "We get it. I just wish my brother knew I was okay."

Nix nodded. "The best thing to do is to leave them be. Believe me, if I didn't have to involve my nephew in this, if I'd done things differently, he'd be safe. He's in the middle of this mess because of me, and his father. I know what you're going through, but it is our only option right now."

Ann crossed her arms in front of her. "Works for me. You guys are my family."

Nix smiled at her then. "Exactly the attitude that's going to get us all through this. Now, who's working on the camp today?"

The young adults all groaned in unison. Nix chuckled, and looked out at the highway, toward their future. *Ah, the enthusiasm of youth…* It almost helped remove the cold chill that ran down her spine, colder than the air conditioning in August could naturally get. It wasn't normal, no wind could create it. It warned of destruction and death. Something was wrong…

Agent Ryan turned on his laptop and logged into his email, noting he had a new message from Tyrus labeled, "This may be a problem." He clicked on the title, reading the quick message, before clicking the link at the bottom. The webpage loaded and he was inundated with videos, pics, and chat platforms devoted to the remembrance of "Stabby Steve." There was even T-shirt merchandise with an acronym that apparently meant, "Avenge Stabby Steve." How colorful. He bookmarked it for later, sighing heavily. This would *definitely* warrant further investigation.

Made in USA - Kendallville, IN
39313_9798988313519
12.05.2023 1257